When the wind blows . . .

Melanie went downstairs to the living room and sat on the sofa where she could hear the slightest sound from the nursery. She hated being alone when a storm set the house wailing. Would Frank never get home!

A cold tremor ran up the back of her neck. The creaks in the ceiling were no longer random like the wind. They now tracked past the nursery. She scrambled up the stairs and slumped down at the top of the stairs feeling foolish until she saw her older boy emerge from the bathroom. She laughed uneasily. If only she were as smart as her own two-year-old, she'd go to bed, and curl up and fall asleep.

Melanie went to the kitchen for a glass of warm milk. When she heard footsteps, she realized Frank was home. She smiled as she saw him emerging from the shadows.

"Hi, dear. Welcome home." She let the glass drop and her hand went to her throat. It was the man who had rescued Tammy in the park. Tammy lay still in his arms. His green eyes glowed with a mad intensity . . .

In the moment before the dark wind carried her off, she heard him laugh softly.

...CRADLE AND ALL

...CRADLE AND ALL

FAY NEDRA ZACHARY

PAGEANT BOOKS

PAGEANT BOOKS
225 Park Avenue South
New York, New York 10003

Cover artwork by Marvin Mattelson

Printed in the U.S.A.

First Pageant Books printing: January, 1989

10 9 8 7 6 5 4 3 2 1

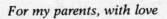

For my parents, with love

What ties this serial killer to his victims? A bond so ancient, so strong, even the latest technology cannot weaken it.

Yet modern technology so warps and clouds this most basic human bond, we sometimes deny it exists. We do so at our peril. For though no such killer has stalked the streets in history or fiction before, he may be wandering, unknown, among us today.

If our technology hasn't created him yet, our blindness surely will.

—Fay Nedra Zachary

...CRADLE AND ALL

Prologue

Death of a Matchmaker

Philadelphia, October

SARAH'S GRAY HEAD rocked on her long, ribbed neck as her unthinking fingers tapped computer code in through the terminal keyboard. The motion, an unconscious habit, signified her wonder at how much the matchmaking game had changed since her mother had played it for sixty years.

Her mother still played matchmaker, when it came to Sarah's and Sarah's brother's and sister's children. Grandparents had a right to try, she and her mother agreed. Especially when the grandchildren showed little interest in matchmaking for themselves—at least not with anything permanent in mind.

Sarah could not, *would* not, make matches for her

1

own three daughters. She wouldn't dream of trying, though at fifty-seven she felt vaguely unfulfilled with no signs of marriage on any of their rich horizons. The thought that even her youngest daughter already made more money at her profession than Sarah did after thirty years as secretary (and now administrative assistant) to the company president, did not comfort her one iota. All her daughters' money could not buy Sarah any grandchildren.

Still, she would not want her daughters to come here to this matchmaking service simply so she could have grandchildren. She was glad they had chosen not to, even though that meant Sarah might waste the rest of her life nodding and bobbing over this keyboard. There, as dusk gathered threatening shadows close around Sarah's thin shoulders, she might go on bringing immortality to others, only to go to her own grave knowing with an awful final ache that, for her, this was the end of the line.

Forever.

Sad as that was, she disagreed with her daughters, who thought that the type of matchmaking she did on The Service's computers was wrong or even immoral. If people wanted to be mated through a data bank, that was their business. As far as she was concerned, though, a man or a woman was more than just a list of physical, mental, and emotional traits you wanted to pass along to your children. A couple—lovers and parents—had to be forged through synergy, that magical force that made one plus one equal more than two.

Human matchmakers sensed things about people, had hunches. Her mother did.

"Look at the eyes," her mother used to say. "The eyes can't lie. And watch out for flashy smiles."

Her mother had common sense and intuition.

But computers had neither sense nor intuition. Artificial intelligence? Impossible! No matter what scientists said, the old rule about data entry prevailed: GIGO—Garbage In; Garbage Out. Sarah sometimes worried that her clients might furnish her with garbage based on a vested interest that no one knew they had.

Of course, human matchmakers could believe garbage, too. Even her mother—one of the best—had been fooled once or twice by a clever con man's lies. But that could happen even when a couple came together without a matchmaker's help: men lied about themselves; deception *always* accompanied courting. Women batted eyes concealing their wariness. They had learned how to play the game face to face, as couples should play it.

But faceless computers effaced the bold outlines of lies. Belief in their electronic genius imparted an aura of truth to their output, and few women—or men, for that matter—ever questioned a computer printout's honesty. The portfolio Sarah prepared from the facts she keyed in to her machine, stood in for the man himself, spoke for him, did all the courting and convincing for him. Some, she knew, would be lies whispered into ever so willing, ever more desperate ears.

And of the women who pored over the portfolio pages, one or more would buy it all, would choose the "him" it portrayed as the perfect one for her. Though Sarah, who had seen his eyes and his smiles, knew he might not be.

This Friday night, Sarah was working late, as a favor to her boss, Ansel Harrington, who had asked her to stay and catch up on the week's work. Portfolio demand had exploded as more and more women in their mid-to-late thirties abandoned hope, afraid that the old patterns of courtship and marriage would resurge too late for them. Sarah could use some help.

She hated to leave the office after dark; and with daylight saving time ending this weekend, even a normal workday's end would find her scurrying down the office corridors, nervously searching the shadows in darkened doorways. On Monday she'd ask Ansel to find her an assistant.

Meanwhile, dusk settled outside and crept into the room through the office's eastern windows. Only a dim square of light from the unoccupied adjacent front office, a bright fluorescent patch from the swing-arm lamp on her desk, and the wavering green glow of her computer screen kept the shadows at bay from her work center. She typed in the codes for physical features of the man preferred by the woman requesting a portfolio: eyes, brown; hair, curly and black; height, six feet even; frame, medium. Mental features: IQ, 135 or better; education, college graduate; socially well integrated and stable; no personal history of addictive behavior or drug use; no history of arrests or commitments to mental hospitals.

How would they know this was all true? So many men who came in to apply for the program fit this description. She always looked into their eyes.

Most men's eyes twinkled shyly, as though they were somewhat embarrassed at their boldness in being there. Some had the faraway intelligent gaze of a man contemplating a significant commitment he couldn't easily withdraw from. Sarah liked these men, didn't hesitate to send them on to The Harrington Service's counselor for screening.

But others' eyes wavered and ducked her scrutiny. And others' burned like coals that wouldn't take much prodding before bursting into uncontrolled flame. She breathed a nervous sigh. One of the men fitting the description this woman had called for might have eyes like that.

Probably not. The counselor screened out most of the bad ones. But not all of them; some passed the psychological tests designed by Dr. Ansel Harrington to protect his clients from one another and themselves.

Still Sarah doubted these tests. She'd have gone strictly by the eyes to decide. She wished the women themselves had a chance to look into those eyes before they were exposed. But under the strict code of ethics that bound The Harrington Service, that was forbidden. All that the women knew, all they apparently cared to know, was the eye color.

She sighed and shuddered and shifted in the one pool of light that remained in the darkening room. The slight click of the keyboard under her fingers, the squeak of her chair back as she adjusted her position, and the dwindling muffled chatter of vehicles passing on Market Street five stories below, masked the stealthy approach of footsteps toward the outer office door.

She typed in the information required by The Service. Family medical history: No known genetic illnesses; no senility last two generations; no suicides; no mental illnesses. Family social history as requested by the client: No special requirements. Religion: No preference.

A siren wailed outside as she fed the final data into the computer. It faded away, and was followed by others as she saved and reviewed the data against the form she had entered it from. She blamed her rising disquiet on the siren's melancholy wail as it floated back from the east.

She discovered an error in her data entry, corrected it, and saved it again. Press the print command, and the computer would retrieve from its files the information on at least three men fitting the profile requested; then the printer would spit out their portfolios. She would lock the portfolios in the library, and on Monday morning, dispatch them in confidence to the woman. The woman's name she'd learn from the coded information in another computer file.

As she touched the key, the printer whined and clattered to life. She leaned back in her chair, then froze.

In the dimly lit doorway stood a man. He took three steps forward. She knew by the way he held his hands that he was going to kill her.

As the printer chattered away, he came closer. He left the blinding backlight of the door. Now she could see his eyes. Rage and pain seethed behind them, as she'd known the first time she'd seen him. She knew who he was, but . . . Oh God . . . she couldn't remember his name.

Sarah knew what he wanted; she had to warn them that for some crazy reason even she didn't know, he was after them . . .

His shadow rose between them. Oh, God, if only she could remember his name. Then her unthinking fingers, with a keystroke, called up her portfolio program. She began to type in the data for physical features: eyes, code 3; hair, code 2; height, code 7 . . .

He stood over her. The printer stilled as her heart did. Not enough data yet, but she didn't have time. She hit the save key. In an instant the program disappeared from the computer screen.

A metallic gleam flashed before her eyes as she looked up at him for the last time. His code 3 eyes glinted as he brought the knife down at her throat. She did not feel it slash her carotid artery; the blood fled too quickly from her brain.

Still she had time enough to realize, with one awful gripping pang, that this was the end of the line.

Forever.

Chapter One

Philadelphia, the following May: Wednesday

JOANNA MICHAELS pushed herself back on the squat chrome stool and swiveled her long legs away from the foot of the examining table. She stood up so she wouldn't have to crane her neck to see around her client's draped legs, which winged back on raised knee supports and obscured Joanna's view of her face.

A question sat for a moment in the client's cobalt eyes, then fled; a smile crossed her pie-plate face. "You're sure?"

Joanna stripped off her lubricated latex glove and tossed it into the aluminum kick pail near the table. She nodded, and felt her short dark brown hair fall softly over her angular cheeks. "Positive, Wendy. No need for a lab test to confirm it."

The woman rose up on her elbows. "How far along?"

Joanna extended the foot of the table and helped Wendy lift her legs down from the supports. She held up three fingers. "Three months, I'd say. Does that sound about right?"

"Yes. At last. After three tries." She sat up, her eyes glistening. "I know I should have come in sooner. But, I'd missed periods the other two times, too."

"You were here last September, weren't you?" Joanna said. "Before I took my leave?"

"Yes. That was after the second try. It took me a while to get up my nerve after the first one didn't take. This baby is so important to me, Joanna. Who knows how long I'll be able to have one? Or *if* I can."

"It looks like you can. And will."

Wendy smiled. Then a troubled look crossed her face. "Of course, there's the question of whether I really *should*. I've really struggled with that one. It's going to be lonely. I'll have to do it all by myself. Not just for the next six months. Probably for the rest of my life. It boggles my mind."

Joanna nodded. She admired Wendy Green, a teacher with an excellent reputation. Wendy had won a statewide award as Second Grade Teacher of the Year. She'd been nominated by pupils and their parents. Joanna knew she'd make a wonderful mother, with or without help from a father. "Just take it a day at a time," she said.

"Well, anyway, thank God you're back. I thought I'd have to go through my pregnancy without you."

Joanna hesitated a moment. "Yes. Well, I'm not the only midwife at the Jordan Martin Birthing Center. I'm sure Monica or Diane would have taken good care of you." She handed Wendy her clothes and a washcloth, then picked up her records and turned to leave the examining room.

"Maybe. But I don't think they approve of what I'm

doing. Most people don't. My parents think it's pretty awful, having a baby without getting married. Even without having sex. Planning to raise it alone on my teacher's salary. But I know what I'm doing, Joanna."

Joanna stopped and turned to face Wendy again. "I know. Most people *won't* approve. Even midwives come complete with biases. You'll just have to learn to live with your choice, no matter what anyone thinks. No matter what I think either."

Wendy knit her brow and brushed a wisp of light blond hair from her eyes. "Still, you're not taking another leave for a while, are you?"

Joanna smiled. She felt a momentary pang of sympathy with her vulnerable client. Wendy was thirty-seven, just Joanna's age. Her flat, dishlike face was not likely a sexual attractant. Marriage would continue to elude her; motherhood needn't. Not with today's technologies and society's changing attitudes.

Still choices like Wendy's . . . like Joanna's . . . weren't easily lived with or lived down. They always brought pain. And sometimes you even lied about choices you made. Joanna admired Wendy. Wendy told the whole truth to everyone. Even to herself.

Joanna walked back and clasped Wendy's shoulder. The paper gown crinkled under her hand. "No. I'm here for as long as they'll keep me." She patted Wendy's shoulder, then walked to the door and opened it. "Now get dressed, and I'll see you in my office. It's nearly nine, and you've got a long drive to Ambler."

"Oh. I forgot the time. I'm keeping you late too."

"It's part of my job," said Joanna. "I'm on call tonight. So, I'll be staying here overnight, anyway." She closed the examining room door and turned to start down the brief corridor toward her office. As she did, she bumped into a tall man in a blue surgical scrub suit and cap. The collision knocked her client's records from her hand and scattered them over the floor.

"Oh! I'm terribly sorry, Doctor. I didn't see you," she said, as she stooped to retrieve them.

She looked up, expecting he would stop and help her. The accident was clearly as much his fault as hers. Instead, he pivoted and ran toward the exit, without so much as an apology.

She watched openmouthed as he rounded the bend at the receptionist's cubicle. He didn't look like any of the Martin Center obstetricians or gynecologists, though something about him was disturbingly familiar.

As she picked up her scattered papers, she reran the scene through her mind: she'd backed out of the door while continuing her instructions to Wendy; she'd turned as she'd closed the door; the man was standing directly outside the door. That bothered her: he was standing there as if he'd been waiting for someone.

Well, maybe he had been. True, she was the only one seeing clients tonight, but though she was on call for emergency deliveries, a physician had to be on call too, in case of a high-risk birth. This man could be a resident starting his obstetrical service and coming in to observe. Or maybe he had just come up from the birthing or operating rooms through the staff elevator, and had stopped just outside her door for a moment. People unfamiliar with the center sometimes accidentally got off the elevator on the fourth floor and became disoriented, then fled, embarrassed.

But his flight seemed less embarrassed than guilty, as if he'd been caught snooping. Joanna ran through the pictures in her mind again: she'd bumped into him; lost her grip on the record folder; watched, dismayed, as the papers scattered; stooped and begun to gather them up; looked up at this face . . .

His face! He'd turned from her in a flash. But she had seen the color of his eyes. His hair had been hidden under the blue paper cap, and his chin had been partially obscured by the mask that dangled loosely from the ties behind his neck. Still the cut of his jaw stood out square and firm in her mind.

"Kevin!" she said aloud to herself. "Oh, my God."

She had seen, in the turning of his body from her, an echo of guilty turnings of the past, and of the agonized turning away from her the last time she'd seen him, last August . . . and the first time she'd seen him, standing over Timmy's hospital bed.

That first time, almost three years ago, he turned away from her too, after turning, surprised, from the child she had come to visit after hours . . . her colleague's child, two days post-op.

"Oh, Doctor. I hope I'm not interrupting. Timmy's all right, isn't he?"

"Yes. Of course. A simple T and A." He pulled the six-year-old boy's bedsheet up over the hem of his hospital gown, covered his thighs, and patted him quickly on the shoulder with one hand, while stuffing his stethoscope into his pants pocket under his lab coat, which seemed caught on the bed's lowered side rail.

"Timmy doesn't look like he thinks having his tonsils out is so simple." She smiled and leaned over the bed. "Mommy asked me to stop over to see you, Timmy. She's working tonight. But she wants you to know she and your daddy will come to take you home tomorrow morning."

Timmy nodded his head. He glanced from Joanna to the doctor and back.

Puzzled by the uneasiness in the boy's eyes, Joanna asked, "They're treating you all right here?"

Timmy's face tightened as he looked at the doctor.

The man laughed, nervous and unsmiling. "I guess I was just one too many doctors poking around. And a little past his bedtime. But he was awake."

Joanna nodded. She bent down and kissed Timmy's cool, damp forehead and patted his arm. "Well, we'll put a stop to that." She looked up at the doctor and smiled. "Doctor . . .?"

"Willman."

Then she saw his name on his badge: Kevin Willman, M.D. "Dr. Willman, why don't you write an order on Timmy's chart that his dad, Dr. Coyne, will do his discharge exam tomorrow?"

"His father?"

"Yes. Didn't you know? Don Coyne, the gynecologist."

"I . . . I'm new here. An intern. I observed Timmy's surgery. That's why I was interested . . ." His explanation trailed off.

Joanna laughed. "You can relax, Dr. Willman. I'm sure they'll forgive you for being concerned about your patients. Besides, I don't have any clout here at all. I'm a midwife at the Martin Center a few blocks away."

"Oh. We toured it in med school." He squinted at her badge in the semidarkness.

"My name is Joanna Michaels."

"Well, I have to get going. Long day." He started out of the room.

She looked at Timmy. He swallowed and then grabbed his throat as tears came to his eyes. "That hurts . . . Oh, honey, I'll get you some ice cream from the cafeteria. OK?"

He nodded, as she looked quickly to the door and saw that Dr. Willman had left. After a fast pat of Timmy's thin arm, she pulled up the side rail on his bed and hurried into the corridor and to the nursing unit.

The nurse at the desk looked up. "Can I help you?"

"I was looking for Dr. Willman."

She looked puzzled as she brushed a loose wisp of blond hair back and fastened it under her cap. She shrugged.

"The intern who was examining Timmy Coyne."

"What was someone examining him for? The resident checked him already tonight."

"He's new. He observed the surgery and . . ."

"Oh. I think I know the guy. He was here last night, too. That one's going to be a pest. Seems to think he knows everything, even though he's still in doctor kindergarten. I chased him away. The evening shift's busy enough without having to put up with overzealous interns." She shrugged and went back to the chart she was working on.

"Didn't he put a note on Timmy's record?"

"Not that I know of."

You probably had the poor guy intimidated, Joanna thought. No wonder so many doctors seemed to lose their caring instincts, with harridans like this taking control of the nursing units. And on a pediatric surgical wing, at that. "I see," she said.

She started toward the elevators, then turned back. "The cafeteria's on the ground floor, isn't it?"

The woman looked up at her lab coat. "Don't you work here?"

"I work at the Martin Center. With Timmy's mother. She's on call and . . ."

"That kid sure gets a lot of attention. Doctor's kid."

"His throat hurts."

"He got his Tylenol an hour ago."

"I was going to get him some ice cream."

The nurse gave her an irritated glance and

shrugged. "Ground floor, down the corridor just to the left of the elevators."

"Thank you." Joanna started toward the elevators.

"But this time of night, he'll probably have to settle for Jell-O. Doctor's kid or no," the nurse called after her.

She was right. Hard cubes of gelatin in clear plastic bowls, globs of yellow-edged cottage cheese on wilted lettuce leaves, stiff-looking plastic-filmed ham and cheese sandwiches waited like street urchins all in a row for someone desperate enough to rescue them from their chilly, bedraggled condition. And in a large hospital after evening visiting hours, someone was always desperate enough. Overworked doctors and nurses sought refuge from patients' demands and gave their stomachs *anything* solid to grind on. Ironically aides, maids, and custodians found breathing in the smell of acrid, burnt coffee in pleasant contrast to the odors of sickness and death.

Joanna didn't think Timmy was desperate enough for the gelatin. But she had promised him she'd be back, and couldn't return empty-handed. She picked up a bowl of red cubes, paid for it, and started out of the cafeteria.

Then she saw Dr. Willman, hunched over coffee and a book in the farthest corner of the dining room. She went over to his table.

"Hello again, Dr. Willman."

He looked up. "Oh, hello." His eyes returned to the book.

"I don't mean to disturb you. But I thought you wouldn't want to forget to write up your examination on Timmy Coyne's chart."

He looked at her again and knit his brow. His eyes smoldered in deep, dark shadows, two small coals in an immense double furnace.

She stepped back. "You look like you've been working hard. Under the gun. I'd hate to see you lose credit for the extras."

His eyes seemed to relax. "I didn't find anything to write about. Just a routine post-op T and A."

"I was just kidding about writing the order."

He looked puzzled. He picked up his coffee and took a sip, watching her over the plastic foam cup rim. His face, square-cut and handsome, looked oddly hollow—maybe because dark shadows of beard emerged from under his cheekbones and made his cheeks appear concave.

"The order that Dr. Coyne should do the discharge exam," she said.

"They'd laugh if an intern wrote an order like that."

"Maybe. But that's a good reason to write it."

He set down his cup. "It's frivolous."

"Well, Doctor, we all need to laugh once in a while. And I've noticed, in the brief time I've known you, you don't."

His mouth opened slightly.

She bit her lip and felt her face grow hot. "Well, I promised Timmy I'd bring something cool for his throat." She glanced at the gelatin.

"You're going back to his room?"

"I'm almost ashamed to."

"What do you mean?" He looked troubled.

"With this." She held out the bowl of rigid cubes. "They didn't have ice cream. But he's expecting me."

He rose, seeming relieved, and picked up his book and coffee cup. "I'll go with you."

They found Timmy asleep. Joanna was relieved that she wouldn't have to make excuses about substituting gelatin for ice cream. Dr. Willman's face seemed to relax when she turned and touched two fingers to her lips. She set the bowl on the nightstand, half hoping the dessert would be tossed out uneaten, and tiptoed out of the room.

Out in the hall, he said, "It's true I don't laugh much."

She looked up at him, realizing for the first time how tall he was. Over six feet. Slim and athletic-looking when straight—as he suddenly was—he'd seemed bowed and uncertain before. Now his cheeks seemed more fleshed out, too. "Why not?"

"Not much funny."

"You are," she said.

"What do you mean?"

She shrugged. "I don't know exactly. You seem so awfully intense. So serious it's funny. I guess that's what I mean." She stopped and held out her right hand. "My name's Joanna Michaels," she said.

He hesitated a moment before taking her hand. His grasp felt limp and tentative, not sure and strong as she thought a surgeon's hand should. "I know. You told me in there." He gestured with his head toward Timmy's door.

"But you didn't seem to hear."

"I did."

They started toward the elevator again.

"You see, that's what I mean by funny."

He stopped and pressed the elevator call button for down. "You mean strange."

"No. Of course not. I mean different . . ."

He grinned at her, embarrassed and fumbling for words.

Well, that's something, at least, she thought. He does have some sense of humor after all.

They got on an empty elevator and she said, "It's different for someone to know someone's name and not call her by it."

"I didn't expect to see you again. You said you don't work here, and I don't plan to go to the Martin Center. At least not for obstetrics. I plan on general surgery. What floor?"

"Lobby. But you have seen me again, and you still haven't called me by name."

He pressed the lobby button. No other, she noticed—just lobby.

She took a deep breath.

"I didn't need to. You're the only one here, so you know who I'm talking to. Why is it so important?"

The door slid open and they alighted into the lobby.

"Usually somebody says, 'Nice to meet you, Joanna,' when I introduce myself. But you're right. I guess it's not important." She stopped just outside the elevator and turned to him. "Unconventional. Not strange. Not different. Just unconventional, that's what I mean by funny. And I guess it's kind of a relief to meet someone unconventional."

"Well," he said, "if you're going home now, I'm sure I'll never see you again. So, goodbye." He paused. "Joanna." He turned and started across the lobby toward the left.

But when she looked back over her shoulder after leaving through the glass lobby door, she saw him turn in the opposite direction and go through the double doors into the administrative wing. His switch seemed deliberate . . . as if he hadn't wanted her to see where he was going.

More than simple curiosity made her turn back and follow him. She suddenly recalled the upset—or was it frightened?—look in Timmy's eyes when she had come into the hospital room. Dr. Willman himself had used the word "strange" to define himself. And the unit nurse had seemed to dislike and distrust him. Maybe unconventional wasn't a strong enough term.

She was worried, too. Worried, because this man intrigued her. Something about him strummed at her sexuality, and she wanted to know why. If her fascination was grounded in his shyness and the restless intelligence burning in his eyes, that was one thing; but if he was sneaky or weird, and the burning in his eyes indicated something sinister, she wanted to shut off her enchantment right now. Before she got into trouble.

When the double doors closed behind him, she crossed the lobby and pushed one open again. The dimly lit corridor was empty, but a shadow flickered a moment at the far end where a second passageway intersected it.

She hurried after him, her soft footfalls lost in the humming of the air conditioning as she passed by darkened, locked offices. When she reached the other hallway, she stopped, pulled close to the wall, and peeked around the corner.

In the second hall some doors had light coming through their glass panels. These rooms, she deduced, would house offices that had to stay open all night. An arrow on the wall of the corridor directed her to a laboratory wing at the far end. The offices designated here included nursing service, maintenance, and housekeeping—sure to be among the lit ones. The mainframe computer room was also down here.

She straightened her shoulders and ran her hands over the front of her lab coat. If anyone besides Kevin Willman should see her here, she wanted to look as if she knew where she was headed. If he should see her . . . well, she would make up an excuse. She might even let him think she was pursuing him; she'd felt he had sensed her interest anyway, and he might be intrigued by a persistent woman.

When she passed Nursing Service, the evening supervisor, alone and on the telephone, just nodded at whatever was being said to her and didn't look up from her desk.

The woman in Housekeeping seemed engrossed in a

paperback novel and didn't raise her eyes as Joanna went by.

As she passed by Maintenance, she heard conversation from the room across the hall. She looked in and saw two men bent over a disassembled computer. The man who was turned toward her was pointing something out to the man who was turned away—Kevin Willman.

They both straightened. The first man, apparently a technician, took Kevin by the elbow and led him across the room to the mainframe system against the wall. She could not hear what he was saying, but Kevin was nodding and pointing.

He turned and looked right toward the door, his eyes incandescent. No . . . fluorescent.

Joanna pulled back, and turned away. She retreated quickly down the corridor. Her blood pounded in her temples. She knew now that what burned in his extraordinary, troubling and troubled eyes was an intense and hungry intelligence. He was far above and beyond most people. That's what made him hide behind his book in the corner of the cafeteria, shy and withdrawn. That's what drove others off, children like Timmy, angry nurses like the charge nurse on pediatric surgical.

But she wouldn't let him be beyond *her*. She wouldn't let him drive her off. He intrigued her too much. She wanted to find out what made him different and why it fascinated her.

Hoping to solve the mystery—at least that's what she told herself—she began haunting the hospital cafeteria. At first he seemed indifferent. Then he seemed to grow comfortable with her. He'd push aside his books and make room for her as soon as he'd see her sliding her fiberglass tray along the food service line.

"Don't you have a home?" she asked one day. She had realized during the three months she'd been dropping in that, though he was always at the hospital, he wasn't always on duty.

"Apartment," he said.

"Why don't you study there? Don't you get tired of this place? This food?" She screwed up her nose and waved at her tray.

"It stinks there," he said.

"You mean literally?"

"It stinks every way. It's crummy and noisy till all hours."

"Well, why don't you move?"

"The rent's cheap."

"Well, if it's so bad . . ."

"Do you know how much it costs to go to medical school at University?"

She put down the fork she'd been playing at her dinner with. "But you graduated."

"Sure. But my loans didn't."

"Can't your family help?"

His eyes flashed like knives. She felt impaled.

"I've said the wrong thing."

"There's no right thing to say. I don't talk about my family." He thrust away his tray with his uneaten food.

"Well, you must be able to find a decent apartment."

"I don't care. This place is warm. There's always a place to study and rest, and the food's subsidized."

"But what about privacy?"

"There are private corners."

"I suppose you make love in the linen closets."

He fixed her with steady eyes. "I don't make love anywhere," he said.

"My," she said, flustered and aroused. "You really are dedicated to your calling."

"I try to direct my energy. Medicine—the world—needs *some* good out of me."

"But you do get normal urges," she said.

"I said, I deal with my urges." He stood and picked up his books.

She stood, too. "Wait, Kevin. Don't go. I didn't mean to make you angry."

"I'm not angry. Can't you see I'm just tired? Do you know what I'd give just to be able to go back to my apartment and sleep for a solid week!" He picked up his tray and began walking to the tray dump.

She grabbed her tray and ran to catch up with him. "If you'd give anything, for God's sake, then why don't you just move? The extra rent would be worth it, wouldn't it?"

He dumped the waste and pushed the plastic tray onto the conveyer belt. Then he stopped and turned to her. "Joanna, I owe two hundred thousand dollars."

She gasped and let her tray slip from her hand onto the moving belt. She watched as it was snatched up by a kitchen attendant.

He strode through the cafeteria door and into the corridor. She ran to catch up with him at the elevator door. "Are you working tonight?" she asked.

"No."

"Then where are you going?"

"To the library. It's quiet, and open all night. I can put on headphones in the media center and learn how to do a cholecystectomy in my sleep."

"Thank God my gall bladder's intact!"

He laughed.

"Kevin. I didn't realize . . . That's so much money."

"I try to make do."

"But you have to have sleep. And privacy." The elevator stopped at the lobby. She got out. He did not. The door slid between them. "Oh damn!" she said aloud.

She ran to the information desk. "'Where's the hospital library?" she asked the woman in a volunteer's blue-and-white striped uniform.

"Well, let's see. I don't believe anyone's ever asked to go there before." The gray-haired, pink-cheeked woman peered through steel-rimmed eyeglasses. "What would you want to go there for?"

"To do research."

The woman checked Joanna's clothing, which was civilian. "Well, I don't know if you can go in there if you aren't one of our doctors or nurses . . ."

"Well, *I* know I *can*. If you'll just tell me where it is."

"Well, let me see. I wonder how that would be listed. What department would that be under?"

Joanna let out an exasperated sigh. "Never mind, I'll ask someone else."

A few minutes before, the lobby had teemed with people in hospital garb of one kind or another. Now only a few people wearing mufti wandered toward the information desk or sat reading magazines and watching the elevators open and close.

Joanna caught an elevator door as it was about to close, and went back down to the cafeteria. There she went up to a nurse in a scrub dress and asked directions to the library.

"On the fifteenth floor. You'll see it when you get off the elevator."

It was harder to find than the nurse had implied. When she finally got there, the librarian told her she'd need a pass to use the reference room.

"Oh, shit!"

The woman's eyebrows arched above her stern, shocked features.

"I'm sorry. That was rude."

The woman drew her nostrils in and pursed her lips.

"I hope you can do me a favor. It's important. I've got to see this doctor."

"I can't let you in. You'll have to get a pass."

"I can't. That is, I don't have to go in myself. I just need to get Dr. Willman out. It's an emergency."

"If it's an emergency, he would have been paged," the librarian said.

Joanna was about to say "Shit!" again, but she realized she'd already undermined her position with this woman. "Well, you see, nobody knew to page him. But I know he's in the library."

The woman tilted her clenched nostrils upward. "I don't disturb the doctors when they're in there. It can't be that important if he hasn't been paged."

Joanna let out a forceful breath. She wheeled around and caught an elevator down to the lobby. She would just have to wait till tomorrow.

In the lobby again, she passed the information desk on her way to the door. "Oh, Miss," called the volunteer.

Joanna stopped.

"I found out where the library is. It's on the fifteenth floor, and you need a . . ."

"Yes, I know," Joanna croaked. Then she calmed herself down and said, "Thank you."

The volunteer's telephone rang. The woman picked up the receiver and smiled. Joanna began to leave.

Then, "Telephone!" Joanna said, and whirled back toward the volunteer. "Where are the pay phones?"

The volunteer pointed across the lobby.

Joanna dialed the hospital switchboard and asked for Dr. Willman.

"He's not on the board tonight," said the operator.

"Please have him paged anyway."

"It won't do any good."

"But I know he's in the hospital."

After a moment's silence, the operator said, "All right."

Five minutes later, after several repetitions of "He isn't answering" from the operator and "Please keep trying" from Joanna, she saw Kevin emerge from the administrative wing and pick up a house phone at the admissions desk.

She hung up just as the long-suffering operator was about to patch him onto her line. As she crossed the lobby to where he stood, he held the phone away from his face and looked at it with puzzlement. Then he looked up and saw her. His face lit up with insight, and he hung up the phone. He continued to hold onto the receiver as if to steady his hand.

"They wouldn't let me in the library."

"I wasn't in the library."

"I know. Kevin, I'm not trying to track you down."

"What *do* you want?"

"You can't sleep in libraries. You can't just keep eating from machines and that lousy cafeteria. You can't even be a good doctor—any kind of doctor, let alone a surgeon—if you keep on this way. Look at your hands: they're shaking."

"So are yours."

"Kevin, I have an extra bedroom in my apartment. It's quiet and private. You can even lock the door. You could come and go as you please . . ."

His mouth opened, then closed. He let his hand fall from the receiver and took two steps toward her.

"It's just a couple of blocks from here. Walking distance."

"You're offering to rent me a room."

"No. I don't want any rent. You could help pay for food, of course. It would actually save me money. Living alone, I almost never cook. So that means I have to eat out. And I end up throwing out half of what I do make for myself."

"What's the catch, Joanna? Sex?"

"The catch is, you might eventually turn into a decent human being and a half-decent surgeon, instead of a glassy-eyed zombie that wanders University Hospital looking for innocent people to growl at."

He seemed to swell with anger. "Just what do you mean by that?"

She felt herself grow hot as the juices drained from her mouth. "I've seen you. I've heard you growl. I don't think you're even aware of it. I see how people avoid you. Even the first time I met you I saw it."

He snorted. "That's why you keep coming over here."

"No. It's something else. It's . . . something in your eyes. Not in them. Behind them. I bet you have an IQ of 250—if there is such a thing. And there's something else, too. It's burning back there and you can't let it out, and I think it's going to burn you right up. And everyone around you. And the way you're doing things, you and the rest of us are going up in smoke in the next week and a half or so." She stopped and her mouth fell open. She couldn't believe her own words.

For a few moments he said nothing and just stood there, his eyes fixed on hers.

Finally hers wavered. Drained of emotion, she felt weak and foolish.

At last he said, "I sometimes feel exactly like that. Burning up. Burning out. Wishing I would. Get it over with and out. But what do you care? When I pop, you'd be glad. So would everybody."

His words stirred her again. "That's not so. I wouldn't."

"Plenty would." He shrugged. "Well, I do need some rest. If you're serious about the apartment, I guess I could use it at least as a place to crash once in a while."

"There's really no catch. I won't keep track of you.

If you don't want to eat with me, I'll just slide a tray through your door."

She kept her word. Though his stops at her apartment were infrequent at first, she no longer went to the hospital at mealtime. She kept a studied distance from him when she found he'd come in and gone into his room to read or sleep during her absences.

Then, after a month, she could see by the casual strewing of his possessions—a few books left on a living room table, a jacket hung on the back of a kitchen chair, a case of beer in the pantry cupboard— that he had moved in. Because of their work hours, though, they were seldom both in the apartment at the same time.

Even in his absence, she could sense his presence. The print of his hand on a dusty chair back gave dust a purpose—to record his leaning there. She would trace its pattern with her dustcloth, leave a border around it, stay in the room with it as she never dared stay with him.

Memories of his shadow in her bedroom doorway as he left for the hospital before dawn, gave substance and life to the darkness during nights when he didn't return. They played at the edges of her dreams, then taunted her during those few empty moments when work could not distract her from her yearnings.

She noticed he seemed to be haunted by shadows sometimes, too. Not dream shadows like hers ... which she'd gladly reveal to him if she dared ... but nightmare shadows that drove the light from his eyes and increased the distance between them.

She longed to leap over that distance, ask him what was wrong, what hurt him so. Still, she kept her word and resigned herself to living with his ghost, preserving and cherishing his imprints on the surroundings he shared with her. Someday her dreams would spring to life.

They did, but not as she'd hoped and imagined. One night she arrived home to find a thick medical text lying on the dining room floor among shards of shattered mirror. Two beer bottles lay like broken clubs in a sticky puddle on the kitchen tile. One bottle neck bled at its knifelike edge. Brownish-red drops and blotches led from the kitchen across the dining area to the brief hallway that ran to the bedrooms and bath.

Following the path of bloodstains, she flew past his clothing—a bloodied scrub shirt, an undershirt, a surgical mask, its ties ripped from the gauze. A cry froze in her throat. She heard him moan; she fled to the bathroom on liquid legs.

His nightmares, not her dreams, had come true. He turned from the washbowl, his arms held before him, dripping, dripping, bruising the white rim of the bowl, bruising Joanna's heart.

"Kevin—No! Why!"

Fear splotched his face. His lips were drawn back, silent; but a cry for help leapt from his eyes.

She tore a towel from the rack and wrapped one wrist tightly. Then she pulled off her blue silk blouse and twisted it around the other. She grasped both his arms and pinioned his wrists against the sides of her heaving chest with her own arms.

He sagged.

"Come on. To a bed." She led him to her room.

He sank, shivering, to the bed.

She clung to his wrapped wrists, pressing her fingers tight against them. The blood seemed stanched; still she did not let go for several minutes.

He lay back on the pillow. She pressed his wrists against his chest. "Hold them there, Kevin," she said.

He nodded.

She let his arms go and took off his shoes. She

removed his scrub suit trousers, then pulled the bedspread and top sheet out from under him and covered
him.

"The bleeding's stopped. You don't need to go to the
emergency room."

"No."

"I won't say anything to anyone. But why? Why,
Kevin?"

He drew a wavering breath, then shook his head. He
swallowed dryly.

She touched his cheek with the back of her fingers.
"I'll get you some water."

He drained the glass she brought him and handed it
back to her without a word. Then he turned on his
side, drew his knees up, cradled his head between his
bandaged forearms and closed his eyes.

She closed the slats of the window blinds and sat in
her chair at the side of the bed until his breathing
grew quiet. She rose silently, bent over him, touched
his shoulder.

He shifted and sighed, then resumed the jackknifed
position, all folded up into himself.

Away from her.

But she undressed and got into bed beside him,
folded herself in behind him, and arched her arm over
his waist. They slept that way through the night.

Sleep readied him, stole away his defenses, so that
when she woke him, and turned him hard with her
hand, and plied him with her restless fingers and hungry mouth, and rolled him toward her, onto her, he
did not resist but went right into her.

And when she pleased him, with herself, she made
him hard again and pleased herself again and again
with him. Then afterward they bathed together, and
she washed the dried blood off his arms and kissed the
red wounds on his wrists before she bandaged them

lightly with gauze. And they made love again one more time before she left for work.

He never told her what had tortured him, driven him to such despair; but her love for him seemed to have snatched him from his demons. If they still tormented him, he did not show it. Or maybe they drove him now into love instead of death . . . One or the other was said to tantalize possessed men. Let the love demons drive him forever, she thought. Let them weld him to me, hold him to me forever.

Oh, God, she wondered. Am I the driven one or is he?

She would learn the answer to that over the two years they lived together. Two years that changed her life forever.

Over those two years he lost his reticence and became surly. At first Joanna didn't notice; though she wondered why people she respected still drew away from him even long after they had become lovers. Children especially who, like dogs, were supposed to sense things adults might not.

Well, Joanna could live the rest of her life without dogs. Children were something else. She would not live her life without children. He did not hide from her his disdain for them. (Maybe that's why they pulled away from his touch.)

Though his taciturn nature confused her, and his reticence bothered her and conflicted with her own warm openness, she put aside her discomfiture, and determined that her love and physical passion for him would conquer the fears that seemed to lock him inside himself.

After a year, he relaxed enough to accept her close relationship with her sister, Louise, and Louise's husband David. He even began to share it with her, going to dinner at their house with her once every couple of months. Kevin looked down on David's obsession with sports statistics but joined him in an occasional verbal joust on biomedical ethics. When Joanna and Louise tried to enter in, Kevin would turn his body in such a way as to cut the women off and signal that their opinions—usually contrary to his own—weren't welcome.

Louise would shrug and laugh, but Joanna felt stung and defeated. She would watch the back of Kevin's shoulder curve more and more protectively around the space between him and David, till not even a niche remained open to her. Her fists and stomach clenched in frustration. The bile that crept up her throat soured the entire evening.

Still, she considered as progress Kevin's acceptance of her family. Occasionally he even showed that he noticed their then three-year-old son, Michael. Noticed and did not despise him. That was progress too, and Joanna did everything she could to foster it. She encouraged Kevin to help the boy with his Erector Set in his room. She asked him to read him bedtime stories so that Louise and she could chat in the kitchen over cleanup while David ran last minute errands.

"You seem to like Michael," she said as they arrived back at her apartment one evening.

"He's better company than his father."

She held tight to the doorknob so she would not slam it. "I'd say either one is better company than you right now."

"I know what you're after, Joanna," he said, not facing her.

"I'm after a pleasant evening with you and my family now and then. Either you shut me out altogether, or you're nasty and uncivil to them." She stalked past him into the dining area and slammed her purse on the table.

"No. You're after a little more than that. You're breaking me in, aren't you?"

"That's ridiculous." She expelled an exasperated breath. "For what?"

"For children. Forget it, Joanna. You're not going to trap me, whatever you do. If I ever find out you're pregnant, I'll do more than just walk out on you."

She caught her breath. "I see. You'll try to kill yourself again. Is that it?"

He stared at her a moment before curling the corner of his mouth.

"It won't work, Kevin. You'll never hook me on that one. I love you. Sometimes I wonder why. But it's definitely not because you tried to kill yourself. And if I do become pregnant . . ." She looked hard into his eyes, then away. "Don't worry. I won't."

The curl of his mouth seemed to quiver into a distorted smile. "I'm afraid I've ruined your plans."

"I told you, I didn't have any *plans*."

She *hadn't* planned; though she'd hoped. She'd hoped her love had subverted whatever had driven him to try suicide. She'd hoped his passion for her had replaced his passion for self-destruction. And, yes, she'd hoped that in time he would want to have children, as she did, so she wouldn't have to give him up to have what she must. For though life without Kevin would be painful, life without children of her own would be unbearable.

No, she didn't plan to get pregnant. She wouldn't have forced a child on Kevin. True, time had been running out for her at age thirty-six. She didn't expect to wait more than another year to start a family. And then, if Kevin had not changed, *she* would leave *him*. She would not let his manipulative threats of suicide stop her. She would accept veterinarian Jon Isenson's oft-repeated marriage proposal—if that kind and attractive man had not found someone else in the meantime—and bury her passion for Kevin in a comfortable, if mundane, life with a man who loved her more than she loved him.

She did not have to face or make that choice; technology failed her. Or maybe her diaphragm was not meant to withstand the punishment she and Kevin gave it during the week of vacation that preceded his residency assignment, a week in which all the demands of his medical training were suspended and he seemed to be free of his demons.

She thought about getting an abortion, but knew she couldn't. Nor could she tell him she was pregnant; that would be like telling him to kill himself.

Thank God, he didn't seem to notice the early signs of her pregnancy. The rigors of a surgical residency overcame any concerns he might have for her or her unexplained nausea and fatigue. His unconcern gave her a chance to think, to work out her agonizing decision. How she would leave him without making him blame her—or hate himself. The grounding in psychology her arduous eight year nursing education had given her buttressed her now. But nothing could help her deal with Kevin when his thirty-six hour work days turned his eyes once more to smoldering coals.

As she tried to hide her own agony, to act as if nothing had changed while she searched for her way out, he turned even more surly and ugly. Instead of coming to greet her when she arrived home smiling her carefully built smile, he made it obvious he resented her intrusions. He left whenever she came into the room. When she tried to embrace him, his lips drew back, and he bared his teeth, as if preparing to snarl. One time when she approached him, her arms outstretched, he raised his hand as if to slap her. The gesture alone was enough to sting her; she backed away.

But his behavior gave her a rational reason to leave him, a reason to hate him for what he was doing to herself and her baby.

To leave without telling him she was going would be cowardly. To tell him why she was leaving, where she was going, would be foolhardy. To merely leave a note would be unfair. So, one day when he'd had a few days off and had caught up on his sleep, she told him: "Kevin, I've paid up the lease here until October."

He did not look up from the book he was studying. "I'm not concerned with that."

"Yes. You will be. It will give you a chance to find someplace else to live. I know you can't afford the rent here. And it's larger than you need."

His eyes turned up from the page and flickered and narrowed. "You're kicking me out?"

"No. I'm leaving. Louise and David will arrange to store my furniture."

He let his book slide off his lap. He rose. His face reddened beneath his two-day growth of beard.

She stepped back.

Then he shrugged. The beard became a steel mask, and he seemed to retreat behind it. After a few seconds he said, "I couldn't expect you to stay with me when I need your help most. No one ever does. All women demand and take. You're no different."

There it was again: the implied suicidal threat. She wouldn't give in to guilt. She knew if he did kill himself over her leaving, it wouldn't be her fault. In fact, her leaving without revealing that she was pregnant would be merciful. "I won't demand anything from you."

"You won't get anything, if you do. There won't be anything for you to take."

"Fine!" she burst out, in her anger at his manipulative game. "Fine for both of us. It's how it should be. I have no claim on you. And you have no claim on me. As far as I'm concerned, the last two years never happened. You never happened. There won't be a trace of you in my life when you're gone." She gasped, knowing what the words meant to him, wishing she could take them back.

His fists and lips clenched. His jaw twitched.

Then he turned away, his shoulders slumped. He seemed so weary and discouraged that for a moment she almost changed her mind. She reached out to touch him. "Kevin, you don't need me, and I can't live with you anymore. It will be easier for you, don't you see . . .?"

He stiffened and displayed a silent snarl.

She caught her breath and ran out of the apartment to her already packed car.

Six days later she'd arrived at her parents' home in Phoenix. In March, Cassie was born.

Louise and David flew to Phoenix in April and flew Cassie back with them. Joanna drove back to Philadelphia a week later. She rented an apartment close to the Martin Center, and waited another full week before visiting her sister and her baby.

The adoption story that Louise had spread among friends and relatives was accepted by everyone. Everyone knew that Louise and David Horne loved kids. Everyone knew they had wanted another but hadn't been able to conceive.

Nobody questioned the coincidence of Joanna's six-month leave of absence, and of her return's coinciding almost exactly with Cassie's arrival. She'd concocted an itinerary based on her parents' recent European trip and even had photos and souvenirs to document the fabricated journey. She explained her sudden long leave as arising from a need to get away from a difficult relationship and have one final fling before deciding what she really wanted to do with her life. Friends who knew her romantic nature and her passion for Kevin believed her. They knew how much she loved midwifery and babies; they knew she would be back.

Except for her fear that Kevin would somehow learn the truth, Joanna had seldom thought of him since coming home. Soon he would leave Philadelphia to practice surgery in his midwestern hometown and she could safely acknowledge Cassie as her child. Her friends, she knew, would be happy for her.

But now he had come after her, stalked her to her own office at the Martin Center. He had stood outside her door; and his eyes had not swung away so swiftly when she caught him there, that she hadn't had time to see the old terrors in them. If he learned about Cassie, Joanna would be responsible for what he might do to himself. Or what he might do to her or Cassie. Suicidal people wanted to *kill* as much as they wanted to *die*. The hatred they felt for themselves could turn in a flash against whoever they believed had wronged them.

And she'd wronged him by having his child. She didn't dare let him find out.

She picked up the rest of the papers he'd jarred from her hand when he'd bumped her in his flight. She stuffed them into Wendy Green's folder. In her office she lowered herself into the swivel chair behind her desk.

When Wendy came in moments later, Joanna somehow delivered the routine instructions she gave to all pregnant women. Wendy must have asked her questions; she must have answered them and Wendy must have left, but Joanna couldn't recall.

She paced her office, alternately rubbing her hands

over and over down the front of her lab coat, then twisting a strand of her short brown hair between her fingers. She glanced at the glass front of her enclosed bookcase, and saw her own eyes glance back in fear.

As she'd backed out of the examining room, she'd said to Wendy, "I'm staying here overnight."

He had heard her. She knew he had heard her. He knew about Cassie. Knew her baby was staying with Louise and David.

No, he couldn't have known. Nobody knew but Louise and David. And they would never tell anyone.

She ran to her desk and picked up the telephone. She tapped in her sister's number, let it ring once, then hung up. Suppose he was still here, listening in.

"Stop being foolish, Joanna!" she snapped at herself. "How could he tap your private line?" She picked up the phone again, pressed automatic redial, and waited.

As soon as her sister answered, Joanna's reason deserted her. "Louise. Cassie . . . is she all right?"

"Joanna? Of course she's all right. David's giving her her ten o'clock bottle."

"Put her up to the phone. I want to hear her."

"Joanna, what's wrong?"

"Nothing. I just want to hear my baby."

After a brief hesitation, Louise said, "Hold on a minute. I'll get David to take an extension upstairs."

Joanna heard some muffled sounds in the background. She could picture Louise shaking her red head in bemusement as she ran to the foot of the stairs and hollered up to David, who must have been sitting in the nursery rocking chair and holding his two-month-old niece as she took her last feeding of the day. The baby had smiled the other day when Joanna was feeding her. She could imagine that smile now, opening a small wedge around the nipple, breaking the suction as Cassie took a quick breath.

Everyone said that Cassie looked just like Louise, and that no one would guess she was adopted. "That's why we chose her," Louise always said. But the truth was, Cassie looked like Louise because she looked like Joanna. Both women had hazel eyes, and Cassie had got Joanna's. The reddish hair had bypassed Joanna, but it ran in the family and Cassie had inherited it. Of course it was impossible to attribute a baby's nose to anyone. Cassie's probably wouldn't develop Joanna's arched bridge before puberty. It might not develop it at all, but remain short and straight like Louise's. By then, nobody would care, except Cassie, who would be sure to find it objectionable either way.

What was taking David so long to pick up the telephone? Joanna was ready to scream.

"Sis?" his voice spoke at last.

"I want to hear Cassie."

"Sure. About the only thing she has to say is, 'Slurp, slurp'."

"Please!"

"OK. Don't get hysterical. This isn't like you, Joanna."

She heard some shifting around; then some soft sucking noises and a chirp came over the line.

"Mommy loves you, baby," Joanna said. "Oh, Cassie, I love you so much." She listened to the sounds of feeding for a few moments more, then she heard the rustling of the receiver's being moved.

"OK, Sis? Are you convinced I'm not beating her now?"

Louise's voice cut in. "Don't even joke about it, David Horne. It's not funny. Joanna, what in God's name has got into you? You're not worried about that string of murders?"

A click signaled that David had hung up.

She hadn't thought even once today about the bizarre string of Friday night mother-and-child murders that had stunned Philadelphia, even though the last victim had been her client. "No. I saw Kevin," she said.

She heard Louise draw a breath. "But sooner or later you knew you might, Joanna. You both live in the same city. He'll be here another two years to finish his residency."

"You don't understand. I saw him here."

"In your office?"

"In the hallway. Lurking around my office."

After a second of silence, Louise said, "He probably heard you were back and wanted to see you."

"He didn't want *me* to see *him*. He ran away."

"Are you sure it was Kevin?"

"Yes. I'd know him anywhere. You know that."

Louise sighed. "Well, even if it was, it probably doesn't mean anything. He wasn't exactly happy to lose you. He called here at least a dozen times the first few weeks you were gone."

"You never told me."

"What good would it have done? Eventually he gave up. He must have realized I wasn't going to tell him where you were, that it was over between you. At least you know he didn't kill himself."

"But he might do something desperate if he knows about Cassie. The look in his eyes . . ."

"He doesn't know about Cassie. I told him you'd said you were moving away for good, and that you meant it when you said it was all over."

"Then he knows you were lying." Joanna put her fist up to her mouth. "If you told him I was moving for good, and he found out I'm back, he'll . . ."

"For God's sake, Joanna, he'll just think you changed your mind. The worst thing he'll do is try to convince you to come back to him. And you don't have to go. If he's going to kill himself, you're not going to stop him."

Joanna took a deep breath and said nothing.

"You wouldn't, would you, Jo? That's not what you're afraid of, that you'll turn around and get back in his bed . . .?"

"Never! I don't need that kind of relationship, and you know it. In fact I sometimes wonder why I ever did."

After a brief silence, Louise said, "Yes, of course I know. So you don't have anything to be afraid of."

"Except that if he finds out about Cassie, he might kill himself anyway and blame me."

"Joanna, do you hear what you're saying? You mean, *you* would blame yourself."

Joanna sat back in her swivel chair and shook her head. "Well, yes. I would. I had to make a choice about having Cassie. It was her life over his."

"No it wasn't! Now stop doing just what he'd want you to do. You've done all you can to protect him. More than you should, I sometimes think. He couldn't have found out. And he won't. And as far as Cassie is concerned, she's perfectly safe even if he did."

"I'm sorry, Lou. You're right. Seeing him was just such a shock. I couldn't imagine why he'd be here. We don't share any programs with University Hospital, so why would he come here sneaking around in a scrub suit?"

"To see if you were there, without letting you know. He probably knew you'd reject him."

"Yes. You're right." She laughed, chagrined at her senseless fear. "Give Cassie a good-night kiss from me, will you, Sis?"

"Sure. I'll see you tomorrow morning when you get off duty. You can give her her breakfast bottle."

Joanna put the phone on the hook.

A few moments later it rang again. A woman had given birth in a car on the way to the center, and

Joanna was needed in the birthing room to help deliver the afterbirth and check for any lacerations.

The woman's cervix and vagina were intact after a precipitate delivery. Joanna reassured her that all looked well, then visited the neonatal intensive care unit to check on the baby's condition. After returning to the mother with the message that she would have her new baby at her breast in an hour or so, Joanna ran to the cafeteria for a cup of coffee and a cheese sandwich to take back to her desk. She had to finish setting up an obstetrical record on Wendy Green, and put all the sheets back in order in her folder.

Balancing the plastic-wrapped sandwich on top of the plastic foam cup, she ran from the nearly empty cafeteria to try to catch the single operating elevator before its door *whooshed* shut. Too late. She watched the electronic numbers record its halting flight toward the fifteenth floor. She could tell, after its third hesitation in climbing five levels, she would get to the fourth floor more quickly by taking the stairs. Wondering at the logic that led to the idea of closing down the second elevator after eleven P.M., she pushed open the stairwell door.

She looked up. She could see almost to the top of the well, past the fifteen landings above. The door behind her banged shut, and she suddenly felt trapped.

A nervous giggle escaped her, as she realized how irrational her fears were. But, she was annoyed at having to use a stairway at night. She'd thought, after the third of the mother-child murders, they'd take extra care in a birthing facility.

Echoes of echoes of her footfalls followed her up the stairwell. She fled them, trembling in spite of herself, and sighed with relief as she emerged from the heavy fourth-floor steel door. Here, in the peach-colored corridor of the birthing center office wing, she always felt safe even when she was the only one on call. The excitement of imminent new life pervaded the unit night and day, and seemed to impart an atmosphere of invulnerability. The network set up to deal with nature's demands for immediate service quivered with life and didn't sleep.

Still, she felt haunted and chased. And she was. As she approached her office door, she saw Kevin run out of her office toward the staff elevator at the end of the corridor. She let out the scream that had been lodged in her throat since she had first seen him that evening.

He stopped and turned to her. She saw the pain in his eyes; then he smirked and lifted his arm as if to strike her. After a moment, he dropped his arm and laughed. Then he fled toward the opening doors of the elevator and was swallowed up.

Chapter Two

Thursday

JOANNA COULD HAVE changed him, if she hadn't betrayed him as the others had. But like the others she'd brought out the worst in him with her false love, her eager, greedy words of love. She'd insinuated their viscous juices into his ear; traced them with her venomous tongue in the hollow of his neck; trickled them along his sternum in burning droplets of her saliva; etched them in acid pools into his navel; singed the hair of his belly with them; sucked up the milk of his loins . . . then appalled at the taste, gagged and spat it back out at him, spat it into his face. The milk curdled the words, turned the love in them to hate.

Her face, which once had smiled at him, suddenly began to twist with horror when she looked at him. He'd noticed it soon after he'd accosted Michael, her nephew, in the bathroom after they'd played with his Erector Set tower in his room.

She must have known what he'd done to the boy; why else would her face twist in horror?

But if she had only looked at him with love, taken his hand, led it over her body, offered him her body in forgiveness, he wouldn't have gone back to the children again. When she gave herself to him on the day of his greatest despair the children had, for the first time in his life, lost their hold on him. On that day, he'd decided the only way to be free was by killing himself.

He should have done it then; not fallen under her spell as he had under theirs. The horror in her face seeped down into her body; and when he came near her, she curled away from him like burning paper, and shielded her sex with her hands. She bleated like a frightened lamb. The way the children in the hospital sometimes bleated when he told them what they were drinking from him was doctor's medicine. To make them feel better.

He had no choice.

And then she left him, saying their life together had never existed, wiping it out without a trace, saying that's the way it should be.

That left him with only the ugly parts of his life to remember; and the evil rose in him once more. He fell completely under the children's spell once more. And during the long stretches of work without sleep, he watched the gleaming knife in his hand bring mercy and relief to strangers stretched out on his table. Why had she stopped him from cutting out his own pain?

This time she would not stop him. The means would be simple and clean: A surgeon had at his diposal a myriad of remedies for the pain of life, for the horror of living. A swift sleight of hand in the operating room, and he could palm a precious potion and secrete it under his gown. Yellow powders of pentothal, later to be mixed with sterile saline, and injected into his swollen vein by his own hand. He would arrange himself on a table or bed in her apartment . . . it would be ironic when they found him there and called her home to see what she'd made him do. He'd start a drip infusion from a plastic bag, count backwards from . . . what? Zero, perhaps. That's what his life was worth. No life like his should ever have been allowed to exist. Nothing of him should ever remain in the future.

Nothing would, of course. He'd never married, never had children. He'd never had sex with any fertile woman but Joanna. And she had worn a diaphragm and used spermicide. If he'd produced any children, he'd kill them—for their sake and for the world's. He wouldn't want them to suffer as he had, and he wouldn't want the world to suffer from them. Fortunately for the world and its children, his children had never happened.

Fortunately for the world, when he climbed onto a pallet and started a pentothal drip, it would see the last of him as he saw the last of it, as he counted backward from the zero that had been his life.

Over the following week, he'd gathered his paraphernalia: the sack of sterile saline, a few grams of pentothal powder—enough to do the job twice over or more—some tubing and needles; an IV pole to hang up the drip sack; tourniquet to bring up the vein with the help of a few brisk slaps to his forearm. The last pain he'd inflict on himself or any other lost child. He bought a bottle of vodka. An ounce or so would hasten and assure the end.

The week of preparations tested his nerve, his commitment. On the night he'd set for his self-murder his commitment stood tall as the IV pole he set up in Joanna's apartment. A glass of iced vodka buttressed his nerve as, in a few moments, it would fortify the effects of the pentothal . . .

And then he remembered: He had other things to do. There were people who had to die. People he had to kill before he killed himself. Or his pain would live on forever. But he didn't know their names or where they lived.

He knew who could tell him. And if she refused to tell him, he knew how to find them anyway. And he would track them down, make sure that he was right about them, and put them on a list.

Yesterday in Joanna's office, he'd completed the list he'd started in October. Now they were all there, all six of them—the three he'd already taken care of and three more to go. And she belonged on it, he was sure.

He hadn't been sure he was right about her until yesterday, until he had overheard the conversation. He had had to make absolutely certain, had to follow her long enough so there would be no doubt. He wanted to be methodical, to make sure he got every one so he'd finish the job and make sure no one would figure it out until he delivered the *coup de grace* and killed himself too, and left the note and the tape telling them why, telling them all.

Joanna had seen him. She had screamed. But that was all right. She wouldn't know what he was after till it was too late. She wouldn't realize in time who the last one on his list would be.

Three weeks from now, he would get to her, and that would be when he'd do it. When they found the tape beside her, they'd know that he was the killer;

and they'd figure out why. Till then he would leave
them guessing. Joanna looked terrified when she saw
him. They *all* were guessing now; they had been since
he'd killed the dyke two weeks ago, but he threw them
off last week. He snickered at their reasoning. He knew
the system was all against them, all on his side. They'd
never put it together till he spelled it out for them.
Then they'd look back and say "Hey, if we'd only seen
the connection, we could have saved them."

Tomorrow, he'd get the librarian, dedicating her to
The Librarian. Then over the next two Friday nights
he would get the others. He grinned. They were cow-
ering now on Friday nights, looking over their shoulders. He caught them unawares. He set them all up,
and they never guessed. He dedicated each to an appropriate person. None was as poetically right as the
librarian, except for the dyke; but many women in his
life were loathsome and warranted a dedication. He
already knew whom he'd dedicate the last one to. She
deserved a special tribute.

She and The Librarian.

The Librarian, of course, was already dead, so
though he'd salute her tomorrow when he dealt with
Melanie Roberts, she'd never know. Others might appreciate the poetry, though, when it was all over in
the next few weeks. Joe Byrnes might. He was the
other kid involved in the case, the one who didn't talk
and didn't get blamed for what happened to The Librarian's husband.

Kevin and Joe had lived in row houses next door to
each other on North Street. The Librarian lived in the
house on the other side of Kevin's. Joe was four at the
same time Kevin was five, and neither one knew for
sure that the other was involved in what was going
on. Four-year-olds were babies that went to day care

or stayed home with their mothers all day. Five-year-olds went to kindergarten, and were much too smart to have anything to do with babies.

Kevin was smarter than most five-year-olds, smarter than any fiver The Librarian—who let Kevin call her Elizabeth—ever knew. He'd been reading since he was three, and Elizabeth started bringing home books for him before he was four. He whipped through the Golden Readers for six-year-olds before he was five. She began to bring him high school texts only a few months before it happened.

He didn't understand everything he read, of course, but he liked to try to figure it out. Elizabeth encouraged him. Before taking a book back to the library, she asked him how he liked it. After a while she seemed to realize that he didn't like the dumb, made-up stories in the American Literature Books or what she called "real stories" in the history books, and she began to bring him more scientific things to read. He liked the biology books best of all.

She left for work early every morning that fall and winter. Something in his mind would wake him at just the right minute, and he'd scurry out of his bed and scramble to his bedroom window. His forehead pressed to the chilly pane, he'd rub his fists into his eyes to get the grit out. Then he'd watch her come out her front door. She'd pull her coat tight around her tall, skinny body, shudder a little in the cold, and walk to the corner to take the bus to the center of town, where the library and the museum with the dinosaurs were.

He knew Elizabeth was old, older than his mother, even. Nearly fifty, he'd heard people say. Her husband was even older than that, and didn't work because he'd been hurt in an accident. Kevin's mother once said it was a pity that he wasn't in the military service when it happened, so he could at least get help from the Veteran's Administration, instead of just Social Security, which wasn't much since he and Elizabeth didn't have children.

From a distance, Elizabeth's husband, Forest, didn't even look like he was hurt. He walked around the neighborhood every day without a cane. Close up, Kevin could see something was wrong with his eyes. They were watery blue, with a piece missing from one of his irises, like a pie someone had taken a slice from. And they seemed to wander at cross-purposes in pink-veined, bumpy whites.

Kevin thought it must be awful for Elizabeth, being married to Forest, having to get up six mornings a week, go to the library on the shuttle bus, then come home late and take care of the weird old man. And to have to look in those eyes. Back then, before Kevin did what he did, Elizabeth must have wanted children. She even seemed to want Kevin for her child. Almost every Sunday she spent going over the books he had read that week, stroking the back of his head with her long, trembling bones of fingers, occasionally hugging him.

He'd be sitting there in the crook of her arm, running his finger from word to word and picture to picture in the biology book, when suddenly she'd grab him and pull his face into the hard knot of bone between her surprisingly cushiony breasts. Then she'd let out a cry of delight, and plant a dozen wet kisses all over his face. He liked it and hated it at the same time. It sent chills through to his groin.

Kevin's mother seemed to approve. She encouraged him to spend time with Elizabeth. "She needs you, Kevin," his mother often said. "Poor woman. I doubt that she gets any affection at all, at home. Humor her, dear."

He didn't know what "humor her" meant. But the truth was, he loved bony old Elizabeth and all the books she brought him. That was part of the reason he did what he did.

He never expected her to do what she did to him, to make him want to kill himself.

Well, now he *would* kill himself. His list was complete, and the next one on it was a librarian. Melanie Roberts. He knew all about Melanie; he had followed her around for months now. She worked at a high school library in Bryn Mawr. He could tell, from the way she ran to her car after school let out in the afternoons, that she couldn't wait to get home to her three children. She was much younger than Elizabeth The Librarian had been when five-year-old Kevin had loved her. A five-year-old boy, her own, loved Melanie, as did the two others, another boy and a two-year-old girl.

Kevin had his eye on the girl. He had watched from his car or on a bench by a neighborhood park playground, as Melanie played with her on the weekends. Her mother obviously thought she was beautiful, but Kevin had seen her ugliness. He had studied the child; her amber eyes, like her mother's, showed no hint of her father's green. But her hair, thick and brown, must have come from her father. And he could see by the way she handled the seesaw and the swings that even at two, in spite of her ugliness, she showed signs of athletic grace. Her father had never fully developed his athletic propensities, having devoted himself to sharpening other skills.

Like father, like daughter, he thought. Neither had had a chance.

Too bad.

Chapter Three

Thursday evening

JOANNA DIDN'T THINK she'd slept, until the ring of the telephone split itself off from the other sickening gongs in her head. She lay in the dark for a while among the crumpled sheets and wondered how she had gotten back here to her own apartment, and why pain gripped the muscles of her shoulders and neck.

After several rings, she realized she'd been home since seven A.M., and that she'd driven herself to her own apartment instead of to Louise's house, so that if Kevin were following her, he would not suspect that Cassie was Joanna's baby. That is, if he didn't already know.

He hadn't followed her home; at least she hadn't seen him, either during the five-minute drive, or in the secured parking lot at the rear of the building, or in the brief lobby, where she stopped to pick up yesterday's mail and to look over her shoulder before summoning the elevator that took her to her fifth floor apartment.

The pains in her muscles and head must have come from the nightmares she'd been fleeing since she'd fallen, exhausted, into the bed, still wearing her bra and slip.

Another shrill ring sharpened the boundary between dream and reality. She answered the telephone.

"Joanna?" he said. "You sound like I just woke you up. I'm sorry to make such a clumsy reentry into your life."

She didn't recognize the voice; but it wasn't Kevin's. "Reentry?" she said, after a pause.

"Yes. It's been a while. At least it seems like that to me. I didn't mean to wake you."

"Oh, Jon. It's all right. I was having a horrible dream. What time is it?"

"Seven-thirty. You must have worked last night. I'm sorry."

"I did. And it wasn't the best of nights. But I'm glad you woke me up. I'd have slept through till two or three in the morning, and really been off schedule. It's good to hear your voice."

Her mind was beginning to focus on her surroundings. She could see a slim border of dim light around the edges of the blinds on the south-facing window of the bedroom. She stood up, and took a few steps from her bed, then twisted the plastic wand that opened the narrow blind slats. The gray granite north face of the office building across the wide street dulled the ebbing day's glare. The soft light that entered her bedroom allowed a gentle transition for her eyes to adjust to as she surveyed her messy room. She had dumped her skirt, blouse, and panty hose on the floor between her queensize bed and her walnut desk and pulled the striped aqua bedspread off the foot of the bed onto the beige carpet, before collapsing on top of the sheets this morning. Only the neat stacks of papers on her clean-lined desk and the well-organized grooming items on her immaculate walnut dresser reflected the usual orderliness of her life.

"Dave told me last week you were back in town," Jon Isenson said.

Before taking his present job as a marketing vice president for an insurance company, her brother-in-law David had worked for Pharmogenetix Corporation, a drug manufacturer with a home office located in North Wales, a suburb about twenty miles north of Philadelphia. She'd met blue-eyed red-headed Jon Isenson, Pharmogenetix's veterinarian, through David about four years ago when Jon was withdrawing from a long-term romantic involvement with a woman who'd married someone else.

Joanna had suspected that Jon's precipitous passion for her was a result of rebound fever. So she'd entered their relationship with caution. That may have tempered her own passion a bit too much. She allowed herself to like him and enjoy his company. But she turned down his marriage proposals—not just because they came too soon and suddenly, but because he was too "safe".

Her father, like Jon, had been a corporation man in a large established company. He'd spent his entire career playing it safe and climbing the ladder. His only Holy Grail had seemed to be the pension and retirement fund that would give him and her mother lifetime security. He'd reached that goal early enough to retire to Phoenix before he was sixty-two. And her mother seemed satisfied to enjoy the relaxed lifestyle, with its golf and tennis and swimming. Joanna loved her parents; she was glad they were happy and secure. But to her their world seemed dull and uninspiring, too damn risk free.

That's why she'd chosen midwifery. It was *truly* the oldest profession . . . and the newest, too; for only in the last decade had nurses been able to practice it legally and as colleagues with physicians. Her profession was constantly under fire from a jealous medical profession. And capricious Mother Nature constantly threw up hazards and obstacles for her well-honed skills and sharp intelligence to trip over. Each time she did her job, danger hovered over her. And this excited her; she thrived on it.

So how could she even consider marrying someone like Jon Isenson, who'd chosen the safety of an executive position in a research lab rather than the uncertainty of a private veterinary practice? For a while he served as a pleasant counterpoint to the excitement of her job, a warm and considerate lover. But she knew that in the long run they'd fit poorly together. So she kept one eye open for someone a little more exciting and challenging.

Kevin had been all that and more, she thought with some bitterness now, as Jon's secure, calm voice broke through the lingering grip of her nightmare.

She shifted the phone to her other hand and answered his question. "Yes, I'm back," she said.

"And, you've decided what you want to do with your life. Went to Europe to sort it all out, I hear."

She took a deep breath. "That's what David told you?"

"Should he have told me something different?"

"No! I mean, of course not."

"And have you?"

"Have I what?"

"Sorted it out."

"I don't know." Irritation crept into her voice.

He hesitated a moment. "Maybe I ought to call back some other time, Joanna. I got you out of the wrong side of bed."

"No, Jon. I'm glad you called. I really am. Your voice is . . . reassuring."

"My presence would be even more so."

She smiled. "Yes. I think it would be." She hadn't thought of comforting herself with her old friend's company. She'd been hiding herself from anyone who might guess the truth; now she realized she had to begin a semblance of a normal social life. And suddenly she hungered for the safety that Jon represented. As much as she once had its opposite.

"I just want to be sure of one thing, though. That difficult relationship you went to Europe to get away from. That's over?"

She paused. Then she said, "Yes."

"You don't sound sure."

"Jon, I left Kevin because he was acting crazy. The surgical residency was getting to him. I don't think he's emotionally cut out to be a doctor. And I wasn't helping him."

"You still don't sound sure it's over."

"I left him because I was afraid of him."

"Jesus, Joanna. That bastard—did he . . .?"

"No, I was afraid of what he might do to himself. Because of me."

"Stop taking the rap for him."

"I'm not. I just should have known better than to get involved with a crazy man in the first place."

"I'm sure you didn't know he was crazy in the first place. It's hard to see the line between genius and madness sometimes. Anyway, you need to get out of your doldrums. How long will it take you to get dressed to go out to dinner?" he asked.

She looked at her reflection in her dresser mirror. Her short brown hair was matted, her pale skin creased where the crumpled sheets had embossed it. "About half an hour," she answered. "I'll need a good shower."

Jon arrived thirty-five minutes later, wearing a light blue sport coat that highlighted his eyes, beige slacks, and a blue-and-beige plaid shirt that brought out the freckles of his face, making him look more tanned that he could possibly be in May in Philadelphia.

"We have a lot to catch up on," he said, after he'd bent and kissed her unromantically on the lips. Without waiting for her to reply, he helped her into her light tan suede and knit jacket and complimented her on the aquamarine print silk challis dress she had slipped over her head only moments before he arrived.

In his car she told him about her European adventure and promised she'd show him the photos some other time.

By the time they had squeezed themselves into a small red vinyl booth at the rear of a southern Italian restaurant frequented by University of Pennsylvania and Drexel students, she had recited the familiar script and turned the conversation to him.

"What have I been doing? Well, I almost got married," he said, after the waiter had taken their orders and brought them a carafe of vinegar-tinged white wine identified as the house brand.

"Congratulations." She tipped her glass toward him.

He nodded at her half-mocking toast. "Well, you were away, and I got lonely. The lady was in trouble, and I've always imagined myself an amateur detective. So I got involved with her case. I think I saved her life, but I lost her love."

"So you're on the rebound again."

"Right."

"Well, I'm familiar with that. But I just can't imagine you as a detective. Much too risky." She laughed.

The waiter snaked through the nearby tables and set before them two thick, white plates piled with pasta shells bathed in a rich red garlicky meat sauce. She breathed in the steam, which was redolent of memories from evenings with Jon when they had been friends and lovers. Then his boyishness had seemed unsophisticated and naive. She'd taken his warmth and attentiveness for granted, as part of what men did to get into women's beds. Now his grin seemed wonderful and restorative.

He wrinkled his forehead and sniffed at his meal

before taking a great forkful and savoring it. His red eyebrows arched and registered satisfaction.

It's not so farfetched for me to be a detective. I'm always looking for culprits in the Pharmogenetix animal lab. And it's riskier than you might think. I've had death threats from animal rights activists."

"I'm with them," she said, only half joking. "It would serve you right for ordering innocent dogs and cats to the death chamber, then cutting them and their fetuses up to see how the drugs you deliberately overdose them on turn their flesh into cancer and their livers into cottage cheese." She turned up her nose. "You *are* the culprit there, Jon."

"Am I? Is that why our product labels warn your clients against taking our pills when they're pregnant or nursing their babies?"

She put down her fork on her plate and held up her hand, palm toward him, while she swallowed a bite of her pasta. "I know. You've explained it before. I just have a hard time seeing you in that situation. You're just too nice a guy."

"Well, it does make me a detective. I sift through all the evidence and find out just how much of our drug it takes to make dogs and monkeys feel worse instead of better. And which drugs are the bad guys, and how we can stop them."

"Maybe you can stop the bad guy that's running around Philadephia murdering mothers and babies every Friday night." She shuddered, realizing that tonight was Thursday.

He grew solemn. "I wish they'd find the connection on that one. I've tried to figure it out."

"I guess everyone's trying to. It's scary wondering who's next."

"I know the husband and father of the first one."

"Oh, Jon . . ." She reached across the table and touched the back of his hand.

"He works for Pharmogenetix."

"The last one was one of my clients," Joanna said. "The little boy was just two last month."

He looked at her. "You knew them?"

"More like recalled the name. I've delivered over a hundred babies since then. There wasn't anything remarkable about her that I know of."

"Nothing at all?" His expression was intense.

She knit her brow then shook her head. "She was just a woman having a baby, and he was a normal newborn. It was far more important to them than it was to me. At that time, I figured that lots of women have babies. It's always a miracle, always exciting, but I don't get overly caught up in the moment anymore." She looked away from his face for a second and focused on a breastlike shape that was part of the design of the dirty, high, ornate ceiling, remembering Cassie's birth. Then she looked back at him and smiled weakly.

"You couldn't be expected to. But you do keep records."

"Sure. Everything about a birth is recorded."

"So you could really learn a lot about her background. All sorts of things. Medical, social, psychological."

"Sure. But why should I? I think the police could learn a lot more. Including recent things I'd have no way of knowing. They would know I delivered her and would ask me if they needed my input. So far they haven't."

He leaned forward across the table. The freckles on his face knit together. He squeezed her hands. "Joanna, between us we know an awful lot about two sets of victims. Maybe we could find some connection."

"You really take this detective thing seriously, Jon."

His boyish intensity half amused, half surprised her.

He dropped her hands and sat back, his face darkening with obvious embarrassment. "I guess I do. It's kind of challenging. Especially since tomorrow's Friday."

"That's a chilling thought." She shivered.

"Especially for you," he said.

"What do you mean?" She felt her eyes narrow.

"You're involved with a lot of mothers and babies. That killer could be stalking someone else you know right now."

"Or someone else *you* know, Jon."

"You must be worried about your sister and her baby."

"Sure I'm concerned. But there's hardly a connection."

He made his point: "That's just it. How can we be sure? There's *some* connection between those victims. It's just that nobody's found it. Joanna, we each know a victim. Know something about them anyway, or can find out."

"Well, we know that all of them were naturally born from their mothers. Louise's baby is adopted. So, really, Jon, I think she's safe." She heard a shrill edge on her voice, and took a deep breath as she reminded herself that, yes, Louise and Cassie were safe; nobody knew that Joanna was Cassie's mother.

"Right. So what have we got? The oldest baby was about two; there were two girls and a boy; all of the mothers were natural."

The waiter approached the table and asked if they wanted more coffee and dessert. She nodded at the suggestion of coffee, and he ordered amaretto cheesecake. Joanna's mind was playing with what Jon had just said.

"The lesbian, Jon. She was a natural mother, but did she conceive naturally?"

He smiled. "The press really worked that one over. Till the third pair of victims were killed, they thought some homophobe did it. Maybe a copycat. The, ah, widow told the police they had been harassed by some neighborhood guys for some time since the baby was born. But they came up clean. As to the nature of her insemination—it was artificial. She'd never had a male lover in her life."

Joanna said, "Maybe a homophobe *did* kill her. I imagine some macho guys would be appalled at the very idea of a lesbian having a baby. The others may really be unconnected after all."

Feeling suddenly tired, she sat back and rested her head on the cracked red vinyl upholstery of the booth and closed her eyes. She heard the clink of a dish on the table, and opened them. The waiter had placed Jon's cheesecake in front of him.

"I brought the lady a fork if she'd like to share," he said.

Joanna smiled and nodded. Jon pushed the plate to the center of the table, and their forks nibbled their way toward the center of the slice. When Jon finished the final morsel he checked his watch, declared it was after midnight, and ushered her, yawning, to his silver Volvo.

For a while he drove silently. Then he asked, "My place or yours?"

She tensed. "Both," she said.

He looked at her, his eyebrows copper question marks in the yellow light from the streetlights.

"I'll go to my place; you go to yours."

"I'm sorry. I'm not usually quite so presumptuous."

"The only thing wrong with your presumption is that it's a bit premature." She reached for his arm. "You're not out of line, Jon."

As he began to turn left onto Market Street, he glanced at her with a smile of relief. Then, a bright light suddenly reflected in his eyes, and he swung his glance back toward the road.

"Oh, my God!" he cried, as he twisted the steering wheel.

She felt the car lurch toward the right. The tires screeched. Metal crunched. Her side of the windshield shattered as debris crashed through it.

The car spun, then stopped, as the other vehicle bounced off it. With her breath knocked out by her sudden forward thrust into the seat belt and shoulder harness, she was too stunned to cry out. When Jon looked at her and said, "Oh, my God, Joanna, I'm sorry," she realized the warm fluid running down her face, and the red film that covered her eyes, came from a burning spot high on her forehead.

The deserted street suddenly teemed with people who'd poured out of tall apartment buildings. Jon, who hadn't a scratch, leaned over Joanna. He ripped off his jacket and shirt, and pressed the shirt against her forehead. People jamming around the crashed cars shouted instructions: "Better get her out, in case of a fire," and, "Jesus, look at the guy in the other car!" Joanna felt surprisingly clear-headed. As Jon wiped the blood from her eyes, she watched the milling samaritans with fascination. They scattered as sirens and whirling lights approached; a few minutes later she lay inside an ambulance, with an oxygen tube in her nose, and the harsh radio chatter of the parameds communicating with the hospital in her ears.

She thought that they overdid caution by starting a glucose drip into her vein. She knew she could have walked into the emergency room, instead of having three people wheel her through the parting glass doors on a gurney, and two others help transfer her to a bed. They pulled the white privacy curtains around her as a nurse checked her pulse then examined under the pressure bandage the paramedics had replaced Jon's shirt with against her forehead. The emergency room doctor, a young brunette woman who looked familiar, examined her head and face with exploring fingers, and her eyes with a bright halogen opthalmoscope whose light seared Joanna's retinas.

"Your pupils are equal and reactive. There's no sign of any concussion. It looks like that cut on the forehead is going to need sewing up, though." She stood back from the bed. "OK, let's get a look at the rest of you. I hope that pretty dress can be washed. You'll have to pull it off over your head."

"No," said Joanna. "I'm fine. Something came through the windshield and cut me. I was wearing a seat belt. I didn't bump into anything."

"Look, I can't take a chance on missing something. I've got to check your abdomen. Now that you're here, we're responsible for you." The woman fixed her brown eyes on Joanna. They flickered a moment. "Haven't I seen you before?"

"I don't know."

"Well, let me help you take that dress off. We had a woman in here who fell and cut her face up. We fixed up her face just fine, but we didn't do an abdominal on her, and we missed a bruise. Two weeks later she was in here again for an emergency gall bladder. The fall had broken up gallstones she didn't even know she had." The doctor helped Joanna reluctantly pull her dress over her hips.

"I didn't fall."

"Nonetheless . . ." the doctor began. She pulled Joanna's slip up as Joanna pulled her panty hose down. She began to tap her fingers on Joanna's taut midsection. "Relax. It won't take very long. Everything looks fine." She told Joanna to take a deep breath and pressed down hard just below her ribcage.

"Liver's not palpable." She let go and looked down at Joanna and smiled. "That's good. It's not supposed to be.

"I know," said Joanna.

The doctor studied her face for a second. "You're a nurse, aren't you? I've seen you around someplace."

"Yes. Can I get dressed now?"

"You might as well leave your dress off till we get the surgical resident to stitch up that laceration. The nurse has already called him. Meanwhile, I'll need to take a history. We'll start at the top."

Joanna nodded, pulled her panty hose back on, and tugged her slip back down. She dutifully answered the doctor's questions on all her body systems. As she'd seldom been sick and never had any surgery, the history didn't take long.

"OK, when did your periods begin?"

"I was thirteen."

"Any menstrual problems? Pain, hemorrhage, irregularity?"

"No."

"How many pregnancies?"

"None."

The doctor looked at her quizzically. "No abortions or miscarriages?"

"I told you, no pregnancies."

The doctor looked down toward Joanna's abdomen, and knit her brow. Then she said, "Well, you're not here for that anyway, are you?" She flashed her a knowing smile.

"When will the resident be here? I just want to go home."

"Dr. Willman should be here any minute now. He just finished up an emergency in the O.R."

Joanna felt her color flee. The doctor looked at her again.

"Now I know where I've seen you," she said. "Aren't you the one who used to come to the cafeteria to eat with Kevin Willman when he was an intern?"

Joanna said nothing.

"Yes. That's it. Well, he's been a regular bear since he started his residency. No wonder you don't come to dinner with him anymore."

"Yes," said Joanna, feeling faint.

The woman laughed. "Don't worry about your surgery, though. The man's impeccable with his scalpel, and he's an absolute artist with the sutures. Better than most plastic surgeons. Besides your cut being right at the hairline, he'll do such a neat job, you probably won't be able to see a scar in six weeks."

Dr. Kevin Willman pulled back the privacy curtain that separated Joanna's bed from the others in the emergency room. He looked at Joanna and smiled. "In six weeks, I guarantee, she won't see a thing, Dr. Randolph," he said.

"Just as I told her. I've examined her thoroughly, Kevin. Nothing neurological, that I can see. And her abdomen's negative, too. My findings and the history are all on the form." She held out the records to him.

He brushed them aside. "I'll look at them later, if I have any questions. Meanwhile, would you get the nurse to bring me a prep for her repair." He took a pair of sterile gloves by the inside of the cuffs from a wrapper the woman offered him, pulled them skillfully over his hands, then studied the laceration on Joanna's forehead.

She avoided his eyes and looked away from the scornful curl of his lip.

She tried to read the examination form the emergency room doctor had placed on the stand beside the bed. She knew the woman had seen the *linea negra*—that brown-pigmented line bisecting her abdomen from her navel to her pubic hair, that told unmistakably that Joanna had recently been pregnant. And that her pregnancy had progressed quite far.

As Kevin stitched up the tiny wound on Joanna's face, she prayed that the woman had not written it down on the form. After all, as she'd said, Joanna was not here for that.

Still, a thorough physician wanting to show off her physical examination skills might have written it down.

And a surgeon as impeccable as his colleague said Kevin was might later go over the record and learn the truth.

He put twenty-two stitches on her forehead just below her hairline, then peeled off his gloves, smiled at her, picked up the records, and left without saying a word.

Chapter Four

When the wind blows . . .

MELANIE ROBERTS ESCAPED the overheated high school media center at four-thirty on Friday afternoon. The chill outdoors surprised her; for since noon the early May sun had shone into the high bank of windows that gave the remodeled library at the hub of the forty-four-year-old school building its modern look.

Unprepared for the sudden cold blast that cut

through the stand of ancient oak trees lining the broad cement walk to the parking lot, she hunched her thin shoulders and pulled her lightweight blue suit jacket tightly around her. In the shadows of the gray-and-brown stone towers that, along with the wrought-iron-speared fences, made the school look like a castle, the nearly deserted parking lot looked forbidding.

She ran, keys in hand, to her car at the farthest end of the lot, inserted and turned the key in a single motion, scrambled in, locked the door after her. The cold had settled in before her; it gripped her until she at last pulled away from the school and onto the section of Bryn Mawr Road that led south-westward to the day-care center where she'd pick up her two-year-old, Tammy. The sun soon warmed the car, and thoughts of her daughter—her very own child—warmed her soul.

Melanie loved the two boys, too. Others thought she naturally cared less for them. Tammy just seemed more vulnerable, more exposed. When the boys were smaller, their father had more time for them. Then, he was not on the road three weeks out of four as he was now, handling large accounts for his management consulting firm. Before Tammy was born, he handled only the local market—a computer firm here, a small manufacturer of machine dies there. Now he had been rewarded with more money and a company car and sent to cover the Central Atlantic region that stretched from Maryland to New York. Tammy saw her father only on weekends and during the one week a month when he was home. And, even then, he spent more time with the boys. They were the children of his first marriage, which had ended with the tragic death of his young wife. He knew them better from having to do all the things for them that Melanie now did for Tammy. Like picking her up from day care and taking her to the neighborhood playground after work.

Tammy was waiting by the day-care center gate when Melanie arrived. Five minutes later they reached the playground, which—shaded by tall newly leafed maples at its perimeter—chilled Melanie again. She pulled her jacket tight around her.

Tammy didn't seem to mind the chill. Her dark brown curls danced in the wind that blew across the playground and twisted the unoccupied swings on her either side as she twisted the one she was riding. She turned to her shivering mother and begged her to push her swing higher.

Melanie rubbed her hands together a moment, then pushed harder. Tammy squealed as the swing rose to new heights with every push. Melanie was amazed as always by her daughter's lack of fear. She herself was always reluctant to push as hard as Tammy demanded. The man who often sat on the bench next to the wire trash basket about a hundred yards from the swings would sometimes stare disapprovingly as the fearful mother gave in to the demands of her fearless child.

He stared now as Tammy arced through the air and let go of the chain at the height of her flight, making Melanie gasp. Though the child was secured into the swing by a rod at the waist, there was nothing to keep her from sliding between rod and seat. And as a sharp gust of wind set the empty swings rocking and clacking together, the chains of one tangled around Tammy's and her joyful squeals turned to shrieks.

For a moment the swing seemed to pause; then it dropped, tilted to one side, and rocked stiffly. Tammy slid under the rod and hung half wedged there a few yards above the ground.

As Melanie stood helpless, and cried out, the man who had been watching ran over and set his foot on one of the empty seats. He raised himself up, carefully untangled the chains, and slowly lowered the child's swing to where Melanie could grasp her and loosen her from its grip.

Still shaking, Melanie untangled her baby, then clasped her tightly. Tammy screamed for a few moments, then allowed her mother to carry her to the car and secure her in the car seat. By the time Melanie looked up, the man had disappeared. He left her feeling guilty and vulnerable.

Though Tammy soon shook off the near disaster, Melanie couldn't. She snapped at the boys as she readied them for bed, and hung on to Tammy before putting her into bed, as if she could thereby recapture her from the swing and erase the afternoon's mishap.

She read her a bedtime story. The child, thumb in mouth, fell asleep before it was over, undisturbed by the whining of wind, the creaking of old oak trees, the shudders of lifted roof shingles . . . the sighs of her distraught mother.

Melanie twisted the cloth story book in her hands, then smoothed it before placing it in Tammy's bed. The baby would find it in the morning, and look at the pictures while she waited for her mother to take her downstairs for breakfast.

Melanie raised the crib rails quietly and stood looking down at her baby. She trembled again at the memory of her carelessness and the danger she'd put Tammy in. Tammy, the baby she'd taken such risks to have, because she'd had to have a child of her own; because, as much as she loved the boys from Frank's first marriage, they weren't enough. *They weren't hers.*

She kissed her own hand and placed it on Tammy's cheek. "No more, silly baby. I'll never push you so high again."

Tammy sighed and sucked a few times on her thumb. Melanie crept from the nursery and closed the door softly behind her. Then she opened it a crack, so she could hear the baby.

Melanie went downstairs to the living room and sat on the sofa, where she could hear the slightest sound from upstairs. She tried to read the newspaper, but her ears pricked up at every untoward noise that came from the nursery. The shutters of the old Bryn Mawr house shivered with each damp gust of wind. The ceilings crackled and creaked. Would Frank never get home! She hated being alone when a storm set the house wailing.

A cold tremor ran along Melanie's arms and up the back of her neck. The creaks in the ceiling were no longer random like the wind. They now tracked their way past the nursery down the upstairs hallway. She started up the stairs, tripping in her hurry, then scrambled up the remaining stairs.

The bathroom door slammed.

Her knees grew weak, and she slumped down at the top of the stairs feeling foolish till she saw her older boy emerge from the bathroom and run back to his bedroom.

She laughed uneasily. If only she were as smart as her own two-year-old, she'd forget the incident in the park, go to bed, and curl up and fall asleep. Frank would wake her when he got home.

A warm bath would help. She filled the tub in the master bathroom with hot water and bubble bath, and soaked the anxiety out of her muscles and bones. Twenty minutes later, in her cotton gown and terry-cloth robe, she went downstairs to the kitchen for a glass of warm milk.

The hum of the microwave oven and its timer's beep masked the sounds from the living room. When she heard footsteps overhead, she realized Frank was home.

She smiled and took the cup of milk from the oven.

From the foot of the stairs she called up to him. "Hi, dear."

There was no reply. He was probably in the nursery, checking Tammy, and didn't want to wake her. Yes, that's where she heard his footsteps now.

She smiled to herself again, pleased that he loved Tammy so much, even though he'd argued against letting Melanie get pregnant. She'd not interrupt his intimate moments with their daughter. She sat down on the sofa, listening as his footsteps moved from the nursery into the upstairs hallway and toward the stairs. She smiled as she saw him emerging from the shadows of the stairwell.

"Hi, dear. Welcome home."

She let the glass drop. Her hand went up to her throat. It was the man who had rescued Tammy from the tangled swing. Tammy lay in his arms. Deadly still in his arms.

His green eyes glowed with a mad intensity. Melanie moved her numb arms, reaching out, imploring him with her eyes to give her her baby.

Then, with a curl of his lips, he held out the baby. Only then did she see blood dripping from the baby's blanket. Her baby—her only child—was dead.

She seized the blood-soaked blanket of the child and hugged it to her breast, buried her head in it. He allowed her this final embrace, stood back, watching with obvious pleasure.

Then, as the wind rose outside, rattling the shutters, tossing and tangling Melanie in guilty despair for her heavenward arcing daughter, he pulled a shiny scalpel from under his belt and plunged it into her throat.

In the moment before the dark wind carried her off, she heard him laugh softly.

Chapter Five

Saturday morning

JOANNA BURIED HER nose in Cassie's soft copper hair as she gave her her bottle. She had rushed over here to Louise's the moment she'd seen the Philadelphia *Inquirer* headlines. Her blood still beat against the tight wound on her forehead, but the sound of it in her ears had waned in the comfort of her sister's modern blue-hued living room.

As Cassie drained the bottle and let go of the nipple with a satisfied grunt, Joanna could hear Louise and David in the kitchen, discussing last night's murder with puzzled and horrified but impersonal interest. Their voices wafted in on the safe aroma of toast and coffee. She could hear Michael playing upstairs in his room to the sound of a children's television program. Routine. Normal.

She lifted Cassie to her shoulder, and rose as the antique bentwood rocking chair creaked under her. She carried her into the kitchen and sat down at the table.

"Well, you look a little better than when you came in," said David.

"I feel better. Thanks for being here. I'm not used to living lics. Or of asking anyone clsc to. I should've found some other way to handle this. I didn't have to come back. At least not till Kevin was gone."

Louise got up from the table and poured Joanna some coffee. "Some egg and toast?" she asked, and turned to the business of scrambling an egg for her sister.

David, finished with his breakfast and the paper, shoved his chair back from the table and reached over for Cassie. Joanna kissed the baby's head and gave her up to her uncle. The tiny head bounced on his shoulder. Joanna followed the bobbing wisps of her baby's reddish hair with her eyes till he grasped the wrought iron stair rail and started up the stairs.

Louise brought Joanna's breakfast and set it before her. "This way was best for Cassie and you. She knows who her mother is, and she's getting our love all day. I don't feel any of us are living a lie. Mom and Dad know. No one outside of the family has to know till we're ready to tell them."

"I saw Kevin again," said Joanna.

Louise sat down hard in her chair. "Oh, Joanna! Then he *is* following you!"

"No. It wasn't like that." She described what had happened in the emergency room.

"But he didn't see you undressed."

"No. But the doctor might have written it in the record. Something like, '*Linea negra* present. Denies past pregnancy.'"

"Would that be ethical? Sounds judgmental to me."

"I guess it depends. Something left out of a record can come back to haunt you. Still, as she said, I wasn't there for anything related to pregnancy. In that case, if she put it in, it was gratuitous. She was walking a very fine line." Joanna shrugged and began to eat her egg, which was cold.

"Oh, Jo. I guess I'd feel paranoid, too. But if Kevin was going to kill himself over you, he'd have done it by now. He doesn't suspect about the baby, so even if she wrote something down, he probably never even saw it. He was concentrating on fixing your forehead. If he did want to get even with you for walking out on him, well, your accident must have made him *feel* better. Or at least a bit smug."

Joanna sighed. "You're right, Sis. I'll get hold of myself and go back to a more normal life. I'm going to start seeing Jon again."

"That'll be good for you both. David never forgave you for screwing up his matchmaking plans. Now maybe you won't think some crazy killer is after you."

"I wonder who he *is* after. I only read the headline. Did they find any pattern?" She reached across the table for the newspaper.

"Nothing but the murderer's style. He killed the baby first again. Slashed its throat. In the nursery. Carried it to the mother. They could tell from the trail of blood. Then after he killed the mother, he slashed her abdomen. The uterus again. They're beginning to think that's deliberate. As if he's trying to wipe out her womanhood or fertility or something."

Joanna looked at the woman's photograph. Beautiful. In her mid-thirties. A high school librarian, loved by everyone who knew her, it said. Left a husband and two other children. She shuddered and shoved the paper away. "At least I don't know this one," she said.

"Did you know the others?"

"One of them. A client of mine. I'm glad there's no connection with the Martin Center."

Louise looked at her. "You didn't think there was?"

"No. But Jon and I were talking Thursday night. I mentioned that I knew last week's victims, and he got all excited. He knew the first one's husband. From work. He wanted me to start going through this Kimski woman's records, to see if there was some connection."

Louise laughed. "He's playing detective again. You'd better watch out."

"It's a side of him I've never seen. Kind of intriguing. Anyway, he did make me curious. Somebody'd better discover the relationship between that killer and his victims soon. Now there are four pairs of victims. They didn't live near each other. They didn't resemble one another physically. This woman had dark brown hair, one was blond, the other two had different shades of brown. One came from a wealthy background—the lesbian, wasn't it?" They nodded in unison, as if Joanna were thinking out loud for both of them.

"And the other three were middle class," Louise added. "But none of them poor. Well, poor mothers can breathe a sigh of relief."

"Like me. After six months of unemployment, plus paying for Cassie's delivery ... Thank God I had Mother and Dad to take their wayward daughter in." She looked up at Louise. "And you and David."

"Excuse me, dear sister—Weren't you the one who babysat Michael on your evenings off so I could go back to finish college? Those were the days when David and I were poor."

Joanna smiled tightly and gave a short nod. "OK. I guess it's your turn. It just seems suddenly I'm taking from everybody. And I don't like it."

"Nope. My *independent* sister would rather be poor."

"I wonder if money might have to do with those murders, Louise."

"No money or valuables were ever missing. The man was obviously just out to get mothers and babies. Probably hated his mother. Maybe he was jealous of a sibling."

"Why does it have to be a man? It could be a woman."

"They found bloody footprints. He wears size eleven shoes. They know it has to be a tall man. That's one thing they know for sure. And today's paper says it's the same man in every case. He even wears the same shoes every time. Can you imagine that, Joanna! How can he walk around in bloody shoes?"

"Maybe he wants to get caught. They usually do."

"Jon's not the only one playing detective. Listen to the two of us, Joanna. I guess it helps keep us from being terrified. Finding reasons why we aren't next."

"I think I'm going to check out Irene Kimski's records after all. Maybe I *will* find something," said Joanna.

By Sunday evening, home after a satisfying weekend spent in motherly abandon with Cassie, Joanna found the question of Irene Kimski's background nagging at her. A message from Jon on her telephone answering machine fueled her curiosity further. Instead of calling him back right away, she threw on a light jacket and drove to her office.

The birthing center office wing was quiet. The last light had fled from the sky outside her office window. The on-call staff were gathered in the lounge or the cafeteria.

She switched on her swing-arm desk lamp and slid open one of three horizontal file drawers in the tan unit against her back wall. The drawer was thick with folders; the folders were thick with the minutiae surrounding momentous moments; both the moments and the minutiae would be forgotten in the life's traumas sure to follow. The moments could not be retrieved, but the trivia surrounding it could be searched, researched for meaning.

She flipped through the charts and pulled Irene Kimski's.

Of all medical records, an obstetrical record was one of the most comprehensive; besides the mother's complete health history from birth, it often included genealogical information for genetic screenings. Joanna faced the stack of papers with trepidation.

She recalled the time when she was a poor, graduate nursing student. To help pay her tuition, she worked part-time for a company that produced chemical kits for diagnostic tests. She called on physicians, carrying a large black sample case of testing kits. The company had recently produced a new urine dip stick with possibilities for twelve different tests that covered everything from diabetes to brewing urinary tract infections.

She had just gone through her pitch with an arrogant young family doctor. He had sniffed and curled his mustachioed lip and pushed back his chair. He dismissed her, saying, "What am I going to do with all that data?"

At the time she'd thought him rude and unwilling to see the value of her employer's accomplishments in making his diagnoses. Now she saw that he had meant that too much information was just as bad as too little. The record on her desk was like a multicolored litmus strip that enticed with all its possibilities. But it offered her too many roads to follow at once before she even knew where she was going.

Where should she start? At the beginning, she decided, and just read through to the end.

She took notes on her notes for an hour, then read through her scribblings and shook her head. She still wasn't sure what she was looking for. It was late. She closed up the chart and put it away, taking her notebook home with her. She figured she was a far better midwife than detective. Maybe Jon could make sense of it later this week.

Joanna did not have to wait. To her irritation he was pacing her apartment lobby when she arrived. "How did you get in?"

"It was easy—I grabbed the door behind someone else coming in."

"That took nerve."

"Joanna! I've been trying to reach you since yesterday."

"I got your message on my machine."

"Then why didn't you call?"

She shifted her tote bag from one shoulder to the other. "I planned to call tomorrow. I'm tired."

"I haven't seen you since I took you home after the accident. Don't you think you should have let me know how you were?"

She opened her mouth, then closed it on her intended testy response. "I suppose so. I'm sorry. It was thoughtless. I thought you knew I was fine."

"You didn't seem fine when I took you home. You seemed upset."

She jangled her keys in her hand and started toward the elevator. "I *was* upset. But I was fine, too. Didn't they discharge me? If they'd thought I was in danger, they'd have kept me there overnight."

Jon followed her to the elevator. "I really didn't expect you to disappear for three days."

The elevator door slid open and they entered. "I didn't disappear. I went to work Friday, and caught up on my sleep Friday night. That's why the machine took my phone calls. Then I spent the weekend with David and Louise. It was Mother's Day today, and I wanted to spend it with my . . . with my sister and her kids," she said, and swallowed quickly. She looked away from him as the elevator rose toward her floor. Watch your tongue, she thought.

"I'm glad you had the sense to avoid spending the weekend alone."

"For goodness sake, Jon, I'm perfectly capable of taking care of myself. I'm not a child. I don't need anyone to take care of me." She bit her lip as the door *whooshed* open.

"I'm sorry," he said as he followed her to her apartment. "I know you don't need my protection. But I was hoping you'd care whether or not I was concerned."

"I do care. I just don't like to be . . . hovered over. Or followed around."

"My timing seems to be bad again."

She placed the door key in her lock and looked up at him for the first time. The dismay and confusion on his face made her smile. "Oh, damn it, Jon, now I've hurt your feelings." She pushed open her door. "So I can't not invite you in."

"Weren't you going to?"

"No. I really am tired. I was going to call you in a day or so, though. And I honestly haven't even given a thought to that accident. Which was thoughtless of me. I haven't even asked you how your car is."

"Pretty bad. I had to buy a new one. If you want me to go, I'll go." He started to turn away.

"No. Come in. I don't feel tired anymore. I'll get us drinks. There's a jug of chablis in the fridge." She tossed her tote bag down on the oak dining table at the far end of the L-shaped living area.

He nodded and strode into the room and sat on the brown tweed sofa. "We were lucky," he said. "The other driver died today."

"Oh, no! I'm afraid I've been pretty self-absorbed, haven't I?"

"It's normal in your circumstances."

"What do you mean?"

"You were injured. You did have a bang on your head."

"That doesn't excuse me. I've really been terribly selfish."

"You have a right to be once in a while. Your profession demands you to always think of other people. Then, that man you were living with must have demanded a lot, too."

She tightened her grip on the wine jug she'd brought from the kitchen. "I'll get a couple of glasses," she said. She returned to the kitchen and set the jug down. As she opened the cabinet and reached up for the glasses, she heard him behind her.

"He's the one that stitched you up, isn't he?"

She took the glasses down and set them on the counter.

"I heard them page him," he said. He poured them both some wine. "I figured that had something to do with why you were so upset."

"It did." She tasted the wine and gestured to him to return to the living room.

"It tested your resolve," he said.

"I don't know what you mean."

"Seeing him made you want to go back to him. He tried to talk you into it."

She breathed deeply. "No. Never. He didn't try to talk me into it, and I wouldn't dream of going back to him. I told you I don't need that kind of man. And having him stand over me and sew up my forehead wasn't my idea of fun . . . So that's why you've been following me all weekend. You really thought I'd go back to him."

"I thought he'd put on pressure. Maybe keep after you."

She leaned back and studied his earnest, boyish face. Was it his freckles that gave him that ingenuous air? The short, wavy red hair or cloudless blue eyes? The eyes seemed transparent, as if no unspoken thought could possibly hide behind them.

"He didn't. At least not Thursday night. Maybe he intends to. He was hanging around my office the day before. But he didn't want me to see him. Maybe once he saw I was back—just back to my ordinary business—he decided to lay off. He seemed almost disinterested when he was sewing me up. Almost glad, as if he took pleasure in seeing me hurt. Maybe that was all he really wanted: revenge."

Jon narrowed his eyes. "He's just plain sick, Joanna."

"That's why I left him. I could see that he wasn't going to change. He hated children, and I wanted one—eventually. He accused me of planning to trap him into having one. He said if I did, he'd do more than leave me."

"What? He threatened you?"

"He once tried to kill himself. He was threatening to do it again. So, well, I had to leave him. I thought if I got away, I'd straighten my own thinking out. I mean, if I ever want to have children . . ."

"Oh, Jesus! And now he's threatening to kill himself if you don't come back." He leaned forward.

"I was afraid he might. I didn't want him to know I was back in town."

He reached across the coffee table and clasped her hand. "And I got you in that accident and put you right back in his clutches. He threatened again. They always do, suicidal people. To make you think it's your fault."

She loosened her hand from his. "But he didn't, Thursday night. He didn't say a word. So I think he may be over it."

"At least till he finds someone else to blame for making him hate himself."

They sat across from each other, sipping their wine, saying nothing. She would have liked to tell him she appreciated his concern, but somehow she couldn't. She wasn't ready for that closeness.

"I wanted to tell you, Jon, I went through Irene Kimski's records tonight."

He looked puzzled.

"The one who was murdered last week. That I knew."

His brows rose. "You did?"

"You seem surprised. You're the one who aroused my curiosity."

He seemed positively gleeful. He rubbed his hands together. Where, she wondered, had the worried suitor gone?

"What did you find?"

"I don't know. I've decided you're the detective. I just went through the chart taking notes." She rose and got her tote bag from the dining table.

He followed and stood looking over her shoulder as she opened it and took out the spiral notebook. He reached out. She handed it to him. "If there is anything important in here, it's time someone figured it out. Another black Friday is coming up."

"Well, let's have a look." He sat next to her and ran his finger down the pages of uncertain scribbles.

He moistened his finger on his lip as he reached the bottom of each page and prepared to flip it. A few times he shook his head and scratched it, turned back to an earlier page, flipped forward again, cleared his throat, and grunted several times. Then he sat back, flipped to the first page again and displayed his frustration in two upturned palms.

"No help?" she said, not surprised but disappointed.

He lifted his palms again. "Maybe I can come to your office. Go over the record myself."

"They're confidential, Jon."

"You'd hold me to that? Even though she's dead!"

She hesitated. "Well, let me think it over. I'm still thinking like a midwife. Not a detective."

He made a noncommittal sound and picked up the spiral pad again, as if he might find something that hadn't been there before. "I respect your ethics, Joanna. And you've been methodical, at least. There's hope for you as a detective." He lifted the notebook and rattled the pages, apparently hoping something would fall out onto the table and spark a flash of insight.

Then something did flash in his eyes. He slapped the notebook onto the table and pounded the top page with his index finger.

"What is it? What did you find?" she asked, excitement rising with her voice in her throat.

"It's right here. The first note you wrote. Here at the top of the page. You did it right, Joanna. You started at the beginning. A less astute person might have ignored it as an insignificant part of the record."

She leaned over his shoulder and looked. "It just says, 'referred by Dr. Rose Snyder of the Martin Fertility Center.' I can't claim I thought it *was* significant. It was just the first thing under the identifying information on the record. Why is it important who referred her?"

"It might not be in every case. But in this case, it might be a key. I told you we know things about two people between us, and that we might figure out what they had in common. I know that Hal Thomas, the guy from Pharmogenetix, and his wife had adopted a kid . . ."

"I thought all the mothers were natural."

"That's right. They were the birth mothers of the children who were killed. But Hal and Denise had another kid, an adopted one. In fact they were just planning to adopt another when they learned she was pregnant. One of those things."

Joanna knit her brow. "I still don't see . . ."

"I figure if they adopted a couple of children, they must have gone through fertility studies. Both of them badly wanted a child of their own. They probably tried lots of things before adoption."

"Jon, you don't think the Martin Fertility Center's involved in this!"

"Not likely. The Thomas woman wasn't their client. And neither was the lesbian . . . Grace, I think was her name."

Joanna sat down and began slowly nodding her head. "I see what you mean. All three were somehow involved with fertility problems. Grace was artificially inseminated. The Thomases must have been getting treatment. And Irene Kimski must have been seen by Rose Snyder before she got pregnant."

He flashed her a proud smile. "Your instincts are good. And you have a very logical mind." He leaned forward across the table and kissed her on the bridge of her nose. "It's very slim, Joanna. But it's there. If I can only figure out just how this could tie them together."

Something about his idea didn't quite hang together. Joanna thought about the *Inquirer* story on Melanie Roberts. "No," she said, shaking her head, disappointed. "I remember reading that the victims this week were survived by two other children."

"That's right," said Jon. "They were. But the children were from the husband's first marriage. Maybe Melanie had a fertility problem too. Should we try to find out?"

"How in the world do we do that?"

He patted her folded hands and said, "That's the other part of being a detective that I think you'd do well. We interview the widower."

"But they're grieving. His wife and baby aren't even buried yet. What right do we have . . ."

"It's not just a right, Joanna, it's a duty. Eight people have already been killed by this maniac. Bloody Shoes, they're calling him. We've got a very tenuous lead, not enough to even go to the police with. But if a fourth one was also getting fertility treatments, they'd have to look into it."

"My God!" said Joanna. "What am I letting you talk me into?"

"You said you'd been pretty self-absorbed, didn't you? Well this should get you focused outside yourself."

"I guess there's no doubt about that," she said. Then she laughed.

He stood up and stretched, clasping his hands together above his head. "I'll call you at work tomorrow, if that's all right. We can plan our strategy over lunch in your cafeteria."

Overwhelmed, she nodded and followed him to the door. Long after she heard the elevator doors slide open and closed she stood there. Finally she shook her head. No doubt she had found the cure to her self-absorption. But she wondered if the cure might be worse than the disease.

Chapter Six

Monday

UNDER THE BLUE booties, Kevin's white shoes were bloody. Nobody in the operating room thought it odd; their shoes were bloody, too. A misdirected stream from an excised organ being lifted from a body cavity to a tray sometimes got inside their boots. The boots were meant not to keep blood off shoes but to dampen static electricity, which, if it ever got loose near the anesthesiologist's precious oxygen and other gases, could spark a fire or blast them all to bits.

Kevin had thought of ending it all that way. Off he would go in a fiery explosion, taking the OR staff with him. He pictured the horror on their faces. In their eyes. Their mouths would be hidden as they sucked in great lungfuls of flame from their burning masks. Their gowns would curl away, and the drapes that covered the patient, the bloodied spots cooking and crumbling more slowly than the rest. An acrid smell of flesh would be the last thing that filled his nostrils. His own flesh, mortified, mortifying him.

But that wouldn't be enough. The others would still be there, mocking his life. They had to go first, go with him, or the ugliness, the wrongness of his life would go on forever. Would spoil the childhood gardens of the world forever, as the gardens of his childhood had been spoiled.

Elizabeth's husband, Forest, spoiled the garden the first time. When Kevin was five, playing in the backyard with four-year-old Joe Byrnes, because there was nobody else to play with. The houses they lived in were all attached, all in a row, red brick. Solid red brick, except for the roof which was cracked gray slate. From the front they looked more like a block-long, tall walls with doors and windows spaced at regular intervals. Sometimes one of the upper windows would be open, with a curtain blowing out of it, or someone leaning forward on an elbow and chin. On cold days, the leaners would retreat behind panes made opaque by the glare from outdoors.

Forest was one of the leaners. It seemed all he could do in the daytime was lean from the window in the attic high on the wall, just below the edge of some slipping slate shingles. But in the evening after dinner in the summer, Forest would sometimes come out. He'd watch Kevin and Joe Byrnes play soldier games—hide and seek made respectable for boys, because the object of the games was to kill the guy after you found him under the rotting back porch or behind the trash barrel or among the hollyhocks that hid the hole in the chain link fences meant to separate the tiny backyards.

Forest would come out and work in his small vegetable garden. At least that was what it looked like he was doing. Kevin knew even then the garden was Forest's excuse for being out back when the boys were playing. Kevin knew those lumpy eyeballs were following him as best they could, given Forest's inability to control them.

Forest would ferret out the kids' hiding places while seeming to be picking green beans or tomatoes. Kevin saw him aim one eye at the vegetables while the other wandered loosely around to the logical secluded spots in the limited battleground. He'd watch Forest's eye and try to find some pattern of movement, a second when the eye fixed on a spot where Joe might be hiding. But Kevin never could figure it out. Forest wouldn't give away his secrets.

On the night that Forest spoiled the garden, Kevin was hiding from Joe Byrnes in the hollyhocks that covered the break in the fence between Kevin's yard and Forest's. The hollyhocks' furry leaves and flowers climbed the fence on Kevin's side. He hated them, except for their handy strategic placement. He hated them especially because his sister Rayna loved them. She used to break off the blooms to make dolls of them. An unopened bloom broken off the stem looked like a knob. It could be stuck on the stem end of a full bloom to make a head. Then the long, rose-colored petals would look like a skirt. Rayna, who was two years older than Kevin, could play with these for hours; and that made him hate hollyhocks.

But they helped him win the war and kill Joe

Byrnes, who never figured out that Kevin always hid there. Forest did, though, and this time he worked in his garden right next to where the tomato vines curled tightly on their stakes. So the tomatoes blocked the hole on Forest's side of the fence.

Joe had his eyes pressed against the large oak tree where the seeker counted to one hundred to give the enemies time to run and hide. (Kevin was the only enemy this time, as everybody else on the street had gone to the amusement park for the volunteer fire department picnic. Kevin and Joe's parents seldom took them anywhere, because they never had money. Elizabeth had gone, because a librarian had a civic duty to attend such things, she said.)

Kevin scrambled behind the hollyhocks, tearing away the tendrils that had tangled themselves in the fence since the last time he'd hidden there. The broken section of the fence seemed bigger; the wire edges around the hole were bent further back than before. Now there was space for him to stand up. Before he had had to squat down and hold his arms in so the fence and vines wouldn't scratch him.

He could hear Forest working away with some tool in the dirt right behind him. *Scritch scratch.* It made him feel creepy, as the stooping man came closer and closer.

"One, four, five, a hundred, here I come," piped Joe Byrnes, as he ran from the counting tree. *"Unh, unh, unh, unh! Unh, unh, unh! Hch, hch, hch, hch, hch!"* he rattled as he sprayed imaginary machine gun bullets across the illictly joined backyards.

Forest's cultivator *scritch scratched* closer to Kevin. He heard the old man's breath whistling through the boogers that clogged the stiff gray hair in his nostrils.

Joe made a sweep of the trash cans and old lumber piled under the wooden back porches. He banged into a laundry line, loosening the wooden props that supported it and, sending clothes flapping like injured soldiers toward the ground. They hung there limp, brought to their knees.

Forest scratched and dug only inches from Kevin.

Joe began to cry, as he usually did when he couldn't find his enemy. "I can't find you. It's not fair. You're hiding and it's not fair. You're bigger than me."

Kevin, exasperated, threw up his hands. "Here, stupid baby!" he cried. Suddenly he lost his balance and fell back into the tomato plants. A stake snapped and jabbed the back of his leg as he sat hard among the vines.

Forest leaned over him, his eyes seeming to pick up speed. The eye with a slice cut from the iris focused on Kevin.

He felt his skin come alive. It itched and quivered and prickled all over. Forest's breath whistled as it went into his nose, and sprayed little droplets as it came out of his open mouth. Some of the drops caught in the corner of his mouth where others had dried and stuck on his whiskers.

Kevin had never been this close to Forest. His skin began to burn all over. He pulled himself up on his knees and tried to crawl away through the hole in the fence.

Forest grabbed him by the legs, pulled him out of the garden onto the grass, and began to slap at Kevin's arms and legs. He ran his hands all over Kevin's hair and tore his shirt off and flapped it around in the air.

Kevin began hollering.

Joe ran across the other yards and through the hole in the fence. He began jumping up and down, spraying imaginary bullets at Kevin. "I'll kill them for you. *Hch, hch, hch!*"

Kevin felt the bullets hitting him. His skin felt as if it was on fire. Then Forest pulled off Kevin's dunga rees, and rolled him on the grass. Before Kevin knew what was happening, the old man was spraying water all over him with a garden hose.

Joe kept jumping up and down, saying, "Hch, hch, hch, hch!"

At last the magic bullets seemed to work. Kevin sat dripping in the grass. His skin cooled suddenly, except for a spot on the back of his hand. There he saw a tiny red ant, captured in a drop of water.

He yelped and shook his hand, flinging off the drop and its hostage.

Forest stopped spraying. Joe kept right on shooting him with *hches* for a little while. Then, evidently seeing the excitement was over, Joe dropped his arms and stared openmouthed at Forest.

The old man wound his hose up and dropped it under the water tap in a puddle. It made a couple of sounds like Joe's bullets, then lay there. Now all Kevin could hear was the whistle of air passing through Forest's boogers as the man inspected his dripping skin and ran his finger around the elastic waistband of his soaked underpants.

"Nasty critters," said Forest.

Kevin had never heard his voice before and was surprised that it wasn't cracked and old, but had a clear deep tenor.

"You boys follow me now. I'll show you something."

Kevin stood up. His feet slurped in his soggy sneakers as he and Joe meekly followed Forest toward the garden. Forest pulled aside the tomato vines, and exposed an enormous mound of granular reddish earth. The grains seemed to spill and teem over one another as if they were alive. Some of them were. Kevin's skin began to itch as he realized the whole mound was alive.

"I'll show you boys how to take care of ants."

Joe's eyes widened and bulged, and he giggled behind his hands.

Forest's breath whistled furiously as his face grew intense. His eyes even seemed to work together in their wanderings.

"You got to come close to look," said Forest, grabbing Kevin's arm and tugging him up to Joe. The calloused skin of Forest's hand scratched him. His yellow fingernails curved under and were full of dirt.

Kevin was watching the hand that pulled him, and at first didn't see what the other one was doing. But when a fierce yellow stream cut into the anthill and began foaming among the scattering grains, he realized that Forest was peeing.

For a while he thought the stream would never cease. The force of it sheared the top off the mound. The ants tumbled and scattered away, some of them heading under the fence toward Kevin's yard. Then the bottom of the mound sank, coalesced with the foam, and ran in rivulets toward the tomato plants.

"Good for 'em," said Forest. "Makes 'em redder."

Kevin didn't know whether he meant the ants or the tomatoes. But the garden was spoiled forever for him. When Elizabeth brought over vegetables, Kevin refused to eat them. He never did tell anyone why, even after the other things happened.

Now, standing by the operating table in his bloody shoes, placing the intradermal sutures along the abdominal incision of a patient whose face he had never seen, he thought of Elizabeth's face when she learned about everything and turned on him. How right he had been to dedicate Melanie Roberts to her; for if it had not been for Elizabeth and the others like her, he never would have realized that the twelve people on his list would have to die before Kevin could kill himself.

Two women and their children remained. The rock

singer would be next. He would dedicate her to Katie. Katie, who had made his four years of medical school so miserable, who had driven him mad at a time when he needed peace and quiet. And there had been no way out; the apartment next to hers was the only one he could afford. And he couldn't have afforded that, if he hadn't sold his blood to a blood bank every six weeks. He might have sold his soul that often, if he'd thought it a renewable resource and if someone made an offer.

Katie was a whore, and the landlady was her employer. In fact, the landlady collected more than rent from just about every tenant but Kevin. He never quite figured out why she let him have the apartment without any strings attached; maybe she thought a medical student would bring her place some respectability. She had enough drug dealers, prostitutes, gamblers, and hired guns to keep herself rich for life even at a steep quotient of graft for the local authorities. A high vacancy rate wasn't one of her problems.

So he could harldy complain to her if Katie kept him up at night with her constantly blaring stereo and forced him to do all his studying at the medical school library. His hatred of Katie reverberated in his head every time he heard loud rock music.

When he discovered a rock singer on his list, he thought how poetically just her dedication to Katie would be. Her name was Angela Marietta. And he would kill her on Friday night.

After that he had only one more to go. He grinned underneath his surgical mask as he stood in his now bloody shoes in the operating room and carefully placed the last stitch in his patient's abdomen. He was thinking of how right it would be; and how right the dedication would be. He could picture Joanna's face, the last time he saw her, the blood seeping onto her forehead as he put in that final stitch.

It would be the coup de grace, doing it that way. He would rid the world of so much evil and ugliness, and of the carriers of all that evil, who didn't seem to see the ugliness.

Kevin saw it quite clearly, for he knew where it came from.

Chapter Seven

Monday

SHORTLY BEFORE NOON, Joanna finished up her charting on the morning's clients and crossed from the modern, peach-colored birthing center wing to the narrower aqua corridors of the section that housed the fertility center.

First things first, she had decided during a dread-filled night when she'd contemplated interviewing Melanie Roberts's grieving family. Jon was jumping to too many conclusions. The fact that his coworker's wife had conceived after adopting a child meant little. In her practice Joanna had delivered several babies to women who had had the same experience. Not everyone sought professional fertility studies before giving up and turning their parenting instincts to someone else's orphaned, unwanted, or abandoned child. Some didn't even want to know the truth about their infertility. Neither husband nor wife wanted to take the other's blame—or blame himself or herself—for failure to conceive. What they didn't know wouldn't hurt them.

No—Joanna would not barge in on the Robertses before doing a little groundwork herself; or before Jon did some of his own. She would talk to him about it later. Meanwhile she'd follow her own instincts.

She stopped for a second outside the large opaque black glass door of the fertility center office. The names of the associates, stenciled in gold on the door, proclaimed by their stark square shouldered style that human infertility was a serious and expensive affliction. The blackness teased her. What possibilities lay behind it? Joanna switched Irene Kimski's file folder from her right hand to her left, and pulled open the door.

The opulent aqua waiting room lovingly smothered the nervousness of the clients who waited there. The receptionist smiled from her cubicle. Joanna introduced herself and asked if Dr. Rose Snyder could see her yet.

"She's busy with her last client, Ms. Michaels. But she did ask me to have the cafeteria send up lunch for both of you at 12:15."

"Oh," said Joanna, surprised. "She didn't have to do that."

"I know what it's like in obstetrics," Rose Snyder explained moments later in her office, as she cleared away the jumbled papers on her vast rosewood desk so the receptionist could set down the lunches in their fold-back plastic foam cartons. Fine china and sterling silver would have seemed more appropriate, though the aqua carton matched the color of the walls and thick carpet. "I'm an obstetrician, you know. That's how I got into this business. About ten years ago I began to sense that more of my gynecological patients were having trouble conceiving."

Rose Snyder's neatly coifed silver-gray hair fit well

in this elegant setting. But nothing else about her did. The furniture was massive, heavy, new; she was petite, thin, close to sixty. The rosewood glowed beneath a rich polish; her skin was translucent, powdered, blue veined. She lifted one wizened, scrupulously manicured hand and motioned Joanna to the leather chair in front of the desk. "So, I'm familiar, as I was saying, with the kind of pressures you work under, Joanna. And you sounded a bit anxious. I hope you like tuna salad."

"It's fine." Joanna sat down. "It's what I usually have for lunch."

"Most people like it. Safe, you know. Now, what can I do for you?" She sat behind her desk and took a small bite of her salad as her pale blue eyes turned toward the record that Joanna passed over to her.

"You referred this client to us. Nearly three years ago."

"Irene Kimski? That name does sound familiar." She glanced up. "Oh, yes! The one who was killed."

Joanna nodded and washed down some tuna salad with coffee. "One of the four mothers."

Rose Snyder shook her head. "To tell you the truth, I didn't even start to read those stories until the third one was killed. There's so much sensational news these days. All you usually need to do is change the names and places, and the story's the same. Like a series of cheap formula thriller novels. All with the same old plot. But this one's particularly grisly, isn't it? I have to admit to a certain amount of curiosity. Even if it did take almost a week to wake up to the fact I'd had the third victim as a client." She pushed the file back across the desk to Joanna, and smiled at her own benignity. She turned her attention to her lunch, but kept one eye and ear cocked slightly toward Joanna, indicating some interest, at least.

"It didn't pop right out at me, either. And I didn't think it could have any relevance to the other murders. The fact that she was my client, I mean."

Rose looked up quizzically. "Were any of the others your clients?"

Joanna shook her head. "No. That's why I'm here. I wondered if any were yours."

The thin bones in Rose's face seemed to sharpen under the skin. The paleness fled from her eyes as they focused under the hooded lids at Joanna. "If they were, it wouldn't have anything to do with their murders, I'm sure."

"No, of course, it wouldn't. That is, the fact that they were *your* particular clients. Or mine."

Dr. Snyder drew her thin frame up beneath her lab coat, giving it a stiff appearance. "I gave you this lunch hour interview, Joanna, because I thought you had a professional matter to discuss. My relationship with my clients is confidential. I really don't . . ."

"I know that, Rose. I respect that. That's why I came to you first."

"First?"

Joanna took a deep breath. "Before going . . . anywhere else. You see, I know something about one of the other victims that led me to believe that she had received fertility treatments."

"You seem to know a great deal about these victims."

"No. Not really." Joanna dropped her plastic fork into the carton next to her half-finished salad and lifted her hands in frustration. "I seem to be having trouble expressing myself."

"You do indeed. I'm sure it's because you have no business expressing yourself on this subject. You're a fine midwife, Joanna. I can't understand why you fancy yourself a criminal investigator."

"Neither can I!"

Rose laughed. "Well I guess we agree on that."

"Please, Rose, bear with me. This whole thing is pretty scary. You have to agree that until they find out the relationship between all these victims, they can't prevent another set of murders."

"Of course I agree."

"I deliver babies. A lot of my clients are scared. That means a lot of your former clients are scared. So, it is kind of a professional concern, isn't it? I mean, we're supposed to be caregivers. To relieve our clients' anxieties."

"Come on, Joanna! Aren't you stretching your professional responsibilities a bit far?"

"No farther than you did when you switched from obstetrics to fertility." Joanna sat back.

So did Rose, apparently stunned by Joanna's logic, which Joanna herself realized was getting out of hand.

The older woman laughed again and stood up. "You know, I think I admire you. I don't know why you're doing this, but I'm willing to listen. But please start at the beginning, so I can follow all your strange mental twists and turns. If that all makes some kind of sense to me, then I'll answer any direct questions you might have. But, please . . . no fishing expeditions. I'm not going to answer any questions about any client but Irene Kimski."

"Then the others were your clients, too!"

"Joanna! You're testing my patience."

"I'm sorry. I don't mean to trick you. All right. I'll start at the beginning."

Dr. Snyder sat down behind her desk again and listened intently as Joanna told how her interest began. When she finished, Rose Snyder leaned back in her chair and nodded for a few moments. Then she trilled her fingers on her desk a couple of times as she studied Joanna's face.

Joanna waited.

"All right," she said, at last. "What specifically do you want to know about Irene Kimski?"

"Was her conception through artificial reproduction?"

"Yes."

"What kind?"

She hesitated barely a moment. "In vitro fertilization. In fact, we still have some frozen embryos."

Joanna sighed. "Then Jon must be right."

"Jon?"

"The friend who came up with the theory. He knew the first victim."

"Yes," said Rose. "The theory may have merit."

Joanna rose. "Thank you, Rose. This may be the key the police need. Bloody shoes sure aren't enough." She turned toward the door.

"And, Joanna," Rose said.

"Yes?"

"None of the other victims were clients of mine."

Joanna smiled and nodded. She left the office feeling strangely elated. Maybe she wouldn't be a half-bad detective, after all.

"So you decided it's safe for you to come right here every evening from work again," said Louise.

"I feel so much more relaxed," Joanna answered. "I don't even care if Kevin is following me. So what? He doesn't suspect." She removed the nursing bottle of milk from its niche in the refrigerator door and set it in a warming pan.

Her sister put some finishing touches on a salad and checked the clock. "Now all we have to do is wait for David. He's late."

Joanna heard the front door open.

David came directly in and kissed his wife.

"Hey," he said, "I didn't expect to see you here, Sis."

"She was just saying she's decided not to be paranoid," said Louise.

"How 'bout that. Cassie up yet?"

"Still napping," said Joanna.

"And you're not hanging over her worrying?"

"Isn't that your job, Daddy?" Joanna shot back.

He knit his brow. "It's some father's job. So I guess I'm filling in." He sounded tense.

"Now, David, you know you love it," said Louise.

His eyes flickered. "I'm going to wash up and get Michael away from Mr. Rogers," he said to Louise.

After he left, Louise shrugged and smiled weakly at Joanna. "He probably had a bad day at work."

When they were all seated around the kitchen table eating their dinner, Joanna balancing her well-fed daughter on her shoulder, David seemed more relaxed. He asked, "What was the miracle that changed your life, Joanna?"

"It was something you did."

He looked up from his plate, his gray eyes puzzled.

"You told Jon Isenson I was home."

He grinned broadly. "You're in love?"

"David, don't push," said Louise.

"It's all right. I'm kind of in love, but not exactly with Jon."

"Explain that," said David.

"I'm in love with an idea of his." She explained the idea.

"I see," David said, the tension returning to his voice. "You've thrown yourself into this investigation. Don't you think it's a little bit risky?"

"Why, for goodness' sake? I'm just going through my own client's records and asking a few people some questions."

David flipped his napkin down next to his plate and

looked angry. "Those women and their children were murdered, and you're going around asking questions about their background. Don't you think the murderer would care?"

Joanna began jiggling Cassie on her shoulder. Cassie began to cry.

Louise stood up. "What's wrong with you, David? Joanna knows what she's doing." She began to clear dishes from the table.

"Does she? Well I hope the killer doesn't!" He stood up and took Cassie from Joanna's shoulder.

"Why is she crying, Daddy?" asked Michael, who had said barely a word since bouncing into the kitchen fifteen minutes ago behind his father.

"She probably has a bubble," said David. He stalked out of the kitchen, Cassie screaming loudly from his shoulder.

Joanna started after them, but Louise stayed her with a touch to her arm. "Let him calm down a bit, Jo. Every once in a while, my husband gets this idea that we weak little women need his protection and the benefit of his superior wisdom. He might have a point."

"I don't see what's risky about asking a colleague a few questions. Rose Snyder's not the murderer. I looked at her shoes. They're no more than size five and there wasn't so much as a drop of blood on either of them."

"It's not like you to be sarcastic, Jo." Her sister smiled at her ironically.

"All right. What were you saying?" said Joanna.

"If you interview that woman's husband, you may tip off the killer. Maybe he even *is* the killer."

"But that's ridiculous. He was out of town . . ."

"Technically he was in his car on the road on the way home."

"That's still an alibi."

"One they can't prove."

"Surely," Joanna said, her voice rising and becoming brittle, "you don't think he did it. The police said he's not a suspect. And what about the other three husbands . . . ?"

"Two. The lesbian didn't have a husband."

"I know those husbands aren't the murderers. There's no reason for me not to interview them."

The women were clearing the table in silence when David strode back into the room. "Joanna, I came back to apologize. I guess I just think that a woman with a baby is the last person in the world to get involved in this mess."

"But nobody knows I'm her mother," she said. "How could the killer know?"

"He couldn't," said Louise. "David and I wouldn't tell anyone."

Home at midnight, Joanna found a message from Jon on her answering machine and suddenly remembered she was supposed to have met him for lunch. She called him back immediately.

His voice held no sign of sleepiness, and she knew he had been awaiting her call.

"I'm sorry, Jon. I didn't mean to stand you up."

"I called you at lunchtime. Your office couldn't find you. I even drove out to the center and went to the cafeteria. There wasn't a sign of you. By the time I got to your office, you were cloistered away with a patient. If you don't want to help me with this investigation, why don't you just tell me?"

"I *am* helping you. That's what I was doing at lunchtime. And I found out you were right, Jon. There is some connection." She paused. "Irene Kimski had in vitro fertilization."

"Great," he said. "But it would have been nice of

you to call and let me know. We could have had dinner together. Planned our strategy."

"I went to my sister's for dinner."

"But you spent the whole weekend there . . ."

"Why shouldn't I? I really don't have time to cook for myself."

"Joanna, if we went out to dinner, you wouldn't have to cook."

"I don't much like restaurants. Especially every night."

"I'm not talking about *every* night. Just *this* night."

She sat down on the edge of her bed and began worrying her shoes off with her feet. "I have an idea," she said. "We can have our strategy meeting here tomorrow night. I'll make dinner. I'll just call Louise and tell her I won't be coming. But now, I'm tired, Jon," said Joanna. "About 6:30 tomorrow, OK?"

He was waiting in her apartment lobby when she got home at 5:30, her arms full of groceries. He had brought the wine, an expensive beaujolais that she knew would give her a headache, as red wines always did.

She prepared a stir-fry beef dish in a wok she'd used only three times. They decided the meal was worth the heavy smoke that hovered—redolent of shitake mushrooms and succulent peppers—over them in the two bedroom apartment for the entire evening. But she vowed, as she had the other times she'd used the deceptively simple looking vessel, she would never again use a wok.

In the comfortable domestic tranquility that settled on them, the purpose of their meeting eluded them. They fell into a murmur of reminiscences as they shared kitchen tasks for the first time in years. And she wondered, as he threw open the balcony door and began to wave out the smoke with a broom like the Sorcerer's Apprentice, how she'd ever found him uninteresting. Who else could have turned her mishandling of the simplest of cooking jobs into an excuse to dance a ballet?

She laughed as stubborn strands of smoke escaped through the long bristles and wafted back into the room. He seemed to have as much luck in stirring the air as she had had in stirring the food. It made her think that they reinforced each others' natural ineptness with household matters. They weren't cut out for domesticity.

She retrieved the broom from him and slid it into the recess between the refrigerator and the adjacent cabinet. It fell back against the wall, just out of reach of her fingers. She sighed at this one more thing gone wrong this evening. She peered sideways into the deep crack; then she turned to him and shrugged.

He threw back his head in a silent laugh. Then he grasped her shoulders and pulled her to him. The sweet pungent perfume that still swirled in the kitchen mixed in her head with the thin traces of wine. Their winey breaths merged; their winey tongues tasted each other. Her body cried out for his caresses. But as he began running his hands beneath her blouse, she caught them in her own, moved them up to her face. His fingers, his eyes, she knew, would have lingered around the brown margins of her nipples, exploring their changed color and diameter. Had she allowed his mouth to explore below the hollow of her throat, his tongue would have traced the subtle change in her belly, run it to its source in the soft, newly regrown hairs of her pubis, perhaps even found her episiotomy scar.

She held his face between her tingling palms and lifted it so his eyes locked on hers.

"Not now," she said.

"I've rushed you," he said. He kissed her once more on the mouth and let her go.

"No. I just . . . need a little more time." She straightened her hair.

He followed her to the living room sofa and sat beside her. "I really didn't plan that."

"I know. Our strategy meeting got off track," she said. Lifting his hand, she kissed his fingers. How she would have loved to suck them, one at a time, bring him alive, throw off all caution and unmask herself, bring him into her. Instead, she looked at the freckled, broad hand and gently pressed it.

"Hey, this was to have been a work session." He hugged her suddenly with friendly fierceness. "Let's get to it."

"I'll get us coffee," she said.

"I guess you feel better about interviewing Melanie Roberts's family now that you know there's a connection," he said.

The water in the coffee maker began to hiss and spit as it ran through the grounds in the filter.

"Not quite. Jon, you know the other man . . . Hal Thomas. We still don't know that he and his wife went for treatment. We do know he didn't go to Martin Center. At least not to Rose Snyder. All that we know is that his first child was adopted."

"I also know his wife told him she'd do anything to have a baby of her own. She seemed to think that unless she conceived a child, she wouldn't be . . . *whole* . . . or however it was she put it."

"That still doesn't mean they had fertility studies." She poured them each a cup of coffee and carried them to the table. "I think before we go to someone we don't know at all, you ought to go directly to him. Ask him."

"You're right. But I hate to. I know when he was

going through the adoptions, he was upset a lot. I think he felt it was his fault that Denise couldn't get pregnant. He never said he was the sterile one, but I got the feeling he was. He'd talk about taking cold baths before having sex. He said he'd heard that it kept his body heat from killing the fragile sperm."

"Then he must have known his count was low."

"When she did get pregnant, he said he figured the cold baths finally worked. 'Old icy-balls finally did it,' he said."

"Well, that may mean they went for counseling, and it may not. The theory about lowering body temperature is the kind of thing that gets into magazines and newspapers." Joanna sipped her coffee thoughtfully.

"But it has scientific validity."

"Only in very limited cases, Jon. And there's much better technology than that. They could wash and concentrate his sperm and inseminate her with it directly into her uterus."

"Right," he said. "And if they did, then the pattern would fit." He emphasized his statement with a sharp nod.

She fixed her eyes on him. "Making the automatic assumption that that's what they did sounds like pretty lax detective work to me."

He ducked his head in chagrin. "To me, too."

"Jon?" she said, teasing him out of his faintly embarrassed bow.

His eye flickered up.

"This whole theory was your idea in the first place. You were the one that suggested a strategy meeting."

He grinned. "Well, I thought *I* was the one in charge."

"You are. Well, we both are. So neither of us has to go it alone. I'll go with you when you talk with him. You can tell him my interest's professional. Then when I have to face Melanie Roberts's family, you can come along. With two sets of eyes and ears, we'll see and hear things one of us might miss."

"That sounds like an excellent strategy." He reached across the table and grasped her hands. "And you know what we're going to find out at Hal Thomas's."

Both were surprised by what they found out. The small, darkened living room of the Thomas home in Fort Washington, directly across from an elementary school, still smelled of grief and tears—the cloying scent that dying flowers and rotting fruit left in their wake. After Jon had introduced Joanna, Hal sent four-year-old Mitch off to the family room with the grainy-skinned, shiny-haired woman in a sari. He had hired her to care for Mitch and the house. Though she could not have been with the Thomases more than a few weeks—Denise and the one-year-old son had been Bloody Shoes' first victims—she had given the place her own imprint. Joanna could tell from Jon's expression when Hal led them into the room, that this wasn't what he expected. The thin fringes of oriental cotton throws draped over the sofa and chairs rested limp on the burnt orange carpet. Several pillows decorated with miniature mirrors—something like oversize sequins—added a garish brightness to the shrouded furniture.

Joanna noted the tables and lamps bore an unmistakable modernity, which the new housekeeper . . . or maybe Hal . . . had apparently tried to disguise. Such simple lines, such hard-edged shapes, left no room for the family's overwhelming loss; and they had to be covered, subdued.

In this reality-muffling room, Jon began his gentle probing, while Joanna watched Hal's face and listened to his strangled responses.

His handsome features at first seemed clouded. At first he seemed lost in his chair.

But as Jon's questions hardened and dug in, Hal stiffened, drew himself up. She saw that the man was two or three inches taller than Jon, who was five-foot-eleven. His eyes began to glitter and flash like the green mirrored buttons on the cushions.

His voice crackled now like an ice tray doused in warm water to loosen the cubes. "I don't know why you're asking me this. What I told you during those years was confidential." He shot a green glance at Joanna.

She learned forward in her chair. "Hal, Jon never mentioned it to me before this week."

"She's dead now. What difference does it make anymore? She had the baby she wanted. She had it . . . she had it." He buried his head in his hands.

They sat in silence for several moments. Then Jon cleared his throat and began again. "It may matter very much. The baby . . . how she conceived it may be the reason, or part of the reason, she and the baby were killed."

He raised his head and stared. "What the hell are you talking about!"

"If he was a test-tube baby . . . "

"What do you mean!" His eyes flashed; his fists worked till the knuckles popped.

Joanna explained. "If your wife's egg was fertilized with your sperm in the laboratory . . ."

He stood up, towering over them in his anger. "My wife and I would never consent to such a thing. It's against our moral beliefs. I never allowed it. No matter what. If God intended us to have a baby, he would see that we would, and God finally thought it was time."

Jon started to say something.

Joanna rose before he had a chance. "We're sorry, Hal. I don't know what else to say."

Jon rose. "I'll see you at work."

Hal stood in the middle of the room and continued to work his knuckles as Jon and Joanna let themselves out of the house.

The sun seeped out of the red-rimmed sky as Jon drove to her apartment. Neither said anything for most of the trip.

"I can't understand why he'd deny that he had a problem, now that she's dead. They did have that baby," Jon said.

"I don't think he was denying it. I think he was telling the truth."

"You think my theory's wrong?"

She shook her head, bothered by something she couldn't quite get hold of. "The connection's still there, I think. But I'm just not sure how it fits. They must have gone somewhere for counseling. Someone must have suggested in vitro, and maybe they argued about it and decided against it. He feels very strongly about it. He must have fought passionately for his own beliefs."

"I don't doubt it for a minute." Jon grunted. "Well, where do we go from here?"

She knit her brow. "Melanie Roberts's funeral is tomorrow morning. My office hours don't begin until two P.M."

"Tomorrow's Wednesday. I think I can take time off, too." He glanced over at her. "What time should we set your alarm for?"

"The funeral begins at ten at Barklay's in Bryn Mawr." She looked at him and smiled. "I'll meet you there a few minutes before."

"Joanna . . ." he started to say, Then seeming to think better of it, he sighed and let her off in front of her apartment building.

She leaned across the front seat and kissed him light on the cheek. After stepping inside the building foyer, she stepped out again and watched, hidden behind a gray column, as he drove away.

Chapter Eight

When the bough broke

OUTSIDE THE FUNERAL home Kevin heard someone call Joanna's name. He looked up and saw her turn around and register surprise as her eyes fixed for a moment on Kevin. He wasn't sure she recognized him before the television reporter and cameraman passed between them. But he couldn't take a chance. He fled.

What was she doing there? The librarian was not Joanna's patient. She'd gone to a doctor in Bryn Mawr.

She'd spoiled things for him again. Now he couldn't go into the funeral home.

He'd wanted to see Melanie Roberts and her ugly baby one last time. To be sure. To be absolutely sure he hadn't left something undone. Last night he'd dreamed that he'd killed Elizabeth, The Librarian, instead. Killed her that day on her front stoop in the rain.

Night and day, after the garden spoiling, Kevin had felt Forest's eyes wandering over his body like the ants. He didn't want to go near the old man, but his weirdness kept drawing him to the hole in the fence

behind the hollyhocks. At first he just sat there, looking away from the man, feeling his eyes on his back as
he played with the dirt. The hole in the fence kept
growing bigger. He knew Forest was bending back the
edges during the night, turning the boy-sized hole into
a man-sized hole.

But Forest never came close to the fence during the
day; he just scritched and scratched in his garden.

One day when Forest wasn't out back and Kevin's
bladder ached, Kevin climbed through the hole. He
crept behind the tomato plants to the anthill; he'd pee
on the ants like Forest. But the hill had been flattened
out and the ants were gone. Kevin stood confused, his
aim half taken, thinking it was wrong to pee in somebody's garden if you weren't going to kill the ants.

Suddenly fear came over him and he ran back toward his own yard. A snake of hollyhock vine wrapped
around his ankle and tripped him. He twisted and fell
on his back. When he'd pulled himself half-way up on
his elbows, still in Forest's yard, he saw a squirrel
skitter along a thick maple branch that arched toward
Forest's attic window.

The animal stood just outside the window, brushing the branch with its tail. It lifted its thin hand paws
to just under its chin, then darted them out in a quick
acquisitive motion. Then, it sat back and turned something over in its paws inspecting it with one tilted eye.
Kevin tilted his own eye to the attic window. Forest
was looking out at him. In one swift movement Forest
raised his hand and tossed him a handful of peanuts.

Kevin scrambled to his knees, scooped up the nuts
in his hand, and ran through the hole, across his own
backyard, up three wooden stairs, across his back
porch and into his kitchen. There, while his mother
and sister watched, he wet his pants. The pee ran
down his legs and over his sneakers and puddled
around his feet. Rayna, his sister, from her seat at the

chipped enameled metal kitchen table, sneered through missing front teeth and said, "Ugh."

He hated Rayna then; he never stopped hating her.

That night, in Elizabeth's bony arms, with a large book about reptiles and amphibians open on his lap, its edges cutting into his thighs as his fingers marched under the words, he found solace. Shame fled from the room when Elizabeth entered. So did Kevin's sister and mother: His mother because Elizabeth relieved her of bothering with Kevin; Rayna because she coveted Elizabeth's strokes and glances, and if she would stay it would show in her burning gold-flecked eyes and face. Kevin didn't know how he knew this back then; he just did.

From that time on, when Elizabeth left, shame followed Kevin around like Forest's eyes. It hid with him behind the hollyhocks. It lurked behind the unturned pages of books she brought him. The faster he turned the pages to try to seize it and cast it out, the faster it ran onto the next page, slipped behind the words, poked out its spider-veined nose . . . like Forest's nose.

Reading alone, the book spread open on the floor, he flat on his belly with legs crooked up behind his buttocks—once a glorious experience that filled the room with magic possibilities—now made his head pound. A jungle tangled its thick vines around him. Crawling creatures screeched and chattered, demanding peanuts. Ever larger ants in ever larger armies swarmed over the faded flowers on the rug, bits of wool grasped in their jaws as they wove themselves in and out of threadbare spots. Their hills surrounded him; he readied himself to pee on them.

"What are you doing, Kevin!" His mother pulled his hand away from his privates and slapped it. "You mustn't do that. *Never* ever do that again. You ought to be ashamed of yourself."

Shame. Except when Elizabeth was there reading

to him, pulling his head to her breast, breathing warm though sometimes sour breaths on his neck, stroking his arms with her long bony fingers. Teaching him.

He never thought she'd do what she did. He could not have imagined himself wanting to kill her.

He expected Forest to do what *he* did, though, and he began to look forward to the secret moments in the garden. Forest was not always there, but he was always watching. Shame clung to Kevin in the garden, too; but it was different. There was something delicious about it, clinging to his tongue like honey.

The squirrel visited the attic window every day. Kevin made certain to be there, too, so he could get his peanuts. He saved them in his room, thinking he could use them to bribe the hissing creatures shame sent to him in the night. He made piles of them, like anthills under his bed, where his mother never cleaned, except to shove a mop in and stir it around without looking.

At first Forest tossed large handfuls of the gnarled golden pods. Gradually he tossed fewer and fewer.

One day the squirrel got one and Kevin got none.

The next day the squirrel did not come. Forest just leaned out the window and grinned and held out a nut.

Kevin got ready to catch it.

Forest held it out in his palm a moment, then pulled his head and hand back into the window and closed it.

This happened several times, intensifying Kevin's shame, before he realized what he was supposed to do. Summer was drawing to an end. The tomato plants were tough and gnarled, and the tomatoes—according to his mother and sister who were ignorant of their taint and still ate them—had lost their sweetness and grown pulpy. The pea shells thickened, hardened. Only the peas inside them remained edible. And they, too, had lost their sweetness. A section of garden that Forest had cleared out, now put out quick-growing vines with tiny yellow trumpet-shaped flowers.

"Pumpkins," Elizabeth reported during one of their reading sessions. "Do you realize it soon will be Halloween! You'll have the finest jack o'lantern on North Street, if I have anything to do with it."

In September, before Elizabeth could keep her promise, Kevin started first grade, though his sixth birthday wasn't till February. He'd heard his mother say that was Elizabeth's doing. She knew people on the local school board, and as a librarian, she could influence them. They confirmed her reports of Kevin's superior intelligence by sending a woman to his home to give him a test. It was the first time he'd ever heard anyone refer to him as a genius.

"They wanted to skip you to second grade, but I said, that's moving too fast. Give him a chance to adjust, I said," said his mother.

She and Elizabeth argued about it, and his mother won. Kevin was glad. He didn't want to be in the same grade as Rayna, with her teeth and the black holes in between them reminding him of the chipped enamel kitchen table.

So he started first grade in September, and thanks to Elizabeth's tutoring, quickly got so far ahead of his older classmates that he could spend his school hours planning and daydreaming about what he knew was going to happen with Forest.

At night, the creatures in his room clawed at him, demanding more peanuts. Still he was afraid to do what he knew Forest wanted him to . . . climb up the tree and go in the attic window. Kevin slept with the pillow over his head, his hands protecting the part of him that the creatures were howling and nipping at.

After school every day he ran to the garden, hoping

Forest would relent and toss him some peanuts. He squatted there in all kinds of weather until his haunches ached, even when he heard his mother calling across the backyard, even when the air grew chilly, the sky dark. His mother would stop calling and he heard nothing but the rustle of leaves in the growing wind. The wind began to whistle and slap his face with large flat drops.

One night when he came home wet and shivering and covered with bits of leaves and twigs, his mother made him take a bath right away, and didn't give him his dinner, until Elizabeth came over with a new book, and begged her to feed him.

The librarian embraced him much more tightly that night, as if she'd been entrusted with his well-being when other adults turned against him.

How could she have done what she did? To make Kevin want to kill her?

The next day was crisp and sunny. The maple tree looked stark and skeletal with half of its leaves gone. Kevin waited in his own backyard for Forest to appear at his attic window. He craned his neck until he got a crick. He watched as a flock of sparrows congregated along the eaves, fluttered their wings and quarreled with one another. The sudden flying up of Forest's window sent them scattering.

There was a chatter and rattle and squeal. He saw Forest's arm reach out of the attic window. In his hand was a small wire cage. The squirrel was trapped inside.

The old man grasped the tree branch, pulled it toward the window. He secured it flexed against the sill with one gnarled hand made strong by all his gardening. Then he slung a heavy piece of clothesline over the branch, knotted it in a crook, and let the branch go.

Up flew the branch, carrying the squirrel in its cage with it, flinging the tiny animal against the mesh. It squealed in terror.

Kevin let out a small cry and dashed toward the fence, tore through the dying hollyhocks.

Forest grinned down from his window and held out a nut. Kevin didn't want the nut. He wanted to rescue the squirrel. His squirrel. He knew Forest would allow the animal to hang there in that cage until it died. And Kevin's shame would grow worse.

For just a moment, Kevin though he could tell Elizabeth what Forest had done to the squirrel. Then he realized that Elizabeth would know that he had been sneaking through the fence. Somehow he knew she wouldn't approve. She might stop bringing him books and holding him.

He stared up at the tree. The cage was swaying with the squirrel's frantic movements.

The bark was too rough for shimmying. But knots and the stumps of broken branches provided his sneakers and hands a grip. He pulled himself up to the lowest branches, then inched to the side of the tree that leaned toward the house. He had to stretch as far as he could to reach the next branch. Up to the second story the branches were thick and sturdy. They barely bowed to his weight. Even the bent bough from which the cage dangled gave only slightly as he heaved himself onto it and began bellying himself along it toward the attic window.

It dipped suddenly when he was only halfway there. He threw his arms around the branch, and scissored his legs to keep from sliding headlong into the cage. He had only one more body length to go.

The branch rocked. Dipping, dipping . . . dip-dipping . . . dip-dip-dipping before settling into a slow, soft sway. He held on for several long moments, hardly breathing. All he could hear was the squealing of the squirrel in its pitching prison.

He untangled his legs and inched himself forward again. There were no more sudden dips, just a slow bending downward as he closed in on the cage.

The squirrel was watching him, as if it sensed he was there to rescue it. Or, maybe it smelled his fear.

He crept forward another few inches. The breeze swayed through the leaves. He could almost touch the cage, almost grasp the small wire latch of the door. In a moment he'd be able to open it; in a moment, the captive would be safe. Only another inch along the branch . . .

A crack exploded behind him. The branch seemed suspended for a moment before it crashed down. A second later it caught in the web of branches below. Leaves scattered and spun. Kevin tilted forward. The rope holding the cage slipped off; the cage fell, caught a lower branch, and hung swinging precariously.

Kevin cried out as he felt himself falling. The coarse bark tore at his clinging ankles. He shut his eyes, afraid to look down.

Two rough hands grasped his arms, and he felt himself being pulled upward. He heard Forest's breath at his ear whistling though his boogers. He heard a rattle as the bough he'd been clinging to hit the cage and rammed it through the lower branches and to the ground. The animal screeched once, then was silent.

At first when Forest pulled him through the window into the attic, all he could see were bright colors whirling in his head.

The next time he came there, and all the times after that, he saw things he'd never known about before. Things that taught him how evil he was, how rotten and ugly he was inside. That taught him to hate himself and want to kill himself. That had driven him to

kill the others and to want to kill the woman he once
had loved.

He ran now from the funeral home in Bryn Mawr.
His rage against Joanna was swelling in his groin. He
would have turned his anger on her here, in front of
all the television cameras and mourners at Melanie
Roberts's funeral, but he tore himself away. She
would be the last. There was one more to go before
her. But the suffering he would put her through would
make it worth the wait.

Chapter Nine

Wednesday morning

JOANNA TRIED TO shake off the brutish mob of reporters
and photographers surrounding the funeral home.
They appalled her. So did her own attendance there.
Guilt about invading the privacy of Melanie Roberts
nagged at her. The more she thought about Hal
Thomas, the more conviction gripped her: Jon's theory was on the mark; something about infertility tied
these murders together.

She also believed Hal had told the truth. What
bothered her, keeping her awake most of the night,
was his passion. Some other truth lay frozen within
his unshakable beliefs about what had happened.
What had he said? *"I didn't allow it."*

"Joanna!"

She turned at the foot of the broad sweeping stairs of the white colonial funeral home porch to let Jon catch up with her. He took her elbow, apologized for being late, and guided her toward the door.

Just as she turned, her eye caught sight of a man threading his way casually through the crowds of curiosity seekers and reporters and TV cameramen on the sidewalk in front of the funeral home. A jolt of recognition stopped her as his eyes momentarily locked on hers.

A young woman with long blond hair and perfect red lips thrust a microphone and a smile at Joanna's face. ". . . And what is *your* relationship with the victims?" she asked, as if continuing an earlier conversation.

"What? Oh."

"Friends," Jon interjected.

"This must be a terrible shock." The smile retreated just slightly.

"It is. Now please . . ." Jon tugged Joanna's elbow.

Joanna hesitated as she looked once again toward the spot on the sidewalk where she'd seen Kevin. He'd disappeared. She took a quick breath and allowed Jon to guide her up the stairs, across the white-banistered porch, and into the lobby of the home.

"Please sign the guest book," a formally dressed man requested.

She nodded and took the pen he offered her.

Jon squirmed beside her as she scribbled her name, writing in "Philadelphia" as her address.

Jon whispered, "I wish you hadn't done that," as he led her to the chapel.

"They won't even know who I am, Jon. If I hadn't it'd be conspicuous."

"Conspicuous? You already got your face plastered

all over Channel 3 News. Why didn't you just keep on walking? You practically begged them to interview you the way you turned and stared at them."

"I turned because you called me."

"You didn't have to stand there staring."

She stiffened and drew slightly away from him as she walked beside him up the aisle of the solidly packed chapel and past the open coffins. Against the white satin the mother looked larger than she had expected; the baby impossibly smaller. How clean and neat and perfect mother and child looked in death! How different from the bloody moment of birth she so often witnessed with such elation.

Then she realized their deaths, as described in such detail by the *Inquirer*, had been equally bloody. Had the murderer tasted the same salty wonder and excitement at *his* moment of delivering them? Did their blood gushing forth smell the same to him as placental blood did to her: pungent, rich, brimming with sexuality.

Jon was tugging her arm again. She moved on. She grasped the hand of the grieving husband and father, told him how sorry she was. She told the dead woman's parents she'd lost a dear friend. All bowed their heads and accepted her condolences wordlessly. That they didn't know her didn't seem to matter. Because she was there, sharing their grief, she belonged.

After the interment she and Jon approached Frank Roberts as he helped his two small sons into the family car. She ached to give him solace; but he seemed angry when she asked to talk with him as soon as possible. His every movement cried out, Leave me alone!

"It's important. Friday's only two days away," she said.

"There won't be any more Fridays," he said. "Last Friday was the last." He closed the rear car door and opened the driver's door.

"You wouldn't want it to happen to anyone else," said Jon. "Just give us a chance to talk to you. We think you and your wife may have had something in common with the others."

"Look, I don't know those other people. They don't know me. The police have been over everything. What do you know that they don't?"

"We'll explain if you'll talk with us. We might have something for them to go on," said Jon.

Frank Roberts ducked into his car. "No," he said. He started his car and drove off, his tires spitting gravel onto the perfect emerald grass.

Just as Jon and Joanna started toward Jon's car, an older couple approached. "We're Nancy and Ralph Blair—Melanie's parents," the woman said.

Joanna could see her resemblance to the woman in the casket. Melanie's mother's face had the same oval shape. Though her hair was cut shorter, and pulled up and back from her face, though gray streaked it at the temples and rose from a widow's peak, its color was the same as Melanie's. Of course Joanna had no way of knowing the color of Melanie's eyes, whether they were brown like her mother's or gray-green like her father's.

"We heard what you said to Frank," Ralph Blair said. "She was our only child. The baby was our only grandchild." He looked about sixty, a tall, slim man whose dark brown hair had not receded, though it had begun to gray.

"I'm terribly sorry," said Joanna.

"We love Frank. We always have," Nancy Blair said. "He reminds me of Ralph when he was his age. Even looks like him. I always thought she married him because he had her father's hair and eyes."

Ralph nodded and began to sob.

Nancy, looking tiny and slight next to him, put her arm around his waist. "She and that baby were very dear to Frank. And his first wife died, too. But he hasn't lost everything. He still has his boys."

"From the first marriage," Ralph said. "*Her* parents still have grandchildren."

"They're here too." Nancy Blair gestured with her head to a couple kneeling beside a headstone next to the canopied graves Melanie and her small child had just been lowered into. Then Nancy turned her eyes from the unhappy scene and grasped Ralph's hand. "Of course they're grieving, too. But they still have the boys. And a son who just got married. And another daughter with kids."

Nancy went on, "Their children never had trouble giving them grandchildren. We waited so long! She was trying to get pregnant for more than two years. We didn't put on pressure like some parents do. But we knew how badly she wanted a baby of her own. One day she said, 'It's going to happen, Mother. I'm going to give you a grandchild of your own. I'm working on it. I'm working on Frank.'"

Jon shot Joanna a glance.

"You said you heard us talking to Frank. That's why you came over?" Jon asked.

Nancy and Ralph stopped. "Yes," said Ralph. "We heard you saying that Melanie and the others might have something in common."

They started walking toward the cars in a cul-de-sac parking area.

Nancy looked at Joanna. "You said in the chapel that you were Melanie's friend. I was close to my daughter. I thought I knew all her friends. You know, she lived with us until she was nearly thirty. So she introduced us to everyone she was close to. Women and men, both. I . . . I'm sorry, but what is your name?"

"I'm Joanna Michaels. And this is Dr. Jon Isenson."

"She never mentioned you . . ." Nancy shook her head.

"She didn't know me."

The couple looked puzzled, then angry. Ralph said, "But you said in there she was your friend. Why are you here asking questions?"

"What I said," Joanna explained, "was that I had lost a good friend. I've begun to feel that way about all the victims whether or not I knew them personally. Ever since we discovered"—she looked up at Jon— "Jon and I, that there might be a connection between them. I knew there had to be something, Mr. Blair. Some reason the murderer chose them."

Nancy Blair was nodding. "That's true. Though the police can't seem to find anything. So when we overheard you talking to Frank, we thought you might know something she hadn't told us. If she had a friend she hadn't told us about . . ."

". . . then she might have had secrets with that friend," Ralph finished for her. "What do you know about our daughter? Did she do something wrong? Did she belong to some organization we didn't know about?"

"I'm sure she didn't do anything wrong," said Jon.

"Organizations . . . ?" said Joanna.

"You know something," Nancy said.

"No, no. It's just an idea. She might have belonged to a support group of some kind. That might have been what tied them together."

All four stopped and looked squarely at one another. Then Nancy shook her head. "Our daughter was perfectly well. She had a responsible job, took good care of her children. She didn't have any emotional problems. Neither did Frank, to my knowledge. Why would she need a support group? She could always bring her problems to us. Always did."

"What about her infertility?" Joanna asked.

Nancy opened her mouth. "No! She wasn't infertile. That's pretty obvious. She had a perfectly normal pregnancy."

"Are you sure she didn't have trouble conceiving?" said Jon. "You said a while ago that it took a long time. That she said she was 'working on Frank'. What did she mean by that?"

Ralph rubbed his chin. "I don't think he wanted her to get pregnant. His first wife died from a . . . what do you call it . . . a baby in her tubes."

"Ectopic pregnancy," said Joanna. "I can see why he'd hesitate."

"But it was selfish of him. He had children of his own. He didn't have any right to deny her hers. Not when she wanted that baby so badly. Not when the risk was hers." Nancy shook her head again. "You see, he still has something left. We don't. That's why he wouldn't talk to you. He doesn't really care about anyone but himself. Doesn't care about some other mother and baby that might get murdered."

"Nancy, don't say that. The man's lost two wives in just six years. He's hurting," said Ralph.

She looked at her husband. "And he could go out tomorrow and get a new wife. Just like he did our Melanie. To take care of *his* children." She bit her lip and turned away from him.

He raised his hand toward her shoulder, then hesitated and let it drop by his side. "Come on, Nancy. Let's go to the car. It's no use just standing her blaming someone." He dropped his shoulders and trudged a few steps.

She shivered and straightened her shoulders and started after him.

Joanna touched her arm. "Nancy," she said, "people who want children they can't have for one reason or another always blame someone. Husbands blame wives; wives blame husbands. That kind of thing could poison a marriage. Maybe that's what you unconsciously picked up when she talked to you about working on him. Maybe they knew they had a problem that could be solved with professional help. They could've joined a support group to help them deal with his feelings. Obviously they *did* work it out. And she had her baby."

Nancy locked liquid eyes on Joanna. "Yes."

"And if that's so, then that's where she might have come in contact with the other victims. We know already that all of them had some kind of fertility problem. That's what we think they had in common."

The tears slid over the edges of Nancy's eyelids and ran freely down her face. "Another thing they all have in common is that they are all dead. And so are their babies. And we can never bring back our daughter and granddaughter." She shook Joanna's hand off her arm and followed her husband to the car. He opened the door for her, and she started to get in.

"Wait," said Joanna. She walked quickly to the car. "You can't bring them back. But if you can tell us more, maybe Jon and I can prevent more murders."

Nancy shook her head and got into the car.

Jon said, "Please. You've helped us so much already." He caught Ralph by the arm, just as he was about to close the car door behind his wife. "Mr. Blair, you can't let your grief over this terrible loss cost some other mother and baby—maybe many more mothers and babies—their lives. Think of how you'll feel Saturday morning when the headlines are like last Saturday's, if you refuse to help us now."

"He's right, Nancy. We can't do that."

Nancy looked up at Joanna and Jon. "But what can I tell you? You already know more than we do."

"Just tell me the name of the obstetrician that delivered your daughter's baby. He'd know whether or not Melanie belonged to a support group. I'll get in touch with him tomorrow, so if they all belonged to the same group, the police will know whom to warn, whom to protect."

"Her doctor was Terrence Goldblum," she said.

"David is furious about that TV interview," Louise said when Joanna phoned to see how Cassie was doing. "It's a good thing you're not eating dinner here tonight. Maybe by tomorrow night he'll calm down."

"Tell him to calm down now. Jon and I have uncovered the key to the murders. You and Cassie are safe. You don't think I'd do anything to put her . . . or you . . . in danger, do you?"

"Frankly, I'm not sure what you'll do anymore. I've never seen you so obsessed with something that's completely out of your realm of experience. I could kill Jon Isenson." She stopped for a moment and caught her breath. "How do you know you've got the key?"

Joanna explained what happened at the cemetery. "There's only one thing that worries me. Dr. Terry Goldblum doesn't exactly feel kindly toward nurse-midwives. He's definitely from the old school. No natural childbirth; no husbands in the delivery room; no interference from the mother."

"Doesn't sound like he's the kind of guy who'd encourage reproductive technology either," said Louise.

Joanna paused. "I hadn't thought of that. But, anyway, I have an appointment with him early tomorrow, so I won't be able to come by and give Cassie her breakfast."

"Maybe that's better. I think you'll do better with Goldblum than with David."

Joanna laughed. "Oh, I forgot to tell you. I saw Kevin again this morning. Outside the funeral home."

"Joanna! What was he doing there?"

"Seemed to be casually walking by. At first it upset me again. I thought he had followed me. But then he disappeared. Anyway, if he *is* following me, I'd rather have him tail me to a funeral than to your house and find Cassie."

"Wasn't it just a week ago today that he came to your office?" Louise asked after a pause.

"Yes. Wednesday's the day I have afternoon hours. But that might be just a coincidence. Wednesday might be his day off, too. But I've decided not to worry about him. If he wants to follow me, let him. He saw me with Jon . . ."

"Yes, so did the whole world . . ."

"That's good. It should give him the message that I'm surviving without him. Maybe that's why he disappeared."

"Joanna, I really hope you know what you're doing. And I pray Jon doesn't get you into trouble, the way he did the other woman he played detective with."

"What do you mean, trouble?" asked Joanna.

"Her baby was kidnapped, and one of her friends was murdered trying to find it."

Chapter Ten

Thursday

JOANNA WAS SURE the murderer couldn't know what she was doing. Except for Melanie's family, she and Jon had talked only to people they knew. Why would anyone think their contacts were other than personal or professional? As for the TV interview—she'd watched the eleven o'clock news last night, and her appearance lasted only a few seconds and was overshadowed by interviews with Melanie's family.

And only Dr. Terrence Goldblum would know her visit to him this morning was not professional.

Terry Goldblum's office in an old wing of a recently expanded medical office building in Bryn Mawr, reminded her of the office of her childhood family doctor in Pittsburgh, where she was born and lived until she went away to college in Philadelphia. Creaky worn brown leather chairs lined the edges of a small dull waiting room. The receptionist's cage cast a green glow from the walls and sliding glass window, which was opened only if the receptionist deemed it safe. Otherwise she would speak through a small steel-rimmed circle cut into the glass, like a teller in an old fashioned bank.

The receptionist had arrived before Joanna, though the posted morning office hours wouldn't begin for two hours. Joanna suspected he'd called her in early to set a tone of distance and diffidence. Indeed, she spoke to Joanna through the hole, and didn't slide open the window, even when she returned to it after consulting her boss.

"Doctor says you can come back," the receptionist said, nodding at a brown wooden door. Her purpose obviously did not include ushering Joanna in. That would have implied she was welcome.

Terry Goldblum sat stiff and crisp in his lab coat behind a worn mahogany desk in a room painted an institutional green. His thick round steel-rimmed glasses looked like a protective cage. His face had a ruddiness that looked as if it had resulted from a scrubbing with a wire-bristled brush. His white hair, perfectly waved and cut short, might have been groomed with the same ruthless brush.

She hated to think of the treatment his patients received at his hands; but that was probably what they came to him for. Doctor, as the receptionist referred to him, knew best. Don't think for yourself, take Doctor's word for what's good. Lie down on your back for Doctor; lift your heels into the cold steel stirrups for Doctor; slide back on the table for Doctor.

Then the Doctor would wordlessly insert his cold speculum into them—wordlessly because he couldn't bring himself to think of this part of a woman as anything but ugly and shameful, a necessary evil serving as a passage for life. Doctor might occasionally grunt or demand, "Now, relax!"

From what little Joanna knew of Melanie Roberts, she couldn't imagine the woman having gone to this doctor. As she took, in response to his curt nod, the hard chair across the desk from him, she breathed a prayer of relief that doctors like Terrence Goldblum were becoming more and more rare. Most were like Jordan Martin, who ran the Martin Center; they looked at their role as care givers privileged to take part in the process of maternity; they honored and were continually awed by the miracle of a woman's body.

Terry Goldblum looked at his watch. "What can I do for you, Miss Michaels?"

"I have some questions about a patient of yours."

"You know my relationship with a patient is privileged. If one of them has come to your center, I'll be happy to release her records. That is, if she'll sign a release. If one of your *doctors* wants a consultation, I'll be happy to speak with him."

"This patient hasn't come to us. Unfortunately she's no longer living."

He drew back and appeared even stiffer. "I practice the most stringent medicine. Though I must pay the same ungodly liability insurance rates as the less careful obstetricians, I've never been sued. I believe that's not so at your center."

"This hasn't anything to do with malpractice, Dr. Goldblum. The woman I'm talking about was murdered."

He looked relieved. Fine with him that she was murdered! Joanna thought.

"Then what does her being my patient have to do with this? Exactly what is the nature of your inquiry?"

"One of my clients was also murdered by the same person. She was Bloody Shoes' victim."

"Ah, yes. That serial killer. You must mean Melanie Roberts." Dr. Goldblum leaned back in his old leather chair and peered through his glasses at her. His eyes seemed to recede as if she were looking at them through the wrong end of a telescope. "Very tragic, of course. But I hardly think it unusual for a mother and her baby to have been in the service of an obstetrician. Or terribly unusual, these days," he said with obvious disdain, "to have been in the service of a midwife. Since most of us in this field of . . . *medicine* . . . have contact with one another, or at least know of one another, one would expect that the murdered women might have gone to someone we know. But that fact hardly involves either of us in their murders."

"Neither of us is involved in their murders. But I've learned a great deal about the background of Irene Kimski, my client, and one of the other victims."

"The background of people in other obstetric practices is really none of my business."

"These women have been killed because of something in common in their background, Doctor. Something that ties them to the killer."

His head jerked back. "I know nothing about my patient that could possibly tie her to that killer. My patients are from the best of homes. Mostly from Main Line families. Second and third generations, at that."

"This has nothing to do with their family background. The problem they all seem to have is one that cuts across socioeconomic classes . . ."

"Yes, I'm sure that a patient who would go to you would not be the same class of patient that comes to me."

She refused to take offense. "Exactly."

"Tell me, then, what is this mysterious problem they all have in common?"

"Infertility."

He knit his brow.

"I learned from Melanie Roberts's parents that she had trouble conceiving."

"How she conceived and how long it took her was certainly none of my business. And I don't see how it's any of yours."

"You mean you didn't treat her for her infertility?"

"That is not my specialty. My specialty is and always has been the treatment of pregnant woman, and their delivery."

"Of course," she said. "But I assumed you were her gynecologist before she got pregnant. Most ob-gyn doctors get their own obstetrical patients from their gynecological service."

"Yes. That's usually the case. However, Melanie

Roberts did not come in that way. She was already six weeks pregnant when she came to me."

It wasn't the answer Joanna expected. "How unusual. She must have gone somewhere else for her gyn treatment before. Do you know who referred her?"

Terrence Goldblum drew himself up and stood up. "I resent your probing into my patient's background. And I certainly would not expose a referring colleague to your impertinence and presumptions, if one of them had sent her to me. However, as she was referred by her husband, whose first wife was my patient, there is no danger of that. So, at this point, I'll just ask you to leave . . . ."

"Her husband referred her . . . ?" Joanna began to rise.

"Yes. He had perfect faith in me. He certainly would not send his wife to a midwife. Not after the efforts of even so skilled a physician as myself could not save his first wife's life when she so carelessly ignored the symptoms of her third pregnancy and did not get into my office immediately. But it was typical of her to be careless."

Joanna stood up and leaned forward, pinioning his eyes with hers. "I see," she said. "It seems your respect for your patient's privacy doesn't extend far enough to prevent you from maligning her once she's dead. Even to a midwife."

His mouth fell open. Then he said, "I really don't know what you mean. I've said nothing against Melanie Roberts."

She smiled ironically. "Of course you don't understand, Doctor. I wasn't talking about *Melanie* Roberts. Thank you for your time." She turned and left, knowing he'd never know what she meant—that he had blamed Frank Roberts's first wife's death on her own carelessness. Neither of us got anything out of this frustrating visit! she thought.

As Joanna escaped the hostile atmosphere of Terrence Goldblum's office it struck her that if the victims *had* been in the same support group, one of their spouses might have realized the fact by now. Joanna and Jon seemed to be on the wrong track with infertility. They had no proof to take to the police. Still, something nagged at Joanna. Something she couldn't pin down.

On her way to Louise's after work, she decided to lose herself in her own motherhood for the night and not think that tomorrow might bring more murders. Maybe the murderer had vented his spleen; maybe there were no more victims on his list.

She was amazed to find Jon sitting in the living room with David and Louise in strained silence. Michael melted from the room when she came in, as if he had been told to do so.

She studied their faces. They looked away.

Fear gripped her.

"Where's Cassie?" she said. "Something's happened to Cassie."

Louise's mouth fell open.

David shook his head sharply.

Jon's brow furrowed.

But from the stairway leading upstairs from the foyer, Michael's small voice announced, "Cassie's upstairs in her bed."

Relieved, Joanna sank into a chair, wondering why a storm was brewing between her family and Jon.

"What are you doing here, Jon?"

"I invited him," said David. The anger was clear in his eyes.

"Demanded my presence, is more like it," Jon said.

She took a deep breath. "It's about the interview, isn't it?"

"It's about your whole stupid involvement in this thing, Joanna," said David. "It wasn't what I had in mind when I told Jon you were home and might go out with him."

"What you had in mind! I suppose what you had in mind is controlling me for the next couple of years until Kevin leaves and I can take . . ." She stopped and covered her mouth with her hand.

Louise cast a warning glance at Joanna. "He's just concerned for your safety. God knows how many people saw you at the funeral. And you've talked to too many people who were involved with the victims. Why shouldn't the murderer notice? He might even have been at the funeral yesterday, watching you."

"That's ridiculous," said Joanna.

"What does Kevin have to do with this?" Jon demanded.

"I saw him outside the funeral home yesterday."

"Why didn't you say something?"

"You dragged me into the chapel. Later I forgot. That's how important it was."

David said, "That's just it, Jon. A week ago she thought it was so important that she stayed away from our house for days so he wouldn't follow her here."

"David!" warned Louise.

"But your damned investigation seems to have made her careless," David went on.

"Joanna, is Kevin threatening to kill himself again? That bastard!" Jon clenched his fists.

"No," she said. "I told you I was frightened when he came to my office. But when he stitched me up after the accident, I realized he didn't care."

"What was he doing in Bryn Mawr if he wasn't following you?" said Jon.

"That's what I asked her," said Louise.

"Maybe he lives there," Joanna said.

Jon said, "Doesn't he live near the hospital?"

"How should I know? I haven't kept track of his living arrangements since he moved out of my apartment. Maybe he has a new girlfriend to support him." She recognized the bitterness that crept into her voice and hated it.

Jon shot her an icy glance. "That bothers you, doesn't it? You're not afraid of him, you're afraid of yourself. You'd go back to him in a minute. Mental abuse and everything. You think you can save him." He took a few steps toward the foyer before turning to David. "I appreciate your invitation. You're right. I don't have any business dragging Joanna into this case, exposing her to unnecessary dangers."

"That's ridiculous," Joanna said, but Jon was already out the door.

Joanna turned on David. "What made you think you had the right to try to protect me?"

"You owe it to Cassie . . ."

"How dare you tell me what I owe her!"

"You owe it to Louise. You've made Louise and me responsible for her, and now you've put them both in danger."

"You're blaming me for making Louise a mother? That's crazy. She doesn't fit the victims' profile. As far as the world knows, Cassie's adopted. In any case, I haven't made you responsible for *me*. I've taken responsibility for myself."

"I don't think you have."

"I'll prove I can take care of myself. Cassie, too. I'll make arrangements to take my baby back."

"Joanna, you can't," Louise cried out. "You aren't the only one involved anymore. What about me? What about Michael? He loves his little sister. Goddamn it, David, why must you be so arrogant, think you always know best?"

Upstairs, Cassie began to cry.

Joanna ran up the stairs and snatched her out of her crib.

Chapter Eleven

Rock-a-bye baby

ON FRIDAY Angela Marietta slept late. It was her duty to the eight-month fetus inside her. From the time she became pregnant, she paid strict attention to her duties to "The Kid", as Phil liked to call it. Six months before that, she'd stopped doing coke, because the fertility doctor warned her it might make her infertile, too. Then Phil would be the only male member of Holy Fathers and Their Virgins not to produce a kid in the three years the rock band had been together. The only one not to prove his virility by having something more than what the guys and their previously disappointed fans deridingly called his "holy ghost".

Tonight she would sing, rocking her baby-filled belly sensuously out over the edge of the stage, while Phil rocked his pelvis back and forth and hit the strings of his electric guitar. The doctor had said the loud music might be bad, but she'd read that rocking back and forth and singing to the kid was good. So she never missed a date, and vowed to appear onstage until she went into labor, if they happened to have a concert or club date that night.

And Phil said, "Hey, if the momma's music is good

for him, his daddy's has got to be the best, dude. Fuck that doctor's shit."

Besides, the other Virgins had appeared till the very end, and nothing had happened to their kids, though Bette's and George's was a little runty and had to be kept in the hospital for a while till it came off the coke.

Angela was the only one who had trouble getting pregnant in the first place, had to give up coke and all that, which damn near bust off her head for a while, so she tried to be careful and sleep late before the concerts, do some early numbers and go home before Phil, who stayed all night to party with the others. He no longer had anything to lose; and as far as they were concerned, he'd done his part for the Fathers.

Her numbers went well Friday night, and she was honestly glad to go home early. She had to admit she was feeling a little heavy. When she was getting ready to go this afternoon, her belly had suddenly dropped. The kid kicked up a storm for a minute, and it scared her. She felt dizzy for a few minutes and had to sit down.

She had never felt more pregnant. Phil's eyes lit up too when she came onstage for rehearsal. It was a difference everyone could see, and it made the whole band proud.

And that guy who came into the club alone almost every Friday night looked at her like he noticed too. He seemed to come to hear her, because he usually left whenever she did. He was kind of different from the fans and the groupies that hung around them. Never tried to grab at her jewelry or purple hairpiece (which everyone knew was not her real hair); never seemed to be smoking or snorting anything . . . just had a drink or two, sat staring at her, but not mean or weird or anything like that. More as if he liked her and respected her and would never move in on her as long as she belonged to Phil. But maybe after, if she and Phil ever split.

Phil never seemed to notice the man. Neither did any of the Fathers and Virgins. But they were too high and too much into their music to care. So were the fans. If she had been on something, she wouldn't have noticed him either. It was just that they were the only ones in the club who weren't high, so they noticed and liked each other, she supposed. She was planning to stay clean awhile after the kid was born, so she could breast-feed him. The idea of feeding a kid your own milk kind of turned her on.

Anyway, this guy did leave again after her last number; and nobody else seemed to notice or care as usual; and she was too exhausted to care. She was hungry; she felt like she weighed a million pounds; and she just wanted to get back to their apartment and to bed.

She parked her car in the slot in front of their apartment and unlocked the door, glad that she had no stairs to climb, even though having a ground-floor window meant she'd see the flash of headlights on her wall from every car that turned into the parking lot. And on Friday night, cars seemed to pull in all night.

On a warm night like this, she'd also have to keep the window open. She couldn't believe how hot she always felt. Someone told her she must be having a girl—they made you feel hotter than boys. And sicker, too. She'd been plenty sick, though she'd never let it affect her singing.

Phil said she should use the air conditioner, that opening the window wasn't safe. She argued with him. Gave in when he was home with her, even though it sent the electric bills soaring. But when she was home alone, she opened the window about four or five inches and used a trick she'd read about in the paper: put a wooden dowel in the window track so no one could slide it over far enough to get in.

That's what she did tonight in both the living room and bedroom windows before climbing into her bed and falling into a restless sleep.

The lights from cars slid soundlessly across the bedroom walls and seemed to drop into a corner behind her bed. A few seconds after the lights passed, she sometimes heard the whisper of tires move by the window. She'd know when Phil was home. A second flash of lights would follow the car sounds as he pulled into his parking space next to hers in front of the apartment. Then the lights would go off in two stages: first the headlamps, then the parking lights; then the motor went into idle, then he cut it altogether. His door opened and closed with its own peculiar *thunk*— the Toyota sounded different from her Chevy—then she'd hear the keys in the apartment door. She knew he'd close the windows before he went into the kitchen to finish a joint and bring himself down enough to sleep.

She'd fall asleep as soon as she heard him close the windows. After that the lights from the parking lot never bothered her.

Till then she awoke at every sound.

Tonight when he pulled into his parking slot his car sounded a little different. The engine whined a little louder, idled a little faster. Had he had it tuned up? She couldn't remember.

The clunk of his car door closing sounded different, too. Sharper. Harder. It could have been George's. Maybe he had to borrow one of the other group members' cars. That had happened a few months ago, when he'd left his lights on and his battery ran down. She thought a minute about getting up to look, but the weight of the baby welded her to the bed. So what if he borrowed a car? They'd get the battery jumped in the morning like they did the last time. No big deal.

She heard him in the living room at the window. He

seemed to be having a hard time closing it. Sounded as if it was stuck. He'd be mad at her for fooling around with that rod. He'd *told* her it was dumb a dozen times. Wouldn't stop anyone who really wanted to get in.

Well why would anyone *really* want to get into their apartment? It wasn't as if Fathers and Virgins were Ozzie Osborne. No one outside of Philadelphia ever heard of them. They hadn't been able to sell a record. The only commercial they appeared in was for a local car dealer, where George jumped up and down on the hood, and she sang in the backseat and got out gracefully to show a pregnant woman could do it.

There was nothing to steal in their apartment. Shit, they barely could pay the rent. And if someone wanted a hank of her purple hairpiece . . .

Well, he seemed to have got the window closed, anyway, She heard it slide shut and click. And if he was mad at her, she'd remind him that he'd let the car battery run down again, so what was so smart about him?

She sighed and turned her back to the bedroom window and closed her eyes again, because she didn't want him to know she was awake when he came in to close the bedroom window before going into the kitchen for his roach. By the time he'd finished that, she'd be asleep for real.

He came in and closed the window. The reek of pot and alcohol wafted over to her as the aluminum window frame latched. She'd got used to its tenacious hold on their hair and clothing; after the first few months of her pregnancy, it didn't make her sick anymore.

She waited for him to go out the bedroom door and close it, as he always did. Instead, he came close to the bed and just stood there. Something in the way he stood felt different, didn't feel like Phil, but felt like someone she knew from somewhere.

He just stood there. The lights from a car turning into the parking lot cast his shadow on the wall in front of her.

The shadow wasn't Phil's.

A chill passed over her as the light dipped and carried the shadow into the corner behind the bed. Her blood pulsed in her ears and neck. She moved her hands down to her belly to protect the suddenly thrashing baby. She felt weak and dizzy.

He bent over her, took her top arm from her belly and pulled her onto her back.

Now her eyes widened. "You!" she said. "What do you want?"

He dropped her arm and did not try to stop it from its instinctive return to her belly. She lay there too terrified to move, her throat too paralyzed to call for help. Without a word he reached into his pocket and pulled out a knife. Not just a knife . . . a scalpel. The lights of another car flashed across her face, backlighting him as he sliced the blade across her throat.

His silhouette swallowed the light, swallowed her body. Uncontrollable lights pulsated for a moment in her head. She did not feel him remove her hands from her belly, nor did she feel the blade slice her abdomen or her baby thrash as he tore it from her womb.

Chapter Twelve

Saturday

THE SWITCH IN Bloody Shoes' tactics sent a chill through the Martin Birthing Center. Joanna received seven calls from pregnant clients. A woman in her thirty-sixth week, who had had a perfect pregnancy till now, went into premature labor.

Joanna began to reconsider her plans to take Cassie back. Enough time had passed to cool Kevin's anger; the fact that he had a baby was much less likely to make him carry out his suicide threat. Still, whatever Bloody Shoes' relationship with his victims might be, it seemed clear that he was after gestating, not adoptive mothers. By taking Cassie she would reveal the truth; and that would put her and her baby at risk from him if not from Kevin. Not that the risk would be that great. She was only one among thousands of mothers with newborns in the city. Why should she be a likely victim? But she decided to wait. If infertility of the mothers was the link after all, that would surely show up. If not, the real link could not remain hidden much longer. The data were piling up in the police computers. Something was bound to kick off some artificial intelligence program. Bloody Shoes had to leave some tracks eventually.

When she arrived home from the center, she called Louise and told her she'd changed her mind. She hoped David and she could settle their differences, she said.

"Cassie's the important one," Louise said. Her voice sounded taut and strained.

"She always has been."

"No, Jo. The trouble is *you've* been number one. Cassie's just been . . . well, a pawn."

138

Joanna was dumbstruck. "I didn't know you felt that way."

"I didn't. Your needs were everything to me. I tried to put myself in your shoes. If Cassie was a problem for you at this time of your life, I wanted to help. I still do. I love you both. It's just that you've gone off the deep end on this investigation. And the baby . . . well, you treat her as if she's getting in the way of your life. Give her to Louise and David; no, take her back; no let them keep her awhile. As if we didn't really have anything to say about it. Well, we do."

Joanna's hand began to tremble. "Then you want me to take her."

"That's not what I'm saying. I'm saying she's not just a piece of baggage. She's the rest of your life. And you don't seem to give her a thought. You worry about Kevin and whether he's going to kill himself, but you don't spend a minute worrying about her."

"I think of her almost every minute. I ache for her when I'm away. Don't I run to your house after work almost every day? Don't I come for breakfast when I can't come for dinner? Don't you think it tears me apart to have to live with this lie all the time?"

"Maybe you ought to stop the lying, Jo. Maybe that's the whole problem."

"Kevin's the problem. I'm scared to death of what he'll do. I know if he finds out about Cassie . . ." She clenched her fist in her lap and gripped the telephone. "I know I've sounded irrational. But living with a suicidal person—especially one whose life you saved—gets to you. You know you're not really to blame. But . . . I made the decision to have Cassie, even though he'd warned me what he'd do. Because I didn't know if I'd ever have another child if I aborted her. Having her was my decision. He—what he'd do if he ever found out—was my responsibility."

"I know. You don't have to convince me. It's why I

agreed to take her for you. But you don't have to lie to everyone. You don't have to lie to Jon. Why don't you tell him the truth, Jo? Tell him Cassie is yours and Kevin's. That you don't want Kevin to know. Kevin will be gone soon, and you can start having a normal life."

"No, I can't. Not till Kevin moves away."

"What if he doesn't? Do we go on like this forever? You've probably already lost Jon. Tell *him* before David blurts out the truth. Or you do."

"I have to wait."

"Has Jon called since Thursday night?"

"No. It's obvious he thinks I'm planning to run back to Kevin out of some kind of guilt."

"I'm sorry. That's David's fault," Louise said, sounding tearful.

"No. It's mine. You're right about everything, Louise. I know it seems like I'm neglecting Cassie. But I just can't help it. I don't want to lie to Jon, but I'm in a bind. I love him. And if I tell him the truth, he'll leave me."

"He won't. He's not like that."

"I can't take the chance. Not yet. I've got to give it time. Please, Louise. Help me. Don't make it harder. Not now. Give me a chance to win his trust."

Louise sniffed. "I don't see how lying to someone wins trust. But I love you. I won't stop you from making your own decisions. You let me make mine when I ran off at age sixteen and got married instead of finishing school. Then you moved here yourself, and stood by me when Mom and Dad were ready to abandon me." She took a deep breath.

"But do me a favor, Jo. Forget about this investigation. Leave it to the police. The whole thing is scary."

"We reached a dead end last Thursday. I'd have told David that if he'd given me the chance."

Louise sighed again. "Well, thank God for that. You're out of it."

"And Jon probably is, too. Though he was going to try to learn more from Hal Thomas, if he could get him aside man-to-man. He also wanted to make some inquiries about the first Mrs. Roberts. Said something about talking to her parents this weekend."

"Even if it does, you'll stay out of it. Promise me. For Cassie's sake if not for your own."

She hesitated. "Yes. I promise."

"Good. Then I'll tell David. He's been unbearable."

"I've really screwed up your life, haven't I? I'm sorry."

Louise did not answer.

"Forgive me."

"I told you I love you."

"I love you, too, Louise. You'll never know how much. If I hadn't had you to turn to, I couldn't have let Cassie be born. No matter how much I wanted her. When this is over . . ."

"Don't say anything more. Are you coming over tomorrow?"

"Yes. I'll be there for dinner." Joanna swallowed hard and looked at her watch. "I can't talk anymore. I'm going to kick off my shoes, pour a glass of sherry and watch *Cable Network News*. At least the national news isn't going to dwell on Bloody Shoes. I almost think I'd rather hear that the Soviets have launched a missile. At least I'll know it'll all be over at once. And Bloody Shoes will go up along with the rest of us."

She'd misjudged, Joanna realized, as she rested back against her bedrest cushion and flicked her TV on with the remote control—the Bloody Shoes story with its macabre new twist had captured the atten-

tion of the national media. Philadelphia's newest outlandish serial killer surpassed in interest even the
1987 killer who'd lured women into his dungeon,
where he raped and murdered them and put one of
their chopped-up bodies in his freezer. Maybe the fact
that the women involved in the 'Eighty-seven case
were retarded and poor made it less frightening.

At any rate, this case was hot enough to bring out
the psychiatric experts to be interviewed on *Cable
Network News*'s Saturday edition, and to bring their
camera and news crews to Philadelphia. As much as
Joanna hated to see any more of the details, she decided not to change channels or turn off the set. It no
longer meant anything to her. She was not involved in
the investigation anymore. She sipped her iced sherry
and watched and listened. An armchair shrink, she
thought, would bring a note of humor to something as
horrible even as Bloody Shoes. And it was time she
stopped dwelling on the horror. But she wasn't
amused at what she heard.

"I think the police should be looking at the obstetric
community for their man," said the owl-eyed, mus-
tached psychiatrist. "You'll note that the baby was
delivered by a perfect Cesarean, according to the medical examiner. The carotids of all mothers and babies
were neatly severed. Not one unnecessary cut. Except
for the stabbing of the uterus of the non-pregnant
women. Which, if what I've been told is true, was
done after death."

"Could it be," asked the female interviewer, "that
the killer simply has it in for women? Especially for
mothers? He seemed to want to leave a signal that he
had destroyed the very source of their motherhood.
Taken the baby, cradle and all, so to speak." She
smiled as though she savored that metaphor.

The psychiatrist nodded thoughtfully. "I thought of
that, of course. Even thought of that metaphor, 'cradle

and all' . . ." His glittering eyes and emphasis co-opted the reporter's right to it. "However, I took the analysis a step further. Beyond the clever catchphrase stage."

"Arrogant bastard," Joanna said aloud. He *was* making the case amusing, in his own perverse way.

"If that were it, if the views of laypersons with just a dangerously little knowledge," he admonished . . .

"Dear God!" Joanna cried out, and set down her glass on the nighttable.

" . . . were to sway our view, then it would rest on insufficient evidence."

"Could you please explain that?" the woman asked stiffly, her smile somewhat off center.

The psychiatrist swelled. "Well, if the killer wanted to kill motherhood, he probably would have planted his scalpel in the undeveloped wombs of those poor little babies who happened to be girls, too."

The interviewer winced. So did Joanna.

"So I don't think it was motherhood in general the killer sought to destroy. I think it was the motherhood of these particular mothers. Moreover, the killer is obviously a man with surgical knowledge and skill, and particularly with obstetrical skill. I'd look for an obstetrician. Or at least someone associated with obstetrics. Go back and see where these babies were delivered. That could be your link."

"Well, thank you, Dr. Wolfe, for your most enlightening analysis," said the woman, obviously flushed with her scoop, though the doctor may have robbed her of the credit of coining the catchphrase that was sure to replace Bloody Shoes in referring to the murders from now on.

Now surely the police would come to the Martin Birthing Center. They would also question Dr. Goldblum, and Denise Thomas's doctor, whoever that was, and the doctors of the other two victims: Grace Heard, the lesbian, and Angela Marietta, the rock singer.

They would learn, most likely, that no two of them had had the same obstetrician or delivered their babies at the same facility. But now there was no question that Joanna could give them some leads. Jon's theory might work with the police following up on it. When they came in to question her, she'd make sure that Jon was there.

Of course that meant she was still part of the investigation. But not in the active way she had been before. David couldn't find fault with that. And Louise couldn't say she'd broken her promise. She couldn't control her involvement if the police came to her.

Now the interviewer had turned the program back to the hour's anchor, and he in turn had directed it to a reporter in Philadelphia who was reviewing the case.

Joanna was surprised to see the brief clip of Melanie Roberts's funeral and the local reporter interviewing her. Why hadn't such an inconsequential piece been edited out? The appearance of a midwife of one victim attending the funeral of another might seem to suggest a relationship to still another. The police would surely go over every film of every funeral to see if the perpetrator might have returned to view his—*or her*—work. And what if the police then went to the others she'd talked to? To Terrence Goldblum and Hal Thomas. They might learn that she and Jon had been snooping around, asking questions. They might assume . . .

"Oh God! David was right! She had put herself in danger."

Her mind raced. What if they decided she was a suspect? What if they thought Jon was Bloody Shoes? He was a surgeon. He dissected animals in his lab. He knew anatomy. Wouldn't he know how to perform a cesarean section? And wouldn't his accomplice, Joanna, be able to guide him?

When the police began their questioning, they'd learn she'd left town for six months, and that the murders began almost immediately after she returned. If the story of her trip to Europe didn't hold water, as it wouldn't because it was a lie, they'd try to get her to tell the truth. Then, when she finally did, they'd be sure that any woman who gave her baby to her sister and lied about it so the baby's father wouldn't find out, had to be a little crazy. If she said she was scared of Kevin, they'd think she was paranoid. Maybe they would get some psychiatrist like Dr. Wolfe to show she was suffering from a severe postpartum depressive syndrome, which had led to a murderous form of schizophrenia. She'd seen a TV special on that subject not long ago. Maybe . . .

On the screen the story rolled on. They showed scenes from the other funerals. They showed wedding pictures of the victims and their husbands. She recognized Frank Roberts and Hal Thomas. When they flashed on the picture of Irene and Igor Kimski, she even recognized Igor. When you've seen a man's eyes above a surgical mask, brimming and glistening with the joy of new fatherhood, you never forget them; they touch you always.

Now the camera showed Phil Marietta. His drawn face grimed with day-old beard, his watery, red-rimmed eyes, his stooped, twitching shoulders suggested a grief compounded by dissipation. The film contrasted sharply with a publicity poster now shown on the screen. In the photo Phil Marietta stood next to his wife, surrounded by the other members of Holy Fathers and Their Virgins. She was the prettiest of the women, with an air of innocence and purity despite a thick streak of purple in her hair. He stood tallest and straightest of the men. His long brown hair rested on shoulders held high.

His chin was firm and clean shaven. His clear eyes sparkled like wide round ponds in the sunlight. The larger-than-life poster enhanced their color, as it did Angela's sky-blue ones.

Taken in happier days, thought Joanna. Before Angela became pregnant.

In the few seconds the poster appeared on the screen, it burned its impression into her mind. She'd become keenly aware of physical details of the victims. She'd mentally photographed each couple, each person she interviewed, and placed the photos in an album in her head where she could compare them. She'd captured their gestures and mannerisms: Terrence Goldblum's ruddy arrogance and stiffness, Hal Thomas's eyes wandering grief-washed in his pale face, Nancy Blair's shoulders firming as her husband's sagged and he turned his eyes hopelessly from her. She never could forget these things; she'd flip through these album pages forever, trying to make sense of them, see why they all belonged in the same family album. Could she really completely divorce herself from this investigation?

She grasped her glass and suddenly sat forward. The pictures had faded from the TV screen, and the news anchor had gone on to another story; but Joanna still saw the afterimage of the Fathers and Virgins publicity poster in her mind. She could not let it go.

Taking another swallow of her now warm and watery drink, she set it down and switched the television set off. She stared into space, where the details of her photo album hung, a collage of flashing images. She got up, went to her desk, and retrieved her small maroon leather address book from the top drawer. Still holding on to her images, she flipped through the book to Dr. Rose Snyder's name.

She took a deep breath and dialed the phone number. "I'm sorry, Louise," she said aloud as the phone at the other end rang.

The woman who answered said Rose was gone for the weekend. Joanna could reach her on Monday.

For a few uncertain moments Joanna paced her room. She had to call Jon. She had to tell him what she saw in her family photographs, the thing they all had in common, the thing no one else seemed to have looked at. On Monday she'd get Rose to tell the rest of the story about Irene Kimski, the part she'd left out before—for a reason Joanna could understand—respect for the rights of her clients to privacy and confidentiality.

Jon's theory *was* right. She picked up the telephone again and tapped in his number.

His phone rang ten times with no answer.

On Sunday she tried again. He must be away for the weekend. With another woman? she wondered. At last she gave up.

On Sunday evening she ate dinner with Louise and David again, and held Cassie in her arms and fed her while she told her sister and brother-in-law another lie. She promised she would stay out of this investigation.

They seemed to believe her. I must be getting better at lying, she decided. But when all this was over—and someday it would be—she'd never tell another lie. Not to them or Jon or even to herself. Never.

Chapter Thirteen

On the tree top

THE FIRST TIME Kevin went into Forest's attic he cried; so Forest let him go home, as long as he promised not to tell anyone he had been in the dark slope-ceilinged room and seen the pictures of children on the walls. Keeping the secret was delicious, like his visits to the garden and his secret collection of peanuts. The pictures made Kevin breathe fast and sent tingles from his fingers up his arms. Especially the pictures of Joe Byrnes and another kid from the neighborhood whose name Kevin didn't know.

The fall days grew shorter and more chill. He grew sick of the war games with Joe, who always guessed his hiding places, since the hollyhock vines had lost their blooms and leaves and left the hole in the fence more exposed. One calm day, Forest, watching the boys—one with each eye—from his attic window, signaled to Kevin to climb up the tree.

By the time Joe had counted to twenty and scrambled through the hole in the fence, Kevin was snuggled between two forked branches of the tree. Joe looked around and began to cry, obviously frustrated at having had the rules changed on him again. He ran bellowing across Kevin's backyard to his own, and slammed his back door behind him.

Forest laughed softly in his window. Kevin climbed the rest of the way, bellied along the branch and into the man's waiting arms.

This time Forest had books in the attic. "Elizabeth brought them for you," he said. "Lots of nice pictures." His breath whistled fast through his boogers as Kevin let out a gleeful yelp and grabbed for the top one. "I'll read the words under the pictures."

At first Kevin didn't understand all the new words. He'd never seen pictures like these; the parts of the grown-ups seemed so much fiercer than those of the children displayed on the attic wall. But after a few visits he began to realize that he and Forest and Elizabeth were sharing some delicious new secrets. He began to hunger for the attic books and Forest as much as he did for the books and Elizabeth in his living room at home. Elizabeth never mentioned the attic books; but Kevin could tell from the way she embraced him as she read, letting her bony fingers stroke the outside of his thigh in her lap, that she knew what he shared with Forest.

That winter Kevin climbed the tree almost every day after school and threw himself into Forest's trembling arms. They'd look at the pictures, and Forest would whisper the words and stroke Kevin and undress him. He took pictures with his Polaroid camera and put them on the wall. Most of the things that he did made Kevin feel excited and good. The old man showed him how to make milk come from the boy, and large, pulsing, sticky, musky mouthfuls of it come from the man.

"Don't tell Elizabeth I'm feeding you the milk," Forest said. "She wants it all for herself."

Kevin began to hate her.

"I don't always just put milk in Elizabeth's mouth. I put it in her ass." He showed Kevin pictures of men and women, men and men, women and women, men and little girls, men and little boys putting the milk in all the different places it could go in.

That was the first time Forest hurt Kevin and made him bleed.

He began to want to hurt Elizabeth.

The pain repelled Kevin at first; that night he could barely sit still in Elizabeth's lap, but whimpered and wriggled and clamped and unclamped his hands which wanted to grab for his anus.

"Now sit still and behave! Be good! I've never seen you so bad," she said.

His love for her, now mixed with hatred and fear, made him control himself, except for one of his legs, which kept kicking. As the leg bounced into her legs and rumpled her skirt, she snapped at him, sighed angrily and slapped at him as if he were a fly. He wouldn't stop, so she dumped him off her lap and stalked out of the room.

"I'll come back when you've learned to behave, young man. First grade seems to have changed you for the worse."

Now he had no one to run to for relief from his shame.

He discovered solace in the bathtub. But an overlong stay there brought his mother's and sister's wrath.

"Mother, he won't let me in."

"Kevin, what's got into you? I thought you hated baths." His mother started to open the bathroom door.

"No!" he cried out. "I'll get out."

She closed the door. "All right. But hurry, young man. Your sister wants to get in."

He started to get out of the tub, but the dry heat blowing from the vent made his sore spot start burning as soon as he lifted his leg over the porcelain rim. He dunked himself again, lay there until the water grew tepid.

"Kevin, I'll send your father in to drag you out if you don't come out this instant!"

He jumped out, pulled his pajamas on over his wet body, and ran to his bedroom.

"Mother, he didn't clean the tub. It's yucky," Rayna whined.

"Fred, will you do something about your son!"

His father burst into his bedroom and dragged him by his arm to the tub. He pushed him to his knees. As Kevin scrubbed the bathtub, his small body looped over the porcelain side, his head down, buttocks up, his father stood close behind him. A chill of excitement ran through him. He wanted his father to do what Forest had done.

He realized at that moment how thoroughly evil he was.

His mother didn't find out until months later, when she discovered bloodstains in his bed and took him to a doctor. The doctor took his mother aside, leaving Kevin alone in the examining room. When he returned without his mother, the doctor asked Kevin if anyone had ever done anything to him "down there".

Kevin shook his head and denied it.

"Do you do things to yourself? Put anything in there?"

A mute, sharp shake of the head.

"You can tell me the truth. Even," the doctor said conspiratorily, "if it's your father."

Again the bowed mute head drove Kevin's chin into his chest. He'd only imagined it with his father. Lately, when Forest did it, he'd pretended it was his father.

The doctor grabbed Kevin's chin roughly, forcing his head up. "Tell me the truth, son. It's important. Who's doing bad things to you?"

Kevin pulled his head back, evaded the doctor's eyes.

The doctor let go of his chin. He stood up stiffly. His face grew stern, dark, ugly as Forest's. "We'll get it out of you, young man," he said. "I'm going to report this to the county health department. They'll send out a social worker."

That night his mother wouldn't let Elizabeth come to read to him. "I won't let you go near anyone decent until you tell the truth. You'll stay in your room alone when you're not in school. No more running off somewhere every day. Where have you been? Where is it you go all the time? You've become so sneaky lately. So disobedient. I've let you get away with it. So has your father. No more. I won't let anyone accuse that good man of teaching you awful things. You learned them yourself. Sneaking around, daydreaming ugly things in the bathtub."

Except for the hours he was in school, he stayed in his room all winter. His parents took away all his books. In the morning he'd watch Elizabeth go to work. Torn between love and hate, he'd long for her touch, the feel of the hard knot between her breasts pressing against his forehead when she hugged him. Sometimes he'd see her turn and look up toward his window, a sad, hurt look on her face. Then she'd pull her coat around her bony, tall frame and walk quickly toward the bus stop at the corner.

He knew he could tell her about Forest, if only he could talk to her for a few seconds. She might be mad for a while that Forest gave him some of his milk, but he'd offer her some of his own, and she'd still love him, and he'd forgive her.

He had his chance early one rainy spring morning. Risking his parents' wrath, he got up early and ran outdoors in his pajamas. He stood on the unsheltered stoop of Elizabeth's house. The huge, chilly raindrops pelted his head, straightening his brown hair so it stuck to his face and directed rivulets down it.

Her umbrella appeared first and opened like a huge shield that almost knocked him down the cement stairs. She came out behind it and swung it up over her head, then with a gasp discovered he was suddenly standing under it with her.

She stepped back through her door and caught a rib tip, before she recovered her composure.

"You're soaking wet! What do you want?" Her voice held an edge he hadn't expected.

"I'll give you my milk," he said.

"I've already had my breakfast. Now please go back home. I have to catch my bus to the library."

"Not that kind of milk. The kind that Forest gives you. I'll give it to you in your mouth or your. . . ."

She screamed, cutting him off, and swung her umbrella at him; once, twice, three times she ripped it across his arms as he hugged his head and eyes. "Filthy child! You filthy, ugly, horrible little boy!"

Then, the ribs of her umbrella bent and dragging, she ran crying through the rain like a bird fleeing with an injured wing.

The county social worker made an emergency call on Kevin and his distraught mother that afternoon. The Librarian had been too upset to work, had come banging on the Willmans' door and screamed that Kevin had tried to molest her. Kevin hadn't wanted to say anything to anyone about Forest, but now he had to.

The police found the photos and books in the attic and arrested Forest. Joe and the other kid whose pictures were on the wall said all Forest had done was take pictures one time and they never went back again.

Kevin finally told about everything that had happened. His family and Elizabeth said it wouldn't have happened if Kevin hadn't wanted it to, if he hadn't gone back again and again. The others hadn't gone back.

Kevin knew that was true. He'd wanted it and he'd liked it, even the pain. He knew he was as bad as they said. If he hadn't been, Elizabeth wouldn't have hated him, wouldn't have taken Forest's side.

It was Kevin's fault Forest went to jail and Elizabeth had to move. He knew it every time he went to the library, and he ducked as he saw her sitting behind her desk, her large curved nose rising, her chin lifting above her loneliness and hurt.

But he wasn't sorry for her. He hadn't expected her to do what she did; he hadn't expected her to desert him, tell everyone how bad he was. He thought she loved him as much as he loved her; he began to hate her as much as he hated himself, to want to kill her as much as he wanted to kill himself.

Chapter Fourteen

Monday

ROSE SNYDER WAS less cordial this time. When Joanna arrived at her office this noon she had ordered lunch only for herself and didn't offer Joanna even a cup of coffee.

"I know the police will be calling on you, Joanna," she said. "And I prefer that you don't drag our facility into this mess. You or your friend, Dr. Isenson. I should not like to be interviewed on the noon television news."

Joanna winced. "I didn't ask to be interviewed, either."

"Why didn't you tell me that Isenson was involved in your investigation?"

Joanna hesitated. "Why should I have told you?"

"You know he's persona non grata here. You set out to delude me." Rose Snyder toyed with her tuna salad, and finally tossed her plastic fork down. She locked eyes with Joanna.

"I don't understand."

"We're aware of some of his past detective work. He seems to like cases involving fertility centers."

"I might have subconsciously known you might resent him. But I only knew vaguely what he'd worked on before. Anyway, I had no intention of involving him with the fertility center. I don't intend to now." She held her eyes steady.

Rose held hers steady, too. "Then why didn't you tell me it was Isenson's theory that infertility was the link between the victims?"

"Would it have made a difference if I had?"

Rose Snyder's eyes flickered.

Joanna smiled and nodded. "It would have. You wouldn't have told me even as much as you did."

"Maybe not."

"I thought that trying to prevent another murder was what was important. And you didn't tell me the whole truth either," Joanna said quietly.

"What makes you think so?" Rose asked.

"You told me that Irene Kimski had in vitro fertilization."

Rose took a deep breath and slowly let it out. Her knuckles whitened. "I told you that because it is true. I said we still have some of her embryos in our freezer."

"That's good news for Igor Kimski, isn't it? It means that his offspring could be gestated by a surrogate. His and Irene's. They could have grandchildren down the line. A memorial to her. A blessing to him."

The doctor looked hard at Joanna. Then she rose and walked to her window, she pulled back the corner of the blind, and stared out. Without turning around, she said, "What exactly are you getting at, Joanna?"

"You know what I'm getting at, Rose. You didn't tell me everything about the Kimskis' fertility problems."

Rose dropped the blind and turned. "I told you more than you had any professional need to know. I value my clients' privacy. You convinced me you might be on to something that tied the murders together. That's the only reason I told you anything at all. As it is, another woman and her unborn child are now dead. So it seems your . . . Jon Isenson's . . . marvelous theory didn't even hold water. There was no infertility link."

Joanna looked at her and shook her head. "But if you had told me everything . . . told me what you held back, there was a chance that rock singer might not have been killed."

Rose's mouth fell open. "You're crazy!"

Joanna stood up. "I'm not accusing you of deliberately lying, Rose. I understand better than you know why you didn't say more than you did. At the time it looked like just knowing about the Kimskis' infertility would be enough to go on. If I'd only known the exact nature . . ."

"Irene's tubes were blocked. The ova had to be fertilized in vitro."

"I figured that out. Why else couldn't she have been inseminated directly intra-utero? Or intra-vaginally? Or through normal intercourse, for that matter?"

The doctor's eyes flashed. "Why else indeed?"

Joanna picked up her small briefcase, zipped it open, and took out a videotape cassette. "I have something here I want you to watch with me. I know you have a VCR in your consultation room. It'll take less than five minutes. I'll show you what I saw."

The doctor's face flushed.

"If you don't see the same connection I did, I promise you you won't have to tell me anything. If you do, I want you to tell me everything you possibly can about the Kimski case. And if you tell me what I think you're going to, I might have enough to go to the police with before they come to me. I might have enough to reassure my clients who think they're at risk. Or to prevent something from happening to anyone *really* at risk."

After a few moments Rose said, "Very well," and led Joanna back to her consultation room.

Joanna slipped the tape cartridge into the VCR slot and turned the machine to play. "I taped a segment of *CNN*'s coverage of Bloody Shoes' escapades and victims. Thank goodness they run the thing every hour. I had to watch it a few times before I was absolutely sure."

"I watched it myself. I saw nothing—"

"Only because you weren't tuned in to what I was. Just keep your eyes on the victims' husbands."

"But . . ."

"There. The wedding picture. Hal Thomas. It's blown up enough so you can see every detail."

Rose leaned forward. "It was just on a second. I don't know what I'm supposed to be looking for."

"I'll play it again if necessary. I want you to see it yourself. If I tell you what to look for, I'd be leading you."

"Stop playing lawyer, Joanna." Rose mocked her.

"But you're a witness. I don't take this lightly. I want to be sure. Now! There's Igor Kimski. I'm sure you recognize him."

Rose leaned forward again. "Yes."

"Frank Roberts," said Joanna as his and Melanie's wedding picture flashed on the screen.

Rose nodded. "For a second I thought it was still the Kimski picture. Her wedding gown's just like Irene's. They must have had similar taste."

"An astute observation. Now look at the rock group's poster. That's the thing that hit me. The colors are all enhanced."

"I see. They are. But that woman surely didn't have the same kind of taste as the others. That purple hair!"

"Are you sure?"

"I don't have to see that hair again to judge her taste. Lovely as she was, otherwise."

Joanna stepped forward and pressed the tape rewind button. "Think about that awhile. I'm going to run this through again. But this time I'm going to pause the tape so you can look at the husbands again. For as long as you need." She started the tape forward again, stopped it for about a minute on each portrait. She held the tape at last on the rock group's publicity portrait.

Rose stared at the screen. Joanna saw her eyes widen.

"I see it now," she said, after a long hesitation. "You can turn it off."

Joanna stopped and rewound the tape. She ejected it and turned to Rose.

"Come back into my office," Rose said. "I'll tell you as much as I can, which probably isn't going to be quite enough for you to take to the police. Your conjecture about what I omitted before is correct, though I think from what you've told me it's a far cry from that to the conclusions you're drawing on the others. But you're right about the relationships. Those victims may have been radically different from one another. But they definitely had similar tastes in men."

"Probably even the lesbian," said Joanna.

Rose Snyder smiled ironically. "Yes. Probably even the lesbian."

Chapter Fifteen

Monday—Kevin

DOCTOR WOLFE'S ANALYSIS delighted Kevin. He knew what would happen next: The police would close in on the obstetricians ... and the one midwife who'd delivered the children or cared for the women during their pregnancies—Joanna. That would bring their noses right up to the candy store windows. They'd see the goodies inside, but wouldn't quite be able to reach them; they didn't have the key.

Their closeness brought exhilaration to his planned final strike. Now anything could happen. Someone might guess the connection, try to keep his last victim from him, maybe start closing in on him as he closed in on her. If this were a movie they'd fabricate a chase scene. First the camera would focus on her as the hero snatched her from danger, which lurked in the form of Kevin in her bedroom. Then it would cut away to him; show him hovering in the closet (he'd never do such a stupid thing!); capture the glint of his scalpel as he pulled it from his pocket. In the movie, they would catch him, and the victim and her baby would get away and fall in love with the hero.

That was not going to happen here. Because he had it all figured out. Even if they finally realized why Kevin had had to kill these evil women and their ugly plagued children, they still wouldn't know who he was. He'd made sure of that long ago. So he'd finish his work on Friday, finish them off ... *Cradle and All.* As the TV reporter had said.

And then he would tell them why.

159

And they would thank him for ending the pestilence he'd visited on them in the first place. He wished he could see their faces. Especially hers. Especially all the ones he'd dedicated them to.

He wondered how Katie would take it. He'd dedicated the rock singer to her. Whore that she was, she'd probably laugh at the irony.

"Holy shit, Kevin," she'd say. "You didn't need to go that far. I mean, let the fuckers take care of themselves. They only got what they paid for. I mean, they knew they were taking a fucking risk."

"I don't know," he'd answer her. "They didn't know everything. Just what I told them."

"Look, Kevin," she'd say, "you think I tell my johns everything? They don't want me talking at all most of the time. My mouth is for other things."

"Don't say that!" he'd snap.

She'd look at him weird. "Sometimes I wonder about you, Kevin. You're all mixed up about sex."

"No. You're the one that's mixed up. I'd never do what you do. Sell it to every stranger that comes along."

"Well, your clientele might be a little classier, Kevin. But whatever, they still pay your rent."

"Angela Marietta wasn't classier. She reminded me of you . . . no class at all. Made loud music all night long. Gave me a headache. Couldn't keep my mind on my work. Had to go to the library to study. And it was all your fault, Katie. You were the one that gave me the idea in the first place. Who else but a whore could have come up with it. After all, a whore . . . Anyway, that's why I dedicated her to you."

"Well, that's one fucking honor, Kevin," she'd say. "But you didn't have to go that far."

And she'd laugh.

*   *   *

His sister wouldn't laugh about the dyke. "Why did you kill her? No. Don't say a word. You're filthy, that's why. Dirty! Evil clear through!"

He'd curl his lip in irony. Say nothing.

Anger would drip from the down twisted corner of her mouth. "You're all filthy . . . all of you. You don't know the beauty of sex. To you it's just a thrill or a commodity." Then she'd turn and stare at him, hate in her eyes. "Something to buy and sell. Something dirty. How could you do it, Kevin? Let that horrible man touch you. You're filthy. Even Daddy. I saw him once, doing it to Mother. In that awful way. Making it so ugly. So disgusting! I'd never let a man touch me anywhere with that ugly, diseased organ. I never have."

"I know that, Rayna," he'd tell her. "That's why I dedicated the dyke to you." His face would glow with the irony.

Hers would blotch purple with anger. "She had a right to bear her own child. She didn't have to dirty herself with a man. I'd do it myself if I wanted the responsibility of children. That's the *only* way I would do it." Then she'd shudder. "But not if I knew . . ." She'd bury her face in her arms and begin to moan. Dramatically, the way she always did, as if she were performing for an audience.

". . . What you know now," he'd finish for her.

She'd look up at him in horror, as she had when he'd first told his family about Forest.

He'd laugh. "But isn't the ending delicious, my sister? And wasn't I right to do it, after all?"

"But you didn't have to kill her. Wouldn't it have been enough just to kill the baby? Only the baby was tainted. Grace Heard had never been touched by a man."

Kevin would grow angry. He'd ball up his fists and long to hit her. Then he'd work them in his pockets for a few moments, try to control his breath. At last he'd whisper fiercely, "No! She was tainted too. There was no other way. It had to be *Cradle and All*.

Joanna would be different. Joanna would feel guilty. The dedication to her would even up the score. Because she would know—he would tell her in his final note—that she was the reason he did it. Because she had betrayed him and left him. When he'd needed her most. Because the awful things were beginning to happen again. His lust for the children had come back. And he'd felt himself spiraling downward for the first time in almost two years.

The way things were at work—the thirty-six-hour shifts, the availability of young boys and girls in the pediatric wing—he hadn't been able to help it. He was just too tired. He had too many things on his mind to fight off his evil desires. But she could have helped him, if only she hadn't been so selfish and devious in those last few months. She'd turned on him, gotten ugly and mean and sneaky.

Just when he'd needed her most.

When she left, he didn't have anyone left but the little boys and girls. It was her fault he went back to them. But it was also because of her he saw the terrible truth. He knew what had turned her so ugly. And he knew what he had to do. There was no other way.

Chapter Sixteen

Monday afternoon—Joanna

"I'M SORRY," SAID Jon's secretary, a quietly attractive blond woman in her mid-thirties. "Dr. Isenson is in the laboratory for the rest of the afternoon."

"May I see him there?" asked Joanna. The woman's lightly restrained sexuality piqued her jealousy. "I have something important to talk with him about."

"The lab is secured. Even I can't get in, Ms. Michaels. I can leave him a message to call you when he's done."

"Maybe I can wait for him here. When will that be?"

The secretary smiled sympathetically, increasing Joanna's irritation. She was obviously any man's dream secretary: patient, efficient, courteous, alert to her employer's every need. "When he does his dissections, he's often there until six or even seven. I leave at five. I'm sorry."

I bet you are, thought Joanna. She sat down and picked up a magazine. "It's three. I don't mind waiting."

The secretary, Angie . . . hadn't Jon said? . . . opened and then closed her mouth. "But . . ."

"It's all right. You don't have to stay. I've known Jon for years. He trusts me."

"Yes. I know." Her eyes flickered a moment. "That's not the point."

Joanna arched her brow.

"You see, he won't be coming back to the office after he's finished. He leaves directly from the lab."

"I thought you said you'd leave him a message to call me."

"On his computer. I'm hooked up by modem." She pointed to a small box under the telephone.

"Oh," said Joanna, feeling foolish and frustrated. Her sudden surge of sexual jealousy unnerved her. She had felt it before when Jon had mentioned he'd almost married the woman he'd been involved with in his past amateur detective work. Neither Jon nor Joanna had ever discussed with each other their past sexual relations with others, though both agreed on the principle of monogamous relationships, even if the liaisons eventually ended. He was one of only five men she'd slept with since she'd lost her virginity her first year of college. And though he couldn't be blamed for some disappointment at their recent aborted love-making episode, she felt they'd embarked on a lasting affair.

But he had been angry with her last Thursday when he'd walked out after David's outburst; and men often got even with women in somebody else's bed; and Angie looked as if she would happily anticipate and serve his needs there, as well as at the office. She was just too damn handy, this woman. And Jon had been too damn angry.

"I really have to talk to him today," she said. "Can't you phone the lab?"

The woman studied her a moment. "I could. Ms. Michaels . . ."

"Joanna."

She nodded. "Joanna, does this have something to do with those murders?"

"Yes. How did you know?"

"Jon told me this theory." She smiled quickly. "I've worked for him for a long time. He tries out ideas on me. Some of his ideas are pretty way out. He trusts me to tell him when I think so."

"What did you tell him about this idea?" asked Joanna.

"That it seemed far fetched. And dangerous. He nearly got killed the last time he stuck his nose into a case."

"I didn't know that."

"And this time he got his face on TV."

"That was my fault," said Joanna. Ten lousy seconds and nobody would stop talking about it! "But I really doubt it put him in danger. At any rate, that *is* what I came here to talk to Jon about. If I could just talk to him on the phone a few minutes, I'd get right out of your hair."

Angie hesitated a moment. "He won't leave an autopsy for even a minute, I know. But I can get a technician to tell him you're here. He should be able to give you an idea of when he'll be done. If it can't wait till tomorrow . . ."

"It can't. I don't mean to sound melodramatic, but Friday's only four days away."

The secretary picked up the phone and punched in four digits. In a moment she nodded to Joanna. "Craig, can you tell Jon that Joanna Michaels is here. She wants to talk to him when he's finished up tonight. I'll hang on."

She nodded at Joanna again, and covered the mouthpiece with her free hand. "It'll just take a minute. Oh, just a second." She uncovered the mouthpiece. Her face registered surprise. "He did? Are you sure? But he's never done that before. Even I . . . All right. I'll tell her."

Angie hung up the phone. She looked at Joanna as if she were a magician who'd just performed some amazing feat. "He's sending up someone from security. They'll take you down to the lab."

A short, lame man dressed in a brown uniform and brass badge and wearing a lisping radio on his hip, escorted Joanna through a subterranean maze to the animal labs. Craig Summers, the head technician, greeted her on the other side of the heavy steel door.

She had expected the cage-lined corridors to smell like a zoo or pet store; but they had no distinctive smell. She might have been walking through a museum hung with moving collages or past dioramas of animal specimens. Some of the monkeys and rats and dogs were glassed in. Others were in metal mesh cages, with not a vestige of food or waste in range of the eye or nose. Their clinical isolation distressed Joanna. Yet, all the animals seemed oblivious to her passage and contented, not bored.

Craig, a short, carrot-haired man who was probably in his late twenties, said, "Jon told me to give you a quick tour before taking you to the dissection room."

Joanna gulped. "You mean I won't be waiting for him in an office?"

He laughed. "It's not so bad. He says you're a nurse . . . a midwife, right? . . . and you've seen worse than an autopsy on a dog."

"Oh, not a *dog*! I love dogs. How can you guys do it, Craig?" she asked.

"How can you deliver babies? My wife and I just had a little girl last month. Maybe I'm chicken hearted, but I had to leave the delivery room. That baby came out looking like a drowned cat. And, my God, the blood!" He shook his head. "No, assisting Jon with a post on *any* animal is cleaner and lots more fun." He held out his arm and gestured her into an intersecting corridor. "This way," he said.

She looked up at the creatures in the glassed cages and gasped. Were those tiny naked human babies perched on bars and shelves in the cages?

Craig's eyes twinkled. "They're albino chimps. Pioneers in the fight against skin cancer in humans."

"I thought they were babies."

"They're young, but not human."

"It's cruel to keep them in there! They look so exposed, so fragile."

He touched her shoulder gently. "It's their fragility that makes them so valuable. And they are exposed. To selected ranges of ultraviolet light. But it isn't cruel, because they're protected with a new drug developed by Pharmogenetix. A few years down the road, more or less, you'll be able to take a dose by mouth in the morning before you leave Philly, then spend the whole afternoon on the Jersey shore baking. And you won't burn."

"An internal sun screen?"

"Right. Those chimps have been sunbathing for a week, and they're not even blushing. It even protects their little pink eyes like UV lenses on your sunglasses. In the long run, we think it'll prevent cataracts."

Joanna took a deep breath. "I still don't think I could get used to seeing those babies locked in cages."

Craig laughed. "At least they look like babies, not drowned cats."

She smiled. "Whatever turns you on, Craig."

"Jon's in the post room right down here. Pick up a gown and mask from the table outside the door."

"At least that should make me feel at home," she said.

"You don't have to keep it sterile. It's just for your protection against splashing fluids." He pushed open the door while she donned the protective garb. "See you later," he said.

She took a deep breath and walked into the small tile and steel room, clamping her nostrils against the smell of draining blood, urine, and stool, fixatives and preservatives. Jon looked up from the collection of animal organs arranged next to an eviscerated dog carcass on the stainless steel dissecting table. A slow stream of water trickled from a hose at the head of the table and carried away a purplish bruise of fluids along a recess to a drain at its foot.

His eyes smiled above his mask. "Not too much worse than high school biology lab," he said.

She hesitated a moment. "Tell me it's a frog, and I'll be OK."

"That wouldn't be ethical. Anyway, right now it's a butcher shop full of meat byproducts."

"Your work has made you insensitive," she said, taking a few steps forward.

He began slicing into the liver. "This is where we find most of our problems," he said, pointing a gloved finger at the softly parting sections. "I can't see anything gross on this. But we might see cellular changes under the scope."

"How delightful!"

"But you're not here for a pathology lesson. I'm sorry I ran out on you Thursday. I'm glad you came. I love you, Joanna."

Her face grew hot. She said nothing.

"I know you're upset about this guy following you around. I also know you aren't a masochist and would never be somebody's punching bag. What I can't figure out is what the hell David is so upset about. The atmosphere in that house is weird. Has something happened between those two?"

"No. Jon, they're just worried about the investigation. I guess that TV interview . . ."

"The question is, are you afraid?"

"No. That's why I'm here. I'm not afraid. I've figured out something that eliminates my risk completely."

He looked up from his work on the liver. "Your risk?"

"I mean, our risk."

He bent his head to his dissection table, picked up

the hose, and washed the lungs clean. "You said you learned something."

"Yes. That all the fathers are tall and athletic looking, and they all have green or greenish eyes and brown hair."

He placed the hose down on the table and looked up. "The fathers?"

"Well, I don't know for sure that the father in the lesbian's case does. But I'm going to find out. I'm betting he does."

"You think the murderer has something in for green-eyed fathers, so he kills their wives and babies? And how would he even know about the father in the Heard case? She was artificially inseminated. Information about the donor is confidential."

"Yes it is. But probably Grace's widowed partner knows. That should be relatively easy to find out."

"You think she told the murderer?"

"No," she said. "I think he found out some other way. Maybe through someone who works in a . . . medical facility."

He looked puzzled.

"Jon, Irene Kimski was artificially inseminated, too. Not directly—in vitro. Her husband, Igor, is sterile. He only agreed to the insemination if the donor's sperm never would touch Irene's body. Her tubes were fine. But she went through a laparoscopic surgery to harvest her ova out of respect for her husband."

"She consented to have a hole cut in her abdomen and a metal tube stuck in, just so she could have her own baby and everyone would think it's her husband's? With all the risks that entails? And it's not even sure to work."

"You know that some women . . . and men . . . do *anything* to have their own children."

He nodded. His blue eyes clouded and grew reflective for a moment. "Yes. I know." He opened up the lung he was working on and peered into the tissue and blood vessels. "So now we have two who were artificially inseminated." He looked up. "Or maybe three, Joanna."

"You mean Denise Thomas was . . ."

He shook his head. "I don't know about her. But I talked to Frank Roberts's first wife's parents on Sunday . . ."

"I was wondering if you had."

"They told me something interesting. After their daughter's death, Frank vowed he'd never put another woman in danger again. He told them he was having a vasectomy."

Joanna caught her breath. She locked her eyes on Jon's. "Do they know whether or not he actually did?"

"They seem to be convinced he did. Though they believe it mustn't have worked."

"Or maybe Melanie persuaded him to reverse it. Maybe that's what she meant when she told her parents she was working on him."

"And maybe the vasectomy couldn't be reversed." He set the second lung aside and picked up and bisected a kidney.

She nodded. "So she pressured him to allow her to be artificially inseminated." Joanna's mind began to race. "And then there's Hal Thomas . . ."

". . . Who refused to acknowledge his own sterility, but whose wife knew she was fertile. She was desperate for her own child, too. Even though she'd adopted one and was in line to get another. So she arranged to be artificially inseminated without his knowledge, knowing she could convince him his cold-water treatments had finally done the trick." He was examining the ideas with the same incisiveness and skill that he was studying the kidneys with. He cut right through to the core.

"That's it, Jon. All of those women were artificially inseminated. And all of them wanted their baby to have their husbands' features, if not their own. Either so other people . . . like grandparents . . . wouldn't figure out the truth, or so the husband wouldn't."

Jon worked quickly on the remaining organs on his table, then he began to separate the skeletal muscle from bone and inspect it before taking sections. "I wonder, just wonder, if all of the sperm came from the same father. And I wonder if maybe someone isn't after this particular father's children. Who would know who he was, though? That stuff is confidential, Joanna."

"It sure is. Even Rose Snyder can't get the information on Irene Kimski. Only the woman's family can get the genetic facts in case the child develops a medical problem and has to get hold of the father. The mother deals directly with the sperm bank and doesn't even tell the doctor who's treating her which bank she got the sperm from. Everything's done by code. The bank keeps all that data and will release it to the men—and there are some—who want visitation rights or want to learn something about their offspring when the kids are eighteen."

"So the only people who could possibly know whether all those mothers got the same donor's sperm would be at the sperm bank," said Jon. He separated his dissected specimens, selected several slices, and placed them in labeled plastic bags. "I'll get these in the refrigerator and leave the rest for the night tech to dispose of. Then I'll take my shower and we can leave for dinner. Dump your gown and mask in the laundry cart over in the corner. I don't think you got close enough to get yourself contaminated. You can wait till you get home for your shower." He stripped off his plastic gloves and dropped them onto the table with the remains. "Unless you prefer to shower here."

"No. I'll wait outside with the chimps. I could use a little sun."

He removed his mask and smiled. "Craig told you about that? Don't tell anyone. That oral sunscreen's top secret. It could put us miles ahead of the competition."

She said, "I still think it's cruel exposing those poor monkeys to overdoses of sun. The albinos don't have any protection at all. It's bound to damage them."

"Quite the contrary. They haven't had an iota of photosensitivity. And for creatures that can't produce natural pigment, that's a miracle. The drug we've developed has given them more protection than a number twenty-nine sunscreen. They could stay in that light for a month. And that means when the last ozone molecule burns out above the atmosphere of Philadelphia, we can go about our business as if nothing had happened. Skin cancer from sunburn will be a thing of the past."

"Then why don't you just let them go back to their jungles with a bottle of pills? I hate what you do here, Jon."

"Is that why you won't take a shower with me?"

She took off her mask and gown and flung them into the laundry cart. "I'll wait outside."

He laughed. "OK. But don't get too fond of the chimps. I have to sacrifice them one at a time every week starting this Friday."

She strode to the door and pushed it open.

"I hate that part as much as you do, Joanna," he said. "But it's the only way we can see if the stuff has hidden side effects at the dosages that work."

"I know that, damn it. I just wish you'd be like other vets and just give shots to dogs or horses."

"I bet if I were just like other vets, you wouldn't love me."

She stopped halfway through the door and stood there holding it open.

"You do love me, don't you, Joanna?"

"Go take your shower," she said, still facing away from him.

"I guess I really should choose a more romantic setting than this to ask that question. Maybe over dinner at my place."

"Yes. That would be better," she said.

He hesitated a moment. "Wait. I just thought of something. How would you like to go to a rock concert?"

"You're kidding!"

"No. I'm serious. It's at a club up Route 309. The kind you'd call a dive. The food's lousy, the music is loud, and a deep breath of the air is sure to make you feel mellow."

"For God's sake, you know I'd never go to a place like that."

"Well, you're going tonight," he said. He left the room through a rear exit. Just before she stepped into the corridor, she heard the hiss of the shower as he turned it on.

When he had finished his shower and met her in the corridor, he explained. "It's not a concert in the strict sense of the word. It's a requiem for Angela Marietta."

"The rock singer?"

He nodded. "I want to talk to The Fathers and Virgins. I've been doing some research. Phil Marietta was the last of the group to prove his manhood by producing a child. The group nearly fell apart a year ago because of his troubles."

"So it could be . . ."

"Maybe. Anyway it's worth a trip up the pike to find out, don't you think?" He held open the door for her and they crossed to the parking lot.

"Right on!" she said. Excitement gripped her stomach and fists.

"But first, I think we'd better find more appropriate outfits. How punk do you think you can look?"

"Try me," she said as she headed toward her car in the visitor's lot. "There's a place at Montgomery Mall that sells just the right stuff. I'll meet you there."

They met at Spencer Gifts and bought garish makeup and Megadeth and Ozzie Osborne T-shirts. She found a long sequined skirt and long looped earrings at a discount clothing store. He bought a pair of faded orange denim jeans. They left her car at the mall and drove back in his to the lab to get dressed. He used a dissection scalpel to cut off and fray the jeans and she split her skirt up one side. Then they both slipped their T-shirts over their heads.

They looked at each other and laughed.

Two extra long lab coats disguised their disguises as they ran giggling to Jon's car. A few minutes later Jon pulled off the road and they combed goop and coloring into each other's hair, and pulled up stiff spikes until they looked as if they had been electrocuted or frightened to death.

She howled with laughter. "We must have looked at each other."

"Before or after," he said, dabbing makeup on her face.

"I'll have to look in a mirror." She put on her earrings.

"Don't you dare. I wouldn't want to lose you."

"How could you? I'd stand out in any crowd, if I look anything like you do." She studied the effect of his makeup. "You remind me of an Arizona sunset, all mountains and pink and purple. Complete with cactus."

"I'd hate to say what you remind me of. But you won't stand out in this crowd."

"Even though I know how punkers dress, I really can't believe they'd look like this at a wake."

She was wrong. Throngs of punkers and heavy metalers poured out of a rutted, unpaved parking lot and through two tall narrow doors into a huge Quonset hut that looked like a former bowling alley or skating rink. Crepe paper ribbons festooned the domed girded ceiling and rippled in the draft from huge uncovered air conditioners that strained against the pungent, smoke-laden air. In the large oval room, which could have housed a three-ring circus and still left space for an audience, the mourners pressed together at tables almost too close together to pass between.

At the center of the room on a revolving stage The Holy Fathers and Their surviving Virgins rent the air. The Fathers' guitars thundered like speeding railroad cars crashing head on. Cymbals and drums sent the smoke retreating in palpable clouds toward the ceiling and sides of the room. The screaming and wailing of the Virgins slashed out at unprotected eardrums.

Joanna clasped her hands over her ears in pain. She flattened herself against the wall just inside the door. "I can't take this," she said. She had to scream it twice into Jon's ear before he understood.

"Stuff a tissue into your ears," he said. He gave her one.

"How do they stand it?" she asked.

"They don't even hear it. Their ears are already damaged. And the drugs and alcohol make them even deafer."

She shook her head and pushed the tissue into her ears a little more firmly.

"OK. Let's go to the stage." Jon grasped her arm.

"Why? Dear God, it's loud enough back here."

"Take a good look." He pointed to the revolving dais.

The spotlights played everchanging colors on the

performers. Their faces reminded her of the startling visages flashed on the walls of haunted houses in amusement parks.

A circle of mourners pressed up against the edge of the stage as it turned. The crowd seemed to curl toward one angle of it as if it exerted a magnetic pull.

"My God!" said Joanna. "They actually have her here. Why didn't you warn me?" An opalescent metallic casket stood mounted on a black-curtained pedestal at the edge of the stage. The open casket was tilted to expose a view of its occupant to the crowds pressing in from the sides.

"I didn't know. I just wanted to talk with the group."

"I think this is one of your less bright ideas. I'm going back to the car." She started to turn toward the door.

"Afraid to venture into the lion's mouth, eh?"

She turned toward him again. "This whole thing's appalling."

"Why did you come?"

"I thought we were going to get information. Talk to the group at an intermission."

"Well, we've got to be here for the intermission." He gripped her elbow. "Come on. It's kind of exciting, too." He guided her toward the stage. Or, rather, the crowd carried him, and he, in turn, carried her.

A man who appeared to be an usher shoved toward Jon as they neared the stage. He held out a sheaf of small plastic bags. "Got a nickel, dude?" he said to Jon as he pressed one of the bags on him. "To support the grieving father."

"Sure," said Jon. He reached into his jeans pocket and pulled out a five-dollar bill, handed the bill to the pusher, and took the bag.

"I can't believe what you're doing," Joanna said as

Jon pushed the packet into his pocket. "That's enough for me."

He took her elbow again. "I'm just ad-libbing. If you want to be a detective, you've got to get a little dirt under your fingernails when you start the real digging. And sometimes you even have to pay a little protection. Now, come on. This is a fantastic opportunity to test your little theory."

"My little theory!"

"Stop being so damn sensitive. Come on. We're almost there."

At this point she had no choice but to move closer to the edge of the revolving stage. The casket and the body of Angela Marietta was moving inexorably closer to them. She could see the woman's heavily made-up face. A swatch of purple hair curled from the part above the forehead of the perfect oval face, framed the face along one side and to the center of the chin. On the other side the hair was pulled back to expose a tiny earlobe. A triple-looped gold earring hung from it and rested on the collar bone. One arm rested to the side of a sequined red organdy bodice; the other rested on the bodice.

"Oh, Jon. How could they dress her . . . make her up that way?"

He tightened his grip on her arm as the crowd pushed them toward the stage while the coffin cycled toward them.

The bereaved father sat on a stool beside his lost love and tore raucous, enraged discord from his guitar strings. His face and his eyes were glossed with fever, dulled by drugs. But he sang, and Joanna could hear the words.

She double-covered her ears; the words were ugly. Words about death and mutilation; words that degraded life and love. She'd heard them all before:

Motherfucking; cock sucking; shit. Over and over, till they lost any meaning. Till the life and death of Angela Marietta lost all meaning, and only the ugly words remained.

She could not shut the words out; and she could not take her eyes off the body.

Joanna felt nausea rise in her craw. "I've had more than enough, Jon. If you want to stay and talk to them, you'll have to do it alone."

"OK. You're right. This wasn't one of my better ideas. Let's go." He turned against the crowd that was crushing in from behind. "Oh, oh," he said.

She turned too. Now, at the center of things, having been pushed through a funnel formed by the burgeoning mob, she saw there was no way out. A cordon of self-appointed guardians had been thrown up around the perimeter of the massive Quonset to control the crowds. Invaders broke through the cordon at the tall narrow doors. The human rope broke down, unraveled, disintegrated.

The horde now held sway at the doors. They threw them wide. Then no one controlled them. Panic reigned. Women and men screamed. Men and women shouted obscenities, improvising lyrics to another anguished dissonant song.

The Fathers ripped at their guitars and bludgeoned their drums. The Virgins screeched with the mob. The mob bludgeoned one another, tore at one another's hair and clothing. Bits of cloth, strands of hair floated into the beams of colored spotlights. The spotlights lost their moorings; they oscillated chaotically, unable to find a meaning to fix on.

A phalanx of mourners bore down on the stage, trampling those like Joanna who had stopped and frozen in terror at the onslaught. A bearded man with bulging eyes and muscles pressed toward her. His eyes were fixed on the coffin behind her head. She was an insect in his way; in a moment she'd fall under his feet; in a moment he would crush her.

She pushed back against the revolving edge of the stage, but it caught her and geared her into its relentless motion, pulled her down. The man—other men and women—lunged at a spot over her head as she fell. She felt the press of their chests and arms and smelled their sweat and rank breath and heard their cries.

Suddenly she felt strong hands closing around her, pulling her free. They pushed her down to the floor, and rolled her underneath a heavy curtain into a small dark space.

"Stay down," Jon said.

She had no intention of moving; she could not, anymore than she could begin breathing again.

The curtain began to sway in toward them. The bottom edge of it lifted. Colored light whirled in with a precious draft of air. Shoes parted the curtain from all sides of the small rectangular swatch of floor on which she and Jon huddled.

She heard a clamor of grunts and shouts and obscenities, a scraping of feet and furniture, a creaking and trembling of the roof that the tilted table formed above them. Then the table and the curtains quivered and settled around them, and the crowd rumbled away like receding thunder after a sudden and fearsome storm.

She felt the stage beneath her turning, turning. She heard the Fathers and Virgins still wresting grief from their musical souls. The sounds of Phil Marietta's guitar and voice, torn loose from their amplifiers, followed the sounds of the crowd. She knew that Angela's coffin had been raised to the mourners' shoulders. It no longer rested on the table under which Joanna and Jon were hidden. Jon lifted the curtain slightly. The spotlights had found their focus on the shimmering opalescent casket and its sad and desecrated occupant. The crowd had found its direction, the tallest and strongest among them relaying from shoulder to shoulder the coffin of their dead madonna. Raised atop other shoulders, Phil, still pounding his hapless guitar with endless crescendoes of grief, balanced himself on his stool.

Screams and moans followed the cortege through the doors as the crowds poured out behind them. The Fathers and Virgins played a strident recessional in the emptying building as the stage circled on past the toppled tables and chairs.

Not all of the moaning from the ravaged hall had ceased, though. Barely audible over the musicians' cries of psychic wounding came the groans of the physically mangled—the trampled mourned only for themselves.

"Oh, God!" Joanna cried out as she struggled out from under the table.

A few dazed people wandered aimlessly through the vast hall, some setting chairs aright, some walking from one injured person to another, looking at their faces, shaking their heads, calling out names in confused and terrified voices. Two men moved more purposefully across the floor toward each of the casualties, offering advice and comfort. A young woman in neon green tights pushed herself up and limped toward the exit. Another victim rolled over and stared at the ceiling.

Joanna ran to a man who had blood running down the side of his face. She looked in his eyes, and saw the pupils were equal and reactive to the beams of circling light. She ripped off a piece of his shirt and sopped up the blood from his cheek. "It's just superficial," she said to him. "Just stay here. I hear some sirens. Someone will come take care of you." But she wasn't certain about the sirens. She couldn't separate the different noises.

The musicians were oblivious of what was going on

below them, and fell into a repetitive, annoying beat. The injured seemed hypnotized by it, and their exaggerated moaning ceased.

Jon came up behind her. "I think they'll be OK, most of them," he said. "It's a wonder no one got killed."

"A miracle."

"Let's go," he said. "This place is going to be crawling with police soon. And I don't think we want to be on television again."

They worked their way toward the door through a shambles of tables, chairs, shirts, shoes, and jewelry. They were almost at the door when Joanna tripped and fell. As she struggled to her feet, she saw that she'd tripped over a leg protruding from under a table.

It belonged to a woman, who lay on her back with eyes open and blank, and didn't stir; but as Joanna reached out to touch her arm, she made a snorting and choking sound, and liquid bowel contents began to seep out from under her in a rise of noxious smells.

"She's dead, Joanna," said Jon. "There's nothing you can do. Come on. We'd better get out."

Joanna stared at the shape of the woman's abdomen. "She's pregnant," she said. She pulled the woman's maternity T-shirt, which bore the legend HEAVY METAL BABY up over her blueing face and pulled down her pants and underwear. Expertly she measured the abdomen with her fingers. The woman's belly moved beneath her hands.

"I think it's alive. And viable. In the last month." She pressed her ear to the abdomen and felt it writhe slightly as the distressed infant turned and kicked. She sat up and looked at Jon. "It is. We've got to do something. Immediately. The baby can't survive much longer."

He turned and called out to one of the men who was helping the injured. "Where's the kitchen?"

The man looked down at the body. "Oh, fucking Jesus," he said.

"Do you know where the kitchen is? We don't have much time."

The man pointed and Jon ran off, jumping over tables, tossing aside chairs. In a few minutes he was back with an assortment of sharp knives.

"OK, you're the midwife," he said. How do we get the kid out without hurting it." He knelt at her side, as she outlined the fetus with her hands.

Its distress had increased; its position changed quickly. But its head appeared to be low, and just short of engaging in the pelvis. "We'd probably do best going in at the top. There's nothing vital up there. You should know when your blade is in. Then you can slice medially and vertically toward the cervix." She drew a line down the center of the abdomen with her finger.

"Right." He chose a well-honed meat cutting knife, tested the blade with his finger, then followed with his finger the path of her own. His first cut through the outer layers of abdominal muscle drew small droplets of blood that oozed out along the edges of the wound. Then he cut transversely across the abdomen to make flaps and stripped the flaps back to expose the thick pink wall of the uterus.

The man who'd directed him to the kitchen leaned forward over his shoulder in fascination.

"OK, this is the hard part," Jon said. He felt the movements of the baby inside its fatal prison. "We'll get you out of there in one piece, kid."

Joanna leaned forward and felt for herself. "OK. It's got a fighting chance."

She heard the running shuffle of heavy feet and looked up. Uniformed men with gurneys were scattering through the room. A pair ran toward them, and set down the gurney beside them.

"Shit!" said one.

"Holy Christ," said the other. "Oh, man."

They knelt down next to Joanna.

"You have an infant mask with you?" she asked, without taking her eyes off Jon's hands. He had begun his cut down the uterus and had drawn a tiny spurt of amniotic fluid.

One of the parameds ran back toward the door.

Jon finished the long swooping cut, and pulled the muscle back. The amniotic sack writhed inside, still intact except for a minute tear.

"OK, she's yours now," he said, looking up at Joanna. He leaned back on his haunches and wiped beads of perspiration off his forehead with the back of his hand.

She placed both hands inside the gaping uterus, then tore the frail curtain of the sack. The fluid burst from it and bathed her hands. Securing the baby's buttocks in one hand, she brought her other arm behind the head and, supporting its back, lifted it out.

She lifted it by its feet and rubbed its back briskly. Its lungs and throat freed of mucus and fluid, the baby took a deep breath and let out a small bleat, followed by another breath and a series of healthy cries.

"Another week and she'd have been out on her own," said Jon.

"Oh, poor baby," said Joanna. She cradled it in her arms for a minute. Then she handed it to Jon, who had already taken off his T-shirt to wrap it in.

She looked up at the paramed. "I'm going to lift out the placenta. Leave it attached till you get her to the hospital. She looks like she's going to be all right."

The paramed nodded. The other man had returned with the infant oxygen mask. They trussed the baby into the gurney and carried it off to their ambulance.

In the continuing confusion, Joanna and Jon made their escape to his car.

*   *   *

He sped along winding country roads, past the small rural hospital that was surrounded by emergency vehicles. Crowds of the curious milled festively around and watched the weirdly dressed injured being carried in.

"They haven't seen anything like this in this town in a lifetime, I bet," said Jon.

Joanna, exhausted as the emotion began to drain from her, just nodded. Her hands and arms felt sticky with placental blood and amniotic fluid. She was overly conscious of the stiffness of her hair and the greasiness of the makeup on her face. She didn't want any part of her to touch the inside of Jon's new car. Yet she couldn't help leaning her head back against the seat and closing her eyes.

Once he'd pulled the car from the narrow back road onto the 309 access and picked up speed, she took a deep breath, and let the hum of the tires along the stretch of good highway lull her. She didn't think about all that had happened; didn't worry about whether anyone had followed them or gotten Jon's license number; didn't even care where he was taking her. Sleep quickly overtook her.

When she woke she found Jon watching her in the dim light from his garage door opener as it flickered out.

"You are a mess, my lovely. Aren't you sorry now you didn't get that shower?"

She put her hands up to her face. Feeling the makeup and stickiness, she was overwhelmed by the enormity of what she had done.

He seemed to read her thoughts. "You are a hundred percent pro. You saved that baby's life. I love you." He kissed her. "But you really have to get a bath. You taste something terrible."

He got out of the car, came around, and opened her door for her. As she stood up her knees began to tremble and she slumped back into the seat. He scooped her up and carried her to his living room. Soon she heard the rush of water upstairs as he drew her a bath.

A few minutes later he came down. He had washed some of the makeup off his face, but a ruddy smudge ringed it. And his hair stood out stiffly around it like a corona.

"I'm OK, now," she said. "I think I can make it." She stood and her knees held firm.

"You know where it is," he said.

"I think I remember." She looked at him and laughed. "You look like the Cowardly Lion in the *Wizard of Oz*." And she went up and got into the tub.

In the bath, the heat of the water suffused her body and relaxed her and stirred her juices.

He had brought up the clothes she'd changed out of in the lab, but when she had scrubbed and shampooed, she put on only her brassiere and slip, and threw a large towel over her shoulder. As he took his shower, she rubbed her hair dry with the towel. A peaceful feeling settled over her as she heard from his bedroom the sounds of the splashing water.

He came out of the bathroom all scrubbed and steamed and sweet smelling, a towel wrapped and secured around his waist. He sat next to her on the bed, took her towel and began to rub her hair. She ducked her head down as he massaged it, and gave in to the luxuriant rubdown. He grasped her head with the towel and wrestled it playfully. She began to laugh. She pulled her head away from him, and rolled to the opposite side of his bed.

With one hand he reached out and grabbed her, pulling her back. He tossed the towel over her face and buffed her head with it. She sat up, and pushed it off her face. She stared at him a moment as his face came toward hers, and then she cried out as his mouth closed over hers, opened against hers. He rolled over on top of her and she felt his tumescence against her.

Her hunger for him drove her hard up against him.

As he began to undress her in the glow of his bedside lamp, her passion fought for a moment with her fear of being revealed. She turned from him slightly, pulled her slip down, to hide her abdomen.

Then she turned her back to him and let him pull it over head. As he unfastened her bra, she let him, helped him remove it from her shoulders. She passed her own fingers over his chest, down into the feathered hollow of his navel behind his fastened towel.

With one quick motion he tossed away the towel, freeing himself to rise, as her hand grasped and stroked him. But as her bra straps fell from her other wrist, she drew her hand sharply back and turned from him again.

"Turn off the lamp," she whispered.

He stood up, surprised.

She grabbed for his towel and pulled it up to cover her breasts and belly.

He stepped back, eyes still on her, and reached for the lamp.

Quickly she let slip the towel. In the dark, she hid everything from him but her driving desire.

He hid nothing at all from her.

In the morning's light, as pleasure receded with the darkness, she basked under his gaze. Then once again, after her morning shower as she stood naked before the lightly steamed bathroom mirror, she realized what she'd revealed to his practiced pathologist's eyes.

But if he had seen the rings her recent pregnancy

had drawn around her nipples, the line it had painted on her belly, the thin white spiderwebs it had stenciled into the fat pad on top of her hips, he said nothing.

Chapter Seventeen

Kevin

KATIE HAD GIVEN Kevin the idea. He should have known better than to trust the idea of a whore. After all, whores thought nothing of selling themselves to pay the rent. And nothing ever came out of what Katie sold. She could sell it again and again, and it was over and done with the minute she brought her legs together.

But he was desperate for money. He couldn't sell his blood often enough to cover the rent; as he headed into his internship his landlady thought he should be able to afford more. Her demands for an exorbitant amount of money for such a small apartment increased his hatred of women; she had betrayed him as the others had. She had seen him as someone she could eventually get something out of. She'd let him live there as a poor medical student because someday he would be a rich doctor.

Still, he couldn't find anything else so near the hospital. At least nothing cheaper or better. So when Katie said he was an asshole for not selling his sperm—since he wasn't giving it to anyone anyway, just batting it off against her wall—he thought she might have a point. Selling some of it would not interfere with what he did with the children. He still considered it just "milk", and as such it was even less a part of him than his blood. And if he didn't bat it off, it would come out anyway in his sleep, like his pee would if he let his bladder get too full. If someone would pay for his pee, he'd sell it by the gallon.

So the seriousness of the people at the sperm bank took him by surprise. The older woman who interviewed him first studied his eyes with her own watery gray ones as if she were trying to peer into his soul. He looked steadily back into hers; not because he was trying to impress her with his calmness and sincerity, but because she had the rings of age around her irises and he was mentally gauging her chances of having a heart attack from too much cholesterol in her blood.

He answered all her questions about his medical, social, religious, and educational background matter-of-factly. If these things were important to her, he wouldn't hold back. He needed the money too badly to stand on principle. Especially about anything so insignificant as his sperm.

Her interview lasted a half-hour. When she was finished, she stared at him long and hard, as if making a difficult decision, before sending him to a counselor. Kevin had expected the counseling to consist of instructions for collecting the sperm. Instead he was subjected to a long written psychological test that included questions about relationships with his parents and siblings. He lied; those details were none of anyone's business. He wasn't here to be counseled for his long estrangement from his family. He was here to sell a commodity that was easier to produce than blood, and for which they were willing to pay a good deal more.

Answering the questions on the written test did prepare him for the interview by the psychologist.

The psychologist, Dr. Bell, a tall, neat young man with an air of studied compassion, motioned him to a seat across the desk from himself. "A medical student," he said, after glancing over the test papers.

"Starting my internship next month," said Kevin.

"Then you're graduating. Congratulations. You've still got a grind ahead of you, though."

Kevin nodded. He was aware that nothing a psychologist said in an interview meant just itself. He would tell both the truth and the necessary lies with the same straightforward casualness. Let the psychologist be the intense and scrutinizing one.

The man leaned back and smiled.

Kevin assumed the same position. He remembered reading something about taking a cue from the body language of others. If you held yourself the same way they did, you'd win their confidence.

"What made you decide to be a sperm donor, Kevin?"

"Frankly, I need the money."

Dr. Bell grinned. "As good a reason as any. Probably the best, in fact. Most of our female clientele don't want the father showing up and demanding custody somewhere down the road."

"I won't do that. Of course I hope the woman who gets the sperm has a good, healthy attitude, too."

"You don't have to worry about that. We deal directly with the women as well as the men. We screen them as carefully as we screen you."

"Good," said Kevin.

Dr. Bell nodded again. He looked at Kevin's forms on the desk in front of him. "I see you're single."

"Yes."

"Involved with any women?"

"No."

Dr. Bell looked up. "None at all?"

"Not on a steady basis. Of course I'm a normal

man," Kevin said. "And in spite of the demands of medical school, I've managed to work in some extra-curricular activities." He smiled conspiratorially.

The doctor smiled back. "So you aren't involved with any one woman, then."

"No."

"Good. Women can have a proprietary attitude toward the sperm of a man they're sleeping with. If you do get involved, I suggest you talk over any further plans you have to donate with the woman. If she objects, you may wish to reconsider."

"Reconsider the donation or the relationship?" Kevin asked.

Dr. Bell laughed. "I guess that depends on how well the woman can afford to support you."

"It'll be a long time before I can afford a woman who can't."

"Then I guess we can count on your for regular donations." He smiled and pushed aside the papers. "Well, if you and your sperm can pass our physical exam, we'll arrange for your first donation. If you haven't had sex more than three times in the last week, we'd like a sample today."

"That won't be a problem," said Kevin.

He'd donated a sample a month until he'd started having sex with Joanna.

She changed his life as he was just about to end it. Despondent at his inability to control himself with the children, constantly fearful of being caught in the act, he'd vowed to destroy himself. The first time Joanna seduced him, she repelled him as all women did. He'd never had sex with a girl over ten; the first signs of emerging breasts and pubic hair repulsed him. Then he found that if he just fantasized her as a child, he could get and maintain an erection. (He let her believe she'd deflowered him.) Once he got used to the hairy and bulbous parts of her, he began to like her. She offered him something no other woman had—her apartment, with no strings attached. And at times, he loved her. At least he loved her love for him. And she satisfied his sexual needs. And that kept him away from the children. He thought he would be able to curb his desires for them. And that made him almost love her.

But her nephew tantalized him. One evening when he had dinner there with Joanna, he went into the bathroom when the boy was taking his bath. He peed, and then held his penis until it hardened.

"Does yours ever do that?" he asked the boy.

The boy's eyes widened, and he looked frightened.

Kevin quickly covered his penis and zipped up his fly. "Don't tell your parents I showed you," he said. Then he fled.

The next chance he had to spend time with the boy, he helped him build a hospital with his Erector Set. He was careful not to act too quickly. By the time he'd helped him construct a whole campus of buildings over the next several weeks, Michael seemed to have forgotten about the incident in the bathroom.

For a month more, Kevin held back his desire for the boy. Then he could bear it no longer. As the boy constructed a simple phalluslike tower, Kevin began to stroke his legs. And soon, Kevin could see, a small phallus constructed itself between them. He worked his hand up under the little boy's shorts.

The boy turned his wide eyes toward him.

"It's all right, Michael," he said. "It's just getting stiff and tall like your tower. I have one, too. Would you like to see it?"

The boy watched with what Kevin knew was mixed fascination and fear as Kevin took the boy's hand and placed it on his exposed penis. Kevin knew the torment that the boy would suffer forever. But he could not, would not, stop.

Nor could the boy stop him. Kevin drew him into his ever more enticing and exciting games.

He might have consummated a coupling and penetrated Michael, but one night David nearly caught them. And afterwards, Michael seemed afraid.

Maybe the boy, guilty and frightened, told someone. Maybe Joanna found out. Because that was when she turned against him. And forced him back to the other children, the ones in the hospital. They were sick and they cried and they sometimes tried to get away from him when he came into their rooms at night. They made him feel bad, made him realize how very evil he was.

The day she walked out, she said that as far as she was concerned, he had never existed. She said that he should never have existed at all. He remembered that she said he should never even leave a trace.

He would satisfy her. He'd destroy every trace of himself.

Chapter Eighteen

Tuesday—Joanna

BY THE TIME Jon had driven Joanna to Montgomery Mall to pick up her car where she'd parked the night before, she was already late for work. The ticket on the windshield jolted her. The fine for overnight parking in the mall parking lot was fifty dollars. But at least the car had not been towed; if it had, she probably wouldn't have made it into work at all. As it was, she didn't arrive until ten, a full two hours late.

Ginny, her secretary, seemed beside herself with worry. "When your sister called and said you hadn't shown up for dinner last night and you didn't answer your phone, I thought something had happened to you." Ginny threw her arms around Joanna.

"Louise! Oh, my God. I forgot all about dinner."

"You look OK. What happened?"

"Oh, Ginny. I should have called and told you I'd be late. But by the time I realized it, I was stuck in a jam on 309."

"Well, I'm just glad you're here. Monica will be, too. She's been doing double duty with your appointments. But your nine-thirty appointment canceled. And your ten o'clock looks like she's going to be late, too. That should give you a chance to call your sister. She sounded absolutely frantic."

Louise still sounded frantic when Joanna phoned her. "I've already called the police. But they said you hadn't been missing long enough to do anything. They'd have to wait till this afternoon, since you were in your office till two yesterday. Why didn't you come last night? Why didn't you at least call?"

"Oh, shit! I'm so sorry. I completely forgot."

"Say nothing about forgetting your sister. You forgot your own baby! Where were you?"

"With Jon. I just went to his office to try to . . . patch things up with him. And he took me out. I'm so sorry."

She heard Louise take a deep breath.

"I guess I can understand that. But, for God's sake, you could have called me afterwards."

"Afterward we went to his townhouse."

"I see. You did patch things up. But still you could've hopped out of bed long enough to make a phone call."

"I just forgot. How's Cassie?"

"I thought you'd never ask. She's fine. It seems she's in good hands. With people who love her and care for her."

"That's not fair."

"You really must come by and see her sometime. How about dinner tonight?"

"I can't come for dinner tonight."

"You're not working. Why not?"

Joanna made a fist and pressed it against her desk. "Something came up. I can't explain."

There was a long pause. "Something more important than Cassie," said Louise.

"Something that's important because Cassie *is* important. Please, Louise. Try to understand. I have to do something that I just can't put off any longer."

"Why didn't you do it last night if it was that important?"

"Until last night, I wasn't sure just how important it was."

"When will you be here?"

"Tomorrow morning. For breakfast. I don't have to be at work till afternoon tomorrow. Louise—"

"I'll see you tomorrow." The telephone clicked into Joanna's ear.

She looked at the receiver for several moments before setting it back into the cradle. She wanted to cry, but she didn't have time. Now that she'd come this far, she couldn't turn back.

Tuesday evening

Pat Reston's eighth-floor apartment in Society Hill overlooked a section of river not spoiled by oil storage tanks on either side. A window wall exploited the view, affording on this soft May night a montage of glimmering reflections of Philadelphia's more prosperous side.

That an apartment shared by lesbians should reflect such prosperity surprised Joanna at first, though she didn't know why. She hadn't thought of herself as prejudiced, and the notion that a man was required in a home to provide any luxury offended her. Yet here she stood, offending herself with her own chauvinism as she looked past the back of Pat's bent shoulders and out over the panorama while the city below screeched its rude cry beyond earshot, behind the thick plate glass.

"I don't know why I agreed to see you, Joanna," Pat said. "It's only reopening the wounds." The woman turned from the window and straightened her shoulders. Tall and honey-haired, she projected an image of patrician glamor suitable to her position as a partner in a prestigious accounting firm. Her eyes were red with unshed tears, but her face showed no sign of puffiness. "You remind me of Grace. Except for the color of your hair. For a moment when I saw you at the door . . ." She stopped and shook her head and smiled bitterly. "I'm sorry. I don't mean to embarrass you."

"I'm not embarrassed," said Joanna.

"Then you're unusual." She held up a hand. "No.

Don't protest. People who aren't gay *are* embarrassed to be with us. To be called attractive by us. At the very least they're uncomfortable. Especially in a setting like this." She took in the opulent mauve-and-gray room with a sweep of her hand. "Why should we perverts have so much when you straights work so hard just to afford your little houses in the suburbs."

"Please, Pat. I can't help being straight. And I'm not here to judge you or Grace. I'm here to find out if she was linked to the other 'Cradle and All' victims."

"She was the victim of a copycat. A dyke-hating copycat!" She bit off the words and spat them out.

"That may be so. And Bloody Shoes might hate lesbians as much as he hates straight women. Mothers."

Pat laughed. "Maybe he found his own mother in bed with another woman. A new twist on the same old story: 'Impressionable tender young male turned off by sordid sex.'"

"We could bring James Dean back to play the part."

"Very good, Joanna. I see you watch late-night TV too."

"Let's not spar, Pat. Neither of us has the time. I have to get back to finding connections. You have to get back to your grieving," said Joanna.

A red splotch rose on Pat's face, as if Joanna had struck her. "I guess I'm being a bit of a bitch. What do you want to know?"

Joanna, overcome by a sudden surge of sympathy, stepped forward and grasped Pat's shoulders. "Oh, Pat, I don't mean to hurt you." She pulled the woman close to her. "I'm sorry."

After a moment of resistance, Pat gave in to the embrace, let herself go, and wept in Joanna's arms.

When she'd cried herself out, she pulled away and crossed the room to the mauve leather sofa.

Joanna sat across from her in an upholstered chair

of matching color with curved black lacquer arms and legs.

"That's the first time I've done that. For some reason, nobody seems to want to hold me." Pat combed her long fingers through her hair and pulled it back from her damp forehead. "OK. Enough feeling sorry for Pat. I'll tell you whatever I can."

Joanna nodded. "Do you know anything about the man whose semen was used to inseminate Grace?"

"His identity is confidential. As Grace's was from him."

"I mean his features. What were the attributes she wanted to pass on to her child? What did she admire in a man?"

Pat smiled ironically. "Very little."

Joanna said nothing.

"Well, she wanted him to be intelligent, of course. And tall. Otherwise she didn't care too much."

"Did she care about eye and hair color?"

"Yes, as a matter of fact, she wanted the baby to look like me. Does that sound strange?"

"No. I had a crush on a female cousin when I was about thirteen. I thought she was beautiful. I kept a baby picture of her for years, thinking how wonderful it would be if my babies looked like her."

Pat looked up at her. "I think if every girl told the truth about herself, she'd find a story like that in her background."

Joanna, uncomfortable about revealing a personal secret, shifted in her chair. She evaded Pat's eyes for a moment, but their color quickly drew her attention back: beyond the red rims, obscured by a light film of tears, the irises were green.

"You're staring. I've embarrassed you again."

Joanna shook her head. "So she chose a man with green eyes and light honey hair."

Pat now shifted her eyes. "I'm forever suspecting

others of suspecting my intentions. Yes, she wanted the man to have green eyes. But her own hair was blond. Practically white. She thought that the baby would have a better chance of looking like me if the father had dark brown hair. She went back a couple of generations into his history, and learned there were blonds on one side." She clenched her fists in her lap and looked down at them. "It worked out just right. Little Ellen . . ."

Joanna waited for Pat to regain her composure. The woman was sending mixed messages that moved Joanna alternately between pity and a sense of mild revulsion. After Pat sighed and issued her a contrite smile, Joanna said, "She got all that information from the sperm bank?"

"They're pretty thorough."

"Which sperm bank was it?"

"I'm sorry. That's all confidential. It's the only way they can guarantee absolute privacy to the donor and the recipient, both."

"But that secrecy may be protecting Bloody Shoes."

"What do you mean?"

Joanna stood up and crossed the room to a console where she'd set down her shoulder tote. "I have a videotape to show you."

When she'd run through the cassette on Pat's VCR and pointed out her findings on the forty-inch television screen, Pat looked up. She went to a built-in mirrored wet bar, and with trembling hands, poured herself a vodka and soda over ice. After taking what looked like much too large a swallow, she turned to Joanna and asked, "Exactly what is it you're getting at?"

"As I pointed out, all of the husbands of the victims resemble one another."

"And what's that supposed to mean to me?"

"It means that all the wives may have been artificially inseminated by the same man."

"And you think that the semen may all have come from the same bank? Which bank was it?"

"That's what I'm asking you."

Pat's eyes flashed. She clutched her drink. She nodded and took another quick draught. "So the others wouldn't tell you. And that's why you came to me. You thought that a lesbian lover might be less circumspect about things like that, I suppose. Well, I have the same scruples about confidentiality that the men do. As a matter of fact, I have more to lose if artificial reproduction is threatened than they do."

Joanna shook her head. "I'm sorry. I don't see how this can threaten a firmly established technology."

"You don't? Well nothing's so firmly established that the threat of AIDS can't rock it. And some women have contracted it through artificial insemination. And you know what AIDS means, don't you, Joanna? It means filthy faggots are contaminating the world with their sins. First the faggots foul the genetic pool, and now the dykes are wallowing in it."

"I see. So this is another case of you against us. Don't you think you're going a little too far? Even assuming I am the enemy you think I am. There are lives at stake. A murderer's loose. Two more nights from now another two people could die."

"The police know that. And they're doing everything they can to prevent it. That's their job, and from what I've heard, they're performing it with zeal. And you know what they taught me, Joanna? They taught me that everybody, including you and my female gynecologist, is my enemy."

Joanna opened her mouth to protest.

"Oh, yes. The police, in their zeal to catch the murderer among *your* colleagues, called on our gynecologist yesterday. She called me last night and told me how they grilled her. She said it was a nightmare. They treated her like a criminal; they interrogated everyone on her staff. They grilled her male associates, insisted on knowing their shoe sizes. Her senior associate was so upset he threatened to fire her from the practice for getting involved with a lesbian client in the first place. It seems we're prone to being victims of irrational crimes that innocent *doctors* might later be blamed for."

Joanna was incredulous.

Pat's voice dropped its stridency and became almost philosophical. "Of course it isn't so. We're probably less liable to be victims of violence than most people. But there have been a few attacks on gay women who openly flaunt their lifestyle, and of course, that's what makes news. And there was speculation when Grace was killed that the murderer was a homophobe." Her eyes flickered. "I got caught up in that myself. But it couldn't have been. We lived quietly. Only the people closest to us even knew we were gay." Pat set down her drink on the bar. "And as for her pregnancy, most people assumed it natural. She hadn't even told her doctor it wasn't. The insemination was done by a friend. Right here in our apartment, while I held Grace's hand."

Her eyes began to glisten again, and she turned away. "We made love afterwards . . . "

Joanna remained silent as Pat crossed the room and looked out over the Philadelphia panorama.

Pat turned toward her again. "You see what happens? Even our doctor is pilloried because she had something to do with us. The sperm bank could be destroyed by association with a lesbian's murder. They could cut off our supply of spermatazoa. Or the donors might begin to develop new scruples. 'If they won't let us fuck them, why should they have kids?' "

"I really don't think—"

"Oh, don't you? Well, you don't have any idea what we had to go through even to get what we did. All sorts of psychological testing. Both of us, because of the nature of our relationship and because we weren't referred by a doctor."

"I thought the doctors weren't even told which sperm bank the semen came from."

"That's true. But you need a doctor's prescription. Doctors don't like letting go of the right to control women's reproduction. Without a prescription, you can't get a pill or a diaphragm. Well, you can't get some homemade semen, either. The doctors control the supply. They control the demand. They even get their own to produce it. So more medical students can pay their way through medical school. They've got a fucking *cartel*!"

She went to the bar and lifted her glass to her reflection. "Here's to Doctor Whatever-His-Name-Is; he'd never have made it without us."

"Then the donor was a medical student."

"An intern. Well, they are the best and the brightest, aren't they? And they have the best financial prospects. Not that we were worried about that . . ." She looked at Joanna in the mirror and stopped in midsentence. "Well, that hardly tells you much. Considering the statistics."

"You're right. I've known as many poor medical students as rich doctors. Still, it might be a clue," Joanna said.

Pat turned from the mirror and said, "Brava! Our intrepid detective uncovered a new clue." She lifted her drink toward Joanna. "Well, you won't get the name of the bank. As I said, they took a risk in the first place in releasing the sperm to us."

"So you're protecting someone there who did you a favor."

Pat turned to the bar and looked at Joanna's reflection. "That's not entirely it."

Joanna leaned forward. "Then what is it? Entirely."

Pat hesitated. "As far as I'm concerned all you've got is another theory. A rather elegant one, to be sure; but nothing much more. I gather from what you've told me"—she turned from the mirror and looked Joanna directly in the eye—"that the men you interviewed before me weren't particularly forthcoming. They didn't even tell you as much about the donor as I have."

Joanna felt her jaw tighten.

Pat smiled. "Aha. They didn't. That doesn't surprise me from what I know about men. So much pride!"

"Yes. They take their manhood rather seriously. But . . ."

"Manhood! What a joke!"

"Exactly what is your point? The relationships between the sexes is hardly what I came here to talk about." Joanna found herself on the defensive and she didn't know why. But she realized that she wasn't going to get the information she came for and she wanted to extricate herself from the conversation as quickly as possible.

"You thought I was an easy mark, didn't you? You were full of misconceptions about what I'd be like. The men wouldn't answer your questions. You don't even know for certain that all the other victims were artificially inseminated, do you?"

"It's true that at first I knew for sure only about Grace. That's what started me thinking. And I'm reasonably sure about the others."

Pat raised her eyebrows. "What do you mean reasonably?"

"One of them was my client. I know she was artificially inseminated."

"And the others?"

"The husband of one had a vasectomy a few years before . . ."

"And he said she had been artificially inseminated."

"He wouldn't talk to us—to me at all."

"You're investigating this with a partner? Well, well. I bet I know who it is. That lovely red-headed man who accompanied you to your debut at the funeral last week."

Joanna grew angry. Pat was trying to save her own skin—and that of the person at the sperm bank who broke medical protocols—by attacking Joanna's theory. And she was succeeding. Joanna realized she and Jon didn't have any information to bear out their theory. The secrecy of the system and the men's aversion to the reality of their own infertility had frustrated them all along the way.

And Pat was right. Joanna had thought that the lesbians were somehow different—that Pat would be more willing to turn against the system that seemed forever turned against her. But she hadn't anticipated that Pat, to defend herself against the system, had learned to manipulate it . . . and someone corruptible within it . . . with far more skill than Joanna had or could have.

She had also manipulated Joanna—ruthlessly. For Joanna now waffled and wavered in the very certainty that had brought her here.

Pat had cut that sureness right out from under her.

She tried to salvage some measure of self respect from the interview. "If you don't want to tell me about the sperm bank, you don't have to," she said.

"Well, thank you for telling me my rights," said Pat. The brows over her green eyes slanted toward her nose in an unmistakable prideful V for victory.

*   *   *

Joanna's own apartment looked cramped and dull when she got home. The granite walls of the buildings across the downtown street depressed her. She could see no river from here, no ambiance of richness and luxury. The buildings she looked at were all taller than the one she lived in, and they seemed designed to remind her of her own inadequacy and foolishness. She shook off the feeling and telephoned Jon. "That woman humiliated me. It's the worst . . . Even worse than last night's concert. At least there I salvaged my professional pride, in my own eyes. I don't like this whole mess. I'm getting in over my head."

"No, you're not. You're getting closer to the truth. You've learned two pretty important things. First, the donor was a medical student or intern. Second, the sperm bank might have something to cover up."

"But," she said, "we don't even know if the others really *were* artificially inseminated. She picked that up right away. I was sure she'd tell us the name of the bank, Jon."

"That's how you should feel when you approach a witness. If you had doubts you wouldn't be a detective."

"I'm not a detective. That's why I'm dropping out of the investigation. If you want to handle it, go ahead. I'm not going to interview anyone else. All that it proves is that I'm wrong."

"No you're not. And I'll prove it to you. I'm coming over." He hung up before she had a chance to object.

"OK," he said, as soon as he came in the door a half-hour later. "I'll tell you why you're right." He pulled her to the sofa, and sat down next to her.

"The theory stinks," she said.

"No, it doesn't." He poked the oak coffee table with his index finger for emphasis.

"The men couldn't all be lying."

"They aren't. They just aren't talking to us. You can't blame them. And Hal Thomas doesn't even know the truth. And what Pat told you makes that fact possible."

She knit her brows and looked at him. "How?"

"Simple. If someone at the sperm bank would look the other way for Grace Heard, they would do the same for Denise Thomas. Remember, if our theory has any chance at being right, there'd have to be a breach there, at the bank. She probably couldn't have convinced a reputable doctor to help her deceive her husband." He smiled and spread his hands and sat back.

She sat for a moment, then nodded slowly. "That's possible."

"Possible, hell! I'd bet on it."

"All right. Maybe . . ."

"And the other thing that makes it make more sense is medical students."

She was puzzled.

"We have five women, if our theory is right, who were all inseminated with sperm from the same guy. Now how much would they buy from one person? If enough women are inseminated with one guy's sperm, you're asking for trouble ahead. I wonder if they warn the kids who their half-brothers and sisters are."

"I hadn't thought of that. That shows how wrong my theory is."

"No." He tapped on the table again. "I imagine the bank cut corners on that side of their ledger, too. Especially where a bright, good-looking medical student was concerned. The law of supply and demand along with the chances of failed conception might make someone say, 'Well, we'll worry about that later. If too many kids come out of this one, chances are it'll be generations later before any inbreeding takes place. By then, it will be diluted. Let's get as much juice from this guy as he's willing to supply.' "

"You could be right. Damn it, you could be."

"*You* could be. You're the one who saw the resemblance of the fathers. You're also the one who dug out the truth about Irene Kimski. Now how can you even think that your theory stinks?"

She reached up and took his hands. Thanks for pulling me out of my self-doubt and proving that I need you." She paused. "But I can't afford to need anyone now. I have too many things to work out."

He pulled her head to his chest. "Maybe I can help there, too."

She shook her head.

He turned her face up to his and began kissing her face and neck. "When you're ready, I'll be there."

She returned his kisses. "I might love you too much to ever be ready to tell you everything."

"Or you might just love me enough to be ready sooner than you think."

Soon they were making love on her living room floor. Later, in her bedroom.

And for the second dawn in a row, his fingers traced the early light's path over her body.

She realized what time it was and jumped out of bed.

"What's your hurry?" he asked. I thought you had afternoon office hours today. And I don't have to leave for work for another hour. Has my supply of love exceeded your demand?"

"I've never experienced such demand," she said, shuddering slightly to dissipate a surge of desire. She returned to the bed and kissed him on the lips, playing with her own passion as much as his.

He rolled over on top of her.

Her lips and tongue toyed with his for another few moments before she pushed him away and got up, giddy and torn between her love for him and her need to keep her promise to Louise. "No," she said hoarsely. "I really have to go."

"Go where, for God's sake? It's only six forty-five."

"I always go to breakfast at Louise's and David's Wednesday morning."

"Even *this* Wednesday morning?"

"I was supposed to go there Monday night. I forgot to call. Louise was upset. She tried to get me all night. And then yesterday morning when I was two hours late for work."

"Oh, oh."

"And I couldn't explain to her why I couldn't come to dinner last night."

"Why not?"

"I promised her I'd get out of the investigation. You know how David feels about it."

"After the way David treated you Thursday, I wouldn't think you'd care how he feels. I don't know why you even want to go back to their house. I sure don't." He raised himself onto one elbow. His eyes dwelt on her naked body.

She turned and ran to her closet and got her clothing. "I have to take a shower," she said.

When she'd showered and dressed and returned to the bedroom, she found him dressed in his slacks and undershirt, waiting with his electric shaver and toothbrush in his hand.

"Why do you have to get there so early?" he asked on his way to the bathroom.

"I like to give Cassie her bottle."

He paused for a moment. "I see," he said. "Joanna . . ."

"What?"

"Nothing. It's just that ... Nothing." He started toward the bathroom again.

A few minutes later when he returned smelling of toothpaste and aftershave, he said, "All right. But I'm going there with you."

"I thought you didn't want to go there."

"I don't. But I do want to be with you till the last possible moment. As a matter of fact, I don't ever want to be without you again. I don't care what outlandish, crazy things you do. Or have done. Or why." He took her in his arms.

The telephone rang.

"Oh, damn," he said. "This isn't my morning to be loved."

"Well, you shouldn't get greedy."

She picked up the phone. "Joanna, it's Ginny."

"What's wrong? An emergency?"

"Not that I know of. A Lieutenant Crosby is here. He opened the place up with me," she said.

Joanna checked her clock. It was ten after seven. "He sure did." She sighed. "All right. Tell him I'll be there in ten minutes." She shrugged and looked at Jon.

He held up ten fingers three times.

She smiled and shook her head. "No."

"What?" Ginny asked.

"I was just talking to myself. I'll be right over. Give Lieutenant Crosby some coffee and make him comfortable. And answer any questions he has as if you don't have anything to worry about."

"Do I?"

"Of course not. By the way, what size shoe do you wear?"

"Seven. Why?"

"I just wondered. You don't have a thing to worry about." She hung up and smiled at Jon. "Want to come?"

"Do you think you need me?"

"You know damn well I need you," she said.

"Then I guess I'll have to call Angie and tell her I'll be late for work," he said.

"That's easy compared to what I have to do."

"What's that?"

"I have to call Louise."

"Oh, oh," he said.

Yet when she called her sister and explained the police had come to her office to question her, Louise seemed to take it calmly.

"They're the ones that *should be* doing the investigation," Louise said. "Good luck. I'll see you tomorrow morning when you get off call."

Lieutenant Bill Crosby, a tall, large-framed, freckled man of about forty with hair the color of poached salmon, smiled as Joanna and Jon approached him in the office waiting room. He rose and put down the magazine he was reading, then extended his hand.

His manner didn't seem either overzealous or intimidating. "I didn't know you would be off this morning, Ms. Michaels."

"That's all right, Lt. Crosby. Actually, I'm glad you came." She introduced him to Jon, and the men shook hands.

"You're the first one I've talked to on this thing that seems glad to talk to me," he said as she directed him to her office and motioned him and Jon to chairs. "Most people don't like to be involved in murder investigations." He turned to Jon. "I've seen you before someplace, Doctor," he said.

"I think you were on a case I worked on."

"A case? What kind of case?"

"Baby stealing."

Crosby studied him a moment. "OK, I gotcha. The horse-doctor detective."

Jon winced. "I guess that's one way of putting it."

Crosby looked at Joanna. "Have you got some problems at the Martin Center, Ms. Michaels?"

"No. That's not why Jon's here."

"Are you here as a horse doctor or detective?"

Jon maintained his composure. "Actually, Joanna's the detective."

Crosby raised his thick eyebrows. His turquoise eyes twinkled. "Looks like I'm surrounded by amateurs. But I don't mind amateur detectives, Ms. Michaels. They can be a big help if they know their place and don't spout off theories on TV. Like this Dr. Wolfe with his theory that the murderer might be an obstetrician or a surgeon. Made it look like we couldn't have come up with a theory like that ourselves. It also put doctors on the defensive. As if they didn't have enough problems with malpractice insurance." He grinned and leaned forward toward Joanna. "I guess you don't have those kinds of problems, though, ma'am. You're just a midwife."

Joanna bridled in spite of herself. "Now look . . ."

Crosby leaned back in his chair and grinned. "OK. I don't have anything against midwives. I saved you for last because we didn't figure you'd do surgery. Our medical consultant told us midwives don't do surgery or deliver high-risk babies."

"I understand," Joanna said.

He nodded and turned to Jon. "Do you do surgery, Dr. Isenson?"

"Not on people," said Jon. "Though I could in an emergency." His eyes did not flicker. "I do cesareans on dead animals on a regular basis. I work for Pharmogenetix in their animal lab doing research."

"Right. I remember that."

"That doesn't make him a suspect in the Cradle

case," said Joanna. "If you think that's what the relationship is . . ."

"That was the farthest thing from my mind. But now that you mention it . . ." He looked from one to the other.

"She's not trying to second-guess you, Lt. Crosby."

"Why don't you stop trying to make *me* second-guess *you*. You're here for a reason, Doctor. Stop playing around and tell me what you have on your mind."

"We'd thought you'd never ask," said Jon.

"I don't like this," Joanna said. "Do the two of you have to play games? Is that the only way you can get the answers you want, Lieutenant? Through intimidation? Pat Reston was right!"

Crosby leaned forward. "You've talked to the lesbian's widow?"

"Yes. Last night. She told me you'd badgered her doctor."

"Jesus Christ!" Crosby stood up. He looked angry.

"I don't understand why you assume people won't answer your questions without being threatened." She looked up at him.

"I don't assume anything. What the hell were you doing talking to the lesbian? She's not your patient."

"I thought there might be a relationship between her and someone who was. Irene Kimski. Please, Lieutenant, I'm not challenging you. Neither is Jon. And we haven't broadcast our theory on TV."

"OK. I have to admit, I'm about at the end of my rope on this case, and we're only two days away from another possible murder. I've taken a lot of shit from the medical society since that shrink got on TV. You doctors seem to feel you're guilty when a finger's pointed at *any* doctor."

"I'm just a midwife," said Joanna.

"I'm just a horse doctor," said Jon.

"OK," said Crosby. "You know what I mean."

"Not all doctors are the same," Joanna said.

"I apologize. You're talking to one overburdened cop." He paused, then he said, "You saw a relationship between the Kimski woman and the lesbian."

"I realized they both had been artificially inseminated. If you'll come to our conference room, I'll show you on our VCR," Joanna said.

After she'd shown him the tape and explained their theory, Crosby said, "You need more than the fathers' all looking alike. You have to *know* the women were all artificially inseminated."

"We've worked on that, too," said Jon. He and Joanna took turns explaining what they'd turned up. "And I even did some research on the rock singer. The group nearly came apart at the seams when her husband couldn't get her pregnant."

"Say, speaking of them, what did you think of that riot?"

"It was quite a scene," said Jon.

"I ... I didn't even see a paper yesterday," said Joanna. "Did I miss something?"

"I'd think it'd be the talk of this place. What with the dead woman's baby being delivered by cesarean."

Jon said, "I'm surprised you *didn't* see it, Joanna. What happened was some mysterious punkers at a concert found a dead woman after this riot that broke out during a requiem for this singer. They used kitchen knives to section her. Delivered a live baby. Then they disappeared."

"With all your investigating, I thought you couldn't miss it. The guy who did it was tall. And he had to be a surgeon to do the job that he did. And the parameds say the woman seemed to know what she was doing, too. We haven't ruled out a connection between those two and the Bloody Shoes thing. Except, of course,

Bloody Shoes seems more interested in killing kids than saving them."

Joanna cleared her throat. "Well, I never got my paper, as I said. And I didn't even turn on the radio all day or watch TV. I thought it didn't get in the news for some reason."

Crosby looked at her.

"I mean, when Jon said it was quite a scene. It sounded like he had seen it. During his research."

"Joanna didn't know about my research on the group. She was busy with the Reston woman."

"Right," said Crosby. "I guess I had you two wrong. You've come up with good information. That shrink is the horse doctor. You two ought to get private eye licenses and go into business together."

"No thanks," said Joanna, as relief at his missing her slip surged over her. "I like what I'm doing. Frankly, detective work scares me. I'm glad to be off this case."

"You two sure don't have to get off any case of mine."

"We want to," said Joanna.

"How's that?" Crosby asked.

"A lot of people saw me in that TV interview. Pat Reston did. One of the doctors in the fertility center did. My sister and brother-in-law are taking care of . . . have a baby and they feel, well, exposed. They think Bloody Shoes himself might have seen me in that TV interview. He might worry that I know something. I don't know just why he has something in for the sperm donor—which it's pretty obvious he does—but I do know he's got to be a pretty desperate man, and if he thinks I'm onto him, and realizes I've been talking to the survivors of his victims, he might come after me. Take it out on my sister and her baby."

Crosby stared at her a few minutes and then nodded. "I can understand your concern."

Joanna nodded. "But I'm worried about something else. If artificial insemination is really the key . . ."

"You *know* it is," said Jon.

"It looks like it might be," said Crosby.

"If it is, I might have a pregnant client at risk."

Crosby leaned forward. "We ought to give her protection. What's her name?"

Joanna hesitated. "I can't tell you that."

Crosby stood up. "What!"

"It's privileged information. She doesn't want the whole world knowing. And she might not be at risk at all. Not everyone who's ever been inseminated got sperm from the same man."

"That's right, Lieutenant. That singer might have been the last," said Jon. "She was pregnant. And Bloody Shoes might have been working in chronological order."

Crosby sat down and drummed his fingers on Joanna's desk. "Good point. The one with the oldest kid was the first one killed."

"I'd thought of that, too," said Jon.

"That singer was about seven or eight months pregnant," said Crosby. "How far along is your client?"

"About three-and-a-half months."

"You ought to give me her name, Ms. Michaels."

"I can't. Look, if you just find out which sperm bank those women got the semen from, and if it is all from the same donor, you'll also find out who the other recipients are. If any."

Crosby sat back in his chair and hooked his fingers in his belt. "There are two reasons I think we don't want to wait on that. One is the lack of cooperation we're likely to get from the fathers . . . you two know about that. That'll take more than two days. The other is, if that lesbian told you the truth about her relationship with the sperm bank, they might not've listed everyone that got the guy's semen. Corruption always leads to a certain amount of cover-up."

"That makes sense." Jon grew reflective.

"Jon, you know I can't reveal my client's name . . ."

"That's not what I was thinking about."

Crosby's brows lifted. "You got an idea?" he asked.

"Whatever happened with that sperm bank murder back in October? Was that ever solved?"

Crosby's lips tightened. "As a matter of fact, no. The killer didn't leave a trace."

"How was the woman killed in that one?" Jon asked.

Lieutenant Crosby leaned forward and nodded slowly. "You might have something there, Doctor. Just might."

Joanna looked from one to the other. Then she turned to Jon. "Tell me. I wasn't in Philadelphia last October."

"Someone broke into a sperm bank and slashed a woman's throat. A neat surgical cut, right through the carotid artery," said Jon.

Joanna drew a quick breath. "And her children?" she asked.

"She was in her fifties, Ms. Michaels," said the lieutenant. "Her youngest daughter was thirty-one. But that doesn't mean it wasn't Bloody Shoes who killed her. She managed all the computer files. If someone wanted to find out what was in them, they'd have to get past her first."

"But even if they did," said Jon, "how would they have known how to use the computer?"

"It wouldn't have been too hard for someone who knows about programming. But this guy made it easy for himself. He got her when the files were open. The program was what they call menu driven. It prompted him through the commands. All he'd have had to

know was the code number of the person he was looking for. Then, with just a little more hacking, he'd
eventually find the list of women inseminated with
this guy's sperm." Crosby sat back and trilled his
fingers on the edge of Joanna's desk.

"Then it might be someone who worked at the
sperm bank," said Jon. "Maybe someone who knows
the donor and has something against him."

Joanna shuddered. "What an awful way to get back
at someone. Killing his children one by one. And their
mothers. Ugh! Why would anyone do that?"

"I can think of at least one reason," said Crosby.
"Blackmail. Maybe the donor knew this guy was cutting corners. You know it takes money to get someone
to look the other way. Those lesbians had a lot of
money."

"And a lot of women who are desperate to have
kids, like Denise Thomas"—Joanna turned and looked
at Jon—"would scrape up the money if they had to."

"And it doesn't take long for the word to spread
from one desperate woman to another," said Jon.

"So when the donor found out what the sperm bank
employee was doing, he demanded a little hush
money. Then the old woman found out, and the employee made her his first victim," said Crosby.

Joanna rose and walked to her office window and
looked out over the crowded street below. "I sometimes wonder about our technology. As soon as eggs
and sperm and embryos . . . and women's bodies . . .
become commodities, somebody wants to get rich.
They forget they're dealing with human lives. Then
something goes wrong, and they stop caring about
lives at all and just want to keep the money coming."
She turned and looked at the men. "Then something
like this . . ." She shuddered.

"If someone at the bank is out to get back at the
donor, why didn't he just kill the donor?" Jon asked.

"Maybe he will," said Crosby. "Maybe he's saving him for last."

Joanna sat down and stared at the ceiling a moment. "Or maybe it *is* the donor."

"That doesn't make sense," said Jon.

Crosby looked from one to the other, then fixed his eyes on Joanna's and held them. "Oh, yes it does. God damn it, it does, all right. That TV shrink may be a horse doctor, Ms. Michaels, but you'd make one hell of a shrink."

"Or a detective, Lieutenant." She turned to Jon. "Don't you see?"

"No," Jon said. "I don't know what you're getting at. The victims didn't have any relationship with the donor."

"But the donor had a relationship with his offspring. A *psychological* relationship. He knew, even if no one else did, that they were his ticket to immortality. And that they wouldn't have been born without him."

"Sometimes it seems like a pretty lousy world to bring kids into," said Crosby. He looked at Joanna. "Sorry—Don't mean to criticize your profession."

"There are times I think that way, too. What does it say on those bumper stickers? 'Life's a bitch. And then you die.'"

"So why are we trying to save lives? What's another murder . . . or suicide . . . more or less? If your client gets it, she gets it, right? She and the kid will be better off than they were before," Crosby said, needling her.

"I still can't tell you her name. But I *can* find out just how much at risk she is. Find out if semen she got came from a man with green eyes and brown hair. And I can *try* to find out where she got the semen."

"OK. But don't scare the shit out of her while you're doing it."

"I think I know how to approach her," said Joanna.

"The woman has a master's degree in education. She'd probably respond to someone stuck for subjects for a research project. But I'll need Jon's help."

"Remember," said Crosby, "it's Wednesday morning. How soon can you get to her?"

Joanna checked her watch. "It's already nine o'clock. She'll be at work, and I can't justify calling her there if it's not an emergency."

"I'd call it an emergency," said Crosby.

"It's not an obstetrical emergency. I can't let her know that it is. I can't, as you say, scare the shit out of her."

"Right." Crosby stood up. "I'll see what I can learn from the Harrington Sperm Service in the meantime. Whatever's going on, I'm sure Dr. Harrington himself doesn't have anything to do with it. He was pretty shook up when Sarah was killed. I'll tell him I think I have a lead."

"The Harrington Sperm Service?" said Joanna. "Isn't that around the corner from here?"

"Couple of blocks," said Crosby.

"I wish it weren't so close," she said. "I'm on call tonight. I have to sleep here."

"We can give you protection."

"No. I trust our own security system."

After seeing her last client at five, Joanna called pie-faced Wendy Green and asked her to come to the center tomorrow afternoon for an interview.

"What we're trying to find out," Joanna explained, "is whether single women using artificial insemination choose the same type of donor traits that married ones do. It's a long-term study that I just became involved in when I returned from my leave. And, frankly, I've been so busy getting reoriented that I put off doing anything until the deadline for enrolling subjects was on me. I happen to have an hour free tomorrow afternoon, and I wondered if you could drop by after work."

"Of course," Wendy said. "I empathize with you, Joanna. No one who gets a master's in education with emphasis on research like mine would dare turn you down. I've spent hours interviewing subjects . . . and twice as many hours putting off the interviews till a month before the end of a semester."

Joanna laughed. She'd counted on that response; and she was glad she always took time to get to know as much as she could about her clients' backgrounds. "We're sisters under the skin, then."

After Joanna had seen her last evening appointment at nine, she met Jon in the cafeteria. There they drank coffee that had been too long on the hot plate and designed a questionnaire fashioned to get the answers they wanted from Wendy—the physical description of her sperm donor and the name of the sperm bank where she got the semen—all without letting her know the specific information they were after.

They completed the form by midnight; Joanna planned to have her secretary, Ginny, type it up in the morning while Joanna was at breakfast with her sister's family. She had a short day tomorrow, starting at three P.M. Wendy was due at four, so she'd be off on time to have dinner with Jon at his apartment.

He said he didn't want to wait till dinner and would meet her at her sister's house for breakfast. And so, after a good night's sleep at the center, during which not a single woman went into labor, she met him there.

David eyed Jon suspiciously. Then he turned to

Joanna. "Louise said the police questioned you yesterday."

Louise handed Cassie to Joanna. Joanna sat down at the kitchen table and reached for the nursing bottle. "That's right."

"You're finally going to get off this thing."

Joanna tightened her hand on Cassie's bottle, and put the nipple in her baby's mouth. The baby began feeding hungrily and Joanna drew her near.

"You *are* getting off it."

"After today I'll be off it."

David shot an angry glance at Jon. "What does she mean 'after today'?"

"Joanna doesn't need me to speak for her."

"You got her started on this, you bastard! You and your smart-assed detective ideas."

"David, please," said Louise. "You're upsetting the baby. He's still upset about last week," she said to Jon.

"You're damn right I'm upset, Louise. Every husband and father has a right to be upset. This crazy killer's lurking around, and Jon puts Joanna in the middle of this mess. It was bad enough endangering Joanna. But with her coming over here all the time, it endangered you, too. You are the mother, Louise, as far as the killer is concerned."

Joanna froze. Jon's eyes found hers and held them. She felt tears spring out and slip over her eyelids.

"That's crazy, David," said Louise. "The killer couldn't know about Joanna. Nobody knew . . ."

Jon interrupted. "Louise is safe, David. So are Joanna and Cassie. All of the victims were artificially inseminated." He looked at Joanna. "Neither Louise nor Joanna were."

"You know!" said Louise. "Oh, Joanna . . ."

"I finally put it together yesterday morning," said

Jon. "It was the only thing to explain the changes in you, and why you came over here so often. And David's outburst last week."

"I'm sorry, Jon. I told you there were things . . ."

"David, look what you've done," Louise cried.

David didn't seem to have heard her or the others. "I heard the news this morning. Nobody said anything about artificial insemination."

"They wouldn't. If everyone knew, it would screw up the investigation," said Jon.

"Then why did they tell you?"

"They didn't. Joanna figured it out."

David spun toward Joanna. "You told us you were going to keep out of this. You swore you wouldn't put Louise and Cassie in any more danger."

Joanna began to tremble. The nipple slipped out of Cassie's mouth, and Cassie began to cry.

Louise quickly walked over and picked the baby up. She took the bottle from Joanna and returned to her chair. In a few seconds she'd quieted Cassie down. The baby began to drink again.

"Louise and Cassie are safe," Joanna said, recomposed. "I wouldn't . . . didn't . . . do anything to endanger them. Or myself. If Jon and I hadn't got involved, they wouldn't be so close to solving the case. Now, maybe the police can stop the killer before he strikes again."

"You're into this up to the hilt, aren't you?" David shouted. "Police trap and all."

Joanna saw Louise tremble, and Cassie began to cry again.

Louise, babe in arms, stood up and left the kitchen. Joanna rose to follow.

"Stay where you are," David cried out. "If you're part of a trap, you owe it to us to tell us."

"It's not a trap. I'd never take part in a trap."

Joanna's eyes followed Louise and Cassie. Her body was half turned to David.

"I don't believe you," David, face flooded with crimson, whirled to face Jon. "Jesus Christ, Isenson, what the hell have you got us into?"

Now Joanna faced David. "I'm an independent person, David. Or have you forgotten? I do what I want to do. I don't belong to you, or Jon, or anyone else. I make my own decisions."

"No, Joanna. You're not just yourself anymore. Not since you decided to have Cassie. Not since you involved us in her care. We've put ourselves on the line for you. We've lied for you. We've hidden the truth from Kevin. I've never been happy about that. He has the right to know he has a baby."

Jon stepped toward David. "What are you trying to say? That Joanna should have exposed herself to Kevin's threats?"

"The man never abused her. I never saw a mark on her. I never heard him raise his voice. His only fault was that he didn't want children. And she did. So she got pregnant to change him and then ran scared."

Joanna stood riveted to the floor, shaking her head in shock.

Louise returned to the kitchen, rocking Cassie furiously to try to still her crying. "No. You're wrong. Kevin didn't just not want children. He hated them. Scared them."

David laughed. "That's ridiculous."

"No. Michael was terrified of him. It took him months to warm up to him. And Kevin must have hit him or said something to him one night. The next time Kevin and Joanna came to dinner he refused to eat with us. He said he had a stomachache. But after Kevin left he was starved, so I brought a sandwich to his room."

"Why didn't you tell me?" Joanna asked, stunned.

"I thought it didn't matter that much. I knew you loved Kevin. And I was sure Michael would get over it."

"Did he?" asked Jon.

Louise shook her head. "No. He was absolutely terrified of the man. I breathed a sigh of relief when Kevin started his residency and Joanna stopped bringing him over. Then when she told me she was pregnant and asked me to help, I couldn't do anything else."

"Just because one kid is scared of him, doesn't make him a monster," said David. "He still has a right to decide if he wants a relationship with his own child. This thing's been driving me crazy since you started it. I'll never agree with it. What you did was dead wrong, Joanna. You made a decision he had the right to know about, too."

Joanna felt weak; sick. She reached for her chair and sat down. "I've told so many lies. I never told a lie like this in my life before." She looked up at her sister. "I don't understand myself anymore. Why did I do it?"

Louise shook her head and held Cassie close.

Jon stepped forward and grasped Joanna's shoulders from behind. "You were damn scared of Kevin, that's why. You saw him try to kill himself. You're the only one here who knows firsthand what kind of abuse a suicidal man can dish out. And that kind of emotional and mental abuse can be just as bad as physical." He turned to David. "Worse, because it doesn't leave bruises or scars you can see."

"I was wrong," said Joanna. "It was an awful mistake."

"Why didn't you say something, David?" said Louise. "I didn't even know you were upset. I thought you felt like I did."

David shrugged. "I didn't think it through at first. It

didn't hit me till Joanna started playing detective. And Kevin started following her around. Then I thought, My God! Why's everybody sneaking around? Why doesn't she just tell the man the truth? He's not going to kill her. If he doesn't like kids, he's not going to fight her for custody. He'll probably be glad she didn't saddle him with a baby."

Joanna said, "You're right." She looked up at David. "I went a little crazy. I exaggerated everything Kevin did in my mind. I was pregnant. I was afraid . . ."

"Michael wasn't pregnant. And he was just as scared. It wasn't you. It was Kevin," said Louise.

"No, Louise," said Joanna. "Don't make excuses for me. David's right. I should have told Kevin. And I will."

"Thank God!" said David. "I knew you'd be sensible, Sis." He walked across the kitchen and poured himself a cup of coffee. Then he came back and sat next to Joanna. His hands trembled slightly. "Now if Jon will just be as sensible, he'll get you out of the police business."

"No," said Joanna. "I still have one more thing to do. We're too close to the answer to quit now."

David put his coffee cup down. His hand shook more visibly. "Then you're much too close to us. Too close for comfort. And if you won't do anything about it, I will. I want this baby out of our house tonight."

Louise stood up. "No! That's unfair!"

"Yes. This time I'm not going to hide how I feel. I'm not going to let you be a sitting duck for this killer. The two of them had their faces all over TV—even national TV; they've been visiting the victims' families and asking questions; the two of them have been talking to the police." He stopped and narrowed his eyes and drew a breath. "And the two of them were at that rock concert the other night. They delivered that dead woman's baby."

Louise blanched. She shook her head mutely.

David's lip curled as he turned to look from Joanna to Jon. "I'm right. It's all over your face. I knew it the minute I read it."

Joanna could not move; could neither admit nor deny the truth.

Jon said nothing. But no one seeing his face would doubt that David was right.

"Now the two of them are here, in our kitchen, early in the morning. And Joanna's the bait in some kind of trap. It stinks, and I won't have any part of it."

"You don't have to," said Jon. He walked over to Joanna and grasped her shoulders. "I'll help you move Cassie to your apartment this afternoon."

"But I work till after six. And that interview . . . it's the last day we have."

"For God's sake, David," said Louise, whose quick glance at Joanna had understood and forgiven her everything. "Give her time to make arrangements. Who's going to take care of the baby?"

"I'm sure she'll find a way. Maybe she can get Kevin to help."

Joanna shook her head. She looked from Louise to Jon for help. "It's too much to think of at once. I . . . I don't know what to do first . . . "

"I do," said Jon. "I'll call Angie and tell her I'm not coming in. I'll get the furniture moved this afternoon. You get someone to cover for you at work. If you have to, cancel appointments."

Joanna's head was whirling. "I don't know what to do," she said. "That interview . . . "

"Cancel the goddam interview," said Jon. He let go of her shoulders and walked away.

"I can't."

"I'll help with the baby," said Louise.

"No, you won't. Didn't you hear what I said?" David's eyes flashed.

"Joanna and I will take care of everything," said Jon. "I don't mind taking off work. I don't mind helping with Cassie till we can find someone to come in."

Joanna reeled still. So much to think of. So much to do. So many details. She'd never even really been a mother, with all that entailed. Now she had to deal with it all at once, unprepared. And she couldn't cancel Wendy's interview. Jon knew that too. Not after all they had been through. Not after their last two nights together.

He grasped her shoulders again. "Joanna, come on. Go out for a walk. Clear your head. Remember, it's Thursday morning. I'll handle everything here. We'll take it a step at a time."

"Yes," she said.

"Good," he said.

"But I have to tell Kevin."

"That can wait."

"Don't let it wait too long," said David. "The man has a right to know."

"For God's sake, David!" cried Louise. "Get off her back for a second. Can't you get off all our backs for awhile?"

"I should have been on them long ago," he said.

Chapter Nineteen

Thursday—Kevin

KEVIN PERFORMED HIS last surgery at ten-thirty Thursday morning. He finished up at almost exactly noon, thirty-six hours after he began his stint at midnight on Tuesday. The schedule fit into his plans. He had today and tomorrow in which to finish the work he'd begun last October.

After tomorrow, he would have the rest of eternity off. And the world would be free of the scourge he had visited on it.

Drunk as usual from the long siege of work broken only by momentary snatches of sleep, he staggered from the hospital onto the street. Friday—just one day away—drugged him with its promise. He vowed not to sleep until it was over. He had too much to do. He couldn't afford to make a mistake. He couldn't afford to leave a single vestige, a single seed of Kevin Willman's evil, a single trace of Kevin Willman himself. From this moment on he'd follow the teacher, Wendy Green, around. And to make sure that everyone would understand why he did it, from this moment on he'd record everything on his tape recorder. Then his mother and sister would know. And Forest moldering in a mental hospital would know. And Katie would know; and his landlady at the old apartment would know, even though he didn't have anyone to dedicate to her.

And Joanna would know. He would dedicate Wendy to her.

Then everyone would know why he'd had to kill the woman at the sperm bank.

He hadn't planned to kill Sarah. But she hadn't cooperated when he asked who'd borne his children.

She'd looked up from her computer after he'd shown her his identification card and given her his four-digit code, which was secret like those used in automatic teller machines at banks. "I'm sorry, Dr. Willman. You knew when you donated your sperm that the recipients' names are confidential. You didn't request visitation rights, or the right to see the children when they're eighteen. Your sperm was distributed with those wishes in mind, to women who reserved the right to contact you only in a medical emergency, and only through a medical agency. Of course, if it's really important to you, we can see if any of the mothers would accept your newly asserted rights ... but that could be a long legal hassle that probably isn't going to turn out in your favor."

"I'm the father of those children. They bear my genetic heritage. I want to assure their future. I want to make sure they never suffer."

"We all want that for our children. And we at the Harrington Service do our best to see that they get what you'd want for them. Your children face less risk of being raised in an unfavorable environment than many naturally conceived children will. The women who conceive through artificial insemination are desperate to have and nurture their own babies. They have higher than average intelligence and education. They have financial stability. We know their genetic and psychological background. Just as we know yours." Her gray head bobbed back and forth on her long crepey neck as she spoke. Her watery gray eyes searched his.

He recalled with self-satisfied irony how he'd fudged his psychological examination. He knew they wouldn't have taken his sperm if they'd known of his abuse at the hands of a pederast ... if they'd known his own hands were those of an abusive pederast, a pedophilic monster.

And what of the women who'd come wailing and whining for his sperm—any man's sperm? What secrets had *they* hidden from the Harrington Service to get their perverted way? At least his intentions in donating his sperm had been simple and straightforward: he'd needed the money. Even the psychologist had admitted that was a good, healthy reason.

The women's motives were selfish, self-centered, grounded in the heart of the evil desires that drove them. He realized that now. Why would a normal, moral woman want to bear the child of a stranger? He knew that dykes like his sister did it, to bring children into their perverted world. He knew that single women more devoted to their careers than to setting up stable families did it. They let hired people raise their children so they themselves could have everything while the children had neither mother nor father. He knew that wives of sterile men did it so that they could fulfill their own genetic heritage at their husbands' expense. Theirs was a betrayal as great as Joanna's of Kevin. Their forked tongues dripped love laced with acid while they drank their husbands' thin milk but nurtured their starving wombs with the milk of others.

He had watched Sarah's head bobbing before him, her eyes darting between him and her veiled computer screen.

He stood up. "It's odd to me that an old woman like you has more right to know about the women who bore my children than I do."

"But I don't, Dr. Willman. I know only their code numbers, sans the secret four digits. Those are listed in a separate computer program that I have no access to. We take no chances on the security of our information."

*   *   *

But the Harrington Service computers were not secure from Kevin. He had known University Hospital
ran as much these days by the artificial intelligence of
its computers as by the human intelligence of its ad-
ministrators and medical and nursing staffs and their
ancillaries. This required the presence of full-time
computer technicians on call 'round the clock. Kevin
had befriended the chief technician long ago. More
than his curiosity about the computers motivated
him, then. He didn't trust most human beings with
the life-and-death decision a doctor made; he trusted
computers less. So he determined to discover and root
out the machines' weaknesses.

He had spent hours in the computer room with the
technician and often hied there at night between
emergencies. He learned to dissect software as readily
as he did human tissue. He learned to diagnose the
bugs that afflicted computer systems almost as
readily as those that afflicted human body systems.
There were times when, sick with disgust at human
behavior, he wished he had pursued a career in computers. He still might have, if it hadn't deprived him
of opportunities to satiate his sexual drives; a doctor
had more access to those most vulnerable to his advances.

Well, even without a career in computer programming, what he'd learned came in handy now.

The night he killed Sarah was the third night he'd
spent in the Harrington Center hacking software.
Though he hadn't planned to kill her, after he found
out how easy she'd made it for him, he wished he had
killed her the first night. She had her files already
open, and the system up and running, and she'd left
enough printed copy around that he easily found the
files listing sperm recipients' secret codes.

Sarah's blood had hardly cooled and clotted on the
carpet around her when he'd printed up the list of

the women impregnated with his sperm, torn the green bar paper from the printer tractor, and escaped into the chilly October night.

Tracking down the women had been more difficult. They had nothing in common. Though most had already borne their children, one was in the early weeks of pregnancy when he first saw her, and he wasn't sure she *was* pregnant until later.

From the records purloined from the Harrington files, he found out where she received her prenatal care. To obtain her medical records there took little skulduggery. He simply walked through the birth center corridors in a wrinkled scrub suit with his stethoscope drooping from his neck, approached the record room clerk, and asked for her files. The clerk asked for his code number, and he gave one he saw on the record room signout sheet under yesterday's date. She produced the record. Angela Marietta's baby was due in June.

He would leave her for next to last—last at that time in his planning. For he learned from Wendy Green's records, obtained from the Martin Center, that the first two attempts to impregnate her had failed.

He knew they would try a third time, so he followed her to her visit with Joanna. Joanna had written it on the chart and sealed Wendy's fate. Pregnant with the last traces of Kevin's evil seed, she would be the last to go.

He would dedicate her to Joanna. And tell the world why.

On the last day of his surgical career, he walked—oblivious of May's gentle air—from the hospital to his apartment. He took an icy shower to wash away the operating room blood stench from his pores and to rehone the edges of his mind. He dressed in a thin white T-shirt and light gray cotton slacks. He pulled his small tape recorder from his desk drawer, carried it to his car, and tucked it into the console between the bucket seats of his Honda Civic. Then he drove straight out Broad Street till it became Old York Road and turned left at Susquehanna where it bordered Jenkintown and Abington. From there it was only five or six miles to Fort Washington Avenue and the elementary school where Wendy Green taught second grade.

He waited, parked on the driveway near the flag pole, until she left the building and crossed to the large fenced-in lot where parents waited in a chugging caravan to snatch up their just-liberated children.

Wendy was trapped in her parking space till the parking lot cleared. Then she headed in the direction opposite from her home in Ambler.

After he had followed her for a few minutes, he realized she was going through Chestnut Hill toward Wissahickon Drive. He kept her in view as she traveled both River Drives and then drove past the Philadelphia Zoo into University City. There, not far from where he had begun the day's drive, he ended it in the Martin Center parking lot.

What had happened? She couldn't be scheduled for a routine prenatal checkup. She hadn't driven as if in a crisis. Had she miscarried? If she had, he couldn't kill her. Her motives for getting pregnant appalled him, but he couldn't kill her for that reason alone. Nature may have already deprived her of her wishes.

But if nature hadn't killed the baby—and he couldn't tell at only three-and-a-half months—he would have to do it himself. He had to follow her into the Martin Center.

He spoke to his recorder: "I'm taking my scrub suit in, I'll dress in the delivery room dressing rooms, just like the last time I followed her here. But I can't let Joanna see me again. She could ruin everything."

His scrub suit in a plastic bag tucked under one arm, his recorder mike pressed to his murmuring lips, he slipped through the heavy steel doors and climbed the fire stairs to the corridor that led to the birthing rooms. As he walked he began to record his bitter tale—beginning with his love for Elizabeth, his deflowering at Forest's hands. He'd end with Joanna's desertion of him, as he moved toward its final resolution.

Emerging on the birthingroom floor, he looked both ways before he ran to the men's toilet. He nodded to a man pissing into a urinal, and slid into a stall. When he heard the door to the corridor breathe shut after the man, he quickly put his scrub suit on over his T-shirt and slacks. He returned to the corridor with his recorder mike secured beneath his chin. Now the people he passed in the passageway leading to the birthing room nodded and smiled at him and said, "Good afternoon, Doctor." He smiled, knowing their naive words would be played back at them once this tape was found next to the body of Wendy Green.

Outside the birthing rooms he picked up a pair of delivery room booties and a mask and cap. He put on the blue booties, tied on his cap and mask, as he stepped up to the stainless steel sinks in the scrub room. He elbowed on the rabbit-eared water faucets and doused his hands with antiseptic red surgical soap.

A man who had followed him in was studying his every move. Kevin felt the hair rise on the back of his neck.

The man said, "Isn't Dr. Shriver delivering Susan?"

"I'm sure he is, if he was supposed to."

"Where is Dr. Shriver?" the man asked anxiously. He eyed Kevin's hands and fell into an awkward scrubbing rhythm.

"I'm sure he'll be here soon."

"She. Don't you know her?"

Kevin felt his face redden. He began to sweat in the steam rising from the sinks. "I know her father," he said.

"Oh. Is he a doctor here, too? He must be in his seventies."

"Well, Doctor," said Kevin. "I thought he might be here. He was my professor of obstetrics. I was surprised when you asked if he was going to be delivering your patient."

"My *wife*. She's delivering our baby. I just thought Dr. Shriver would help me through this scrubbing. I've never watched a baby being born before. It's our first."

"Well," said Kevin, "I'll help you. In fact, you're doing fine. So well, I thought you were a doctor. Just keep scrubbing the way you are. Pay particular attention to your nails. That's right. And don't forget your wrists and forearms. Even though you won't be taking part in the actual delivery, you'll be holding your baby right after it's born."

The man laughed nervously as he fell into a rhythm matching Kevin's.

Suddenly Kevin stopped.

The man stopped, too. "Did I do something wrong?"

"Oh, no. It's just that I forgot something. I have to go back outside." He elbowed the faucets closed and shook the water from his hands.

"What do I do next?"

"Just hold your hands up like this, so the water runs down over your elbows. From clean to dirty, instead of from dirty to clean. Then see the attendant over there. She'll help you."

"Thank you."

"No problem," said Kevin. He turned to leave.

"It's really kind of you, Doctor. I'd like to tell Susan you helped. What's your name?"

"I'd rather be an anonymous benefactor."

The man laughed. "OK. Thanks."

"You're welcome," said Kevin. He walked toward the door, then turned. "On second thought, if you promise to wait until Saturday, you can tell her the man who showed you how to scrub was Dr. Kevin Willman."

"Saturday? Why not today?"

"I'm just completing a special project. It's going to make news. When you see my name in the *Inquirer* on Saturday, you can tell her what happened today. It's something you'll both remember for the rest of your lives."

The man's eyebrows rose, his eyes widened above his mask. "Really? Are you going to get the Nobel Prize or something?"

Kevin laughed. "I doubt it. Though maybe I should. The Peace Prize. For leaving the world a better place than it was when I came into it."

The man scrubbed away, sending suds spattering in an arc from his hands. "Well, whatever it is, you won't win a prize for modesty," he said; and he shook his head. "But anyway, thanks again."

Kevin spoke into the microphone cradled in the surgical mask that dangled beneath his chin: "I took off the booties outside the scrub room door and tossed them into the receptacle. Now I'm on my way to the staff elevator. It's waiting for me, waiting for Kevin Willman, waiting to swallow me up.

"But I'm not ready to be swallowed yet."

The elevator door opened at the fourth floor.

A slim black woman wearing a crisp white lab coat got on, her stiffness brushing the bristling hairs on his arm as he dodged by her and emerged, head down.

"Well, excuse *me*, Doctor!" she said.

He mumbled an apology; she uttered a sarcastic laugh.

As the door sliced between them, he turned to her, glowered with pride. "Remember you saw me today and didn't know me," he growled.

The shock on her face seemed suspended on the current of air puffed out by the closing door. It sat on his shoulder as he slipped down the corridor toward Joanna's office.

Her door was closed. He went to the waiting room. A woman who looked about seven months pregnant glanced up at him, then returned to her magazine. She shifted in her chair as he stared at her.

"Who are you here to see?" he asked.

"Joanna Michaels."

"I hope she hasn't kept you waiting long."

"It's all right. She had an emergency."

"Wendy Green?" he asked.

"I . . . I'm sorry. I don't know her name."

"Oh, you will," he said. "In a few days, everyone will know it."

The woman dropped the magazine. "Who are you?" she whispered.

"A colleague of Joanna's," he said. "We work as a team sometimes. Wendy is the second patient we worked on together. The first one made news, too."

"Oh. I don't read the medical news."

"You should keep informed. Advances in medicine can be life-and-death matters."

"Well, yes. I will from now on. Oh, I think she's coming out now." The woman got up awkwardly with a forward tip and a twist of her belly. When the receptionist told her she could go back to Joanna's office, her face flooded with relief.

Kevin stepped aside to let her pass; then he stepped

to the waiting room window and pretended to look down at the cantilevered entranceway canopy three stories below. But he was actually watching Wendy Green's reflection as she stopped in front of the receptionist's cubicle.

"No charge for this visit, of course, Wendy," the receptionist said. "Everything's included in the obstetrical fee. Joanna will see you again two Wednesdays from now."

Wendy said something Kevin couldn't hear, then left.

He retraced his way down the staff elevator and through the birthing room corridor to the back stairs, and, aided by legs much longer than hers, arrived at his car moments before Wendy Green got into hers. He followed her through the choked rush-hour traffic to her small frame home off Butler Street in Ambler.

She would be the easiest to take care of. She lived alone in her yellow two-story house and seldom had visitors. And never men. He'd been watching her since last October; and he knew that fall, winter, and spring she always threw open the double-hung windows of her bedroom upstairs before climbing into bed and turning out the lights.

Suddenly everything blurred. A soft buzzing sound filled his head.

A woman walking down the street stopped next to his car, which was parked in front of Wendy's house. He sat behind the wheel, ramrod straight, with his eyes closed. She peered at him for several seconds, then started away.

Then she changed her mind and returned to the car, and rapped on the window. For a few seconds he sat perfectly still, his hands still on the wheel, his head poised as if he was fully alert.

Finally he opened his eyes and stared at the woman. He rolled down the window.

"I'm sorry," she said, leaning in. "Are you all right? You were sitting so still and stiff I thought you might be . . . sick or something."

"Or dead?"

She looked embarrassed. "Well, your face did look a little pale."

"I'm fine," said Kevin. "I was just sitting here thinking."

"Oh. Well, I didn't mean to . . ."

"It's all right." He started the ignition while she still had one hand on the side of the car.

She drew back and he drove away.

He knew what had happened. It was what residents knew as mini-sleep. It usually overcame them when they'd been awake for more than twenty-four hours, and then relaxed for a few moments between crises. He had not slept now in nearly forty-eight hours. He had to go home. His travails would end forever, twenty-four hours from now. There would be no more mini-sleeps then. Only one last eternal rest.

Chapter Twenty

Thursday afternoon—Joanna

WHEN WENDY GREEN arrived at Joanna's office at three, she extended her hand and said: "From one sister to another." Her pie-face expanded to look like one of those smile stickers people decorated cheerful messages with; except that the stickers' faces were usually yellow, and Wendy's was always red. "Fire away with your questions. And remember, I'm an expert. When you're done, I'll critique your questionnaire."

Joanna tried to sound light and relaxed. "I'm sure you'll find it adequate," she said. "I can't claim to have designed it." And though she was quaking inside from the morning's events, Wendy didn't seem to notice. After months of practicing deceptions, I'm becoming a master, Joanna thought with a tinge of bitterness.

But this time it was a matter of life and death. And maybe Wendy's life, not her own. So this time lying was justified. Once this was over she'd never lie, never deceive again. And maybe they would all forgive her. Maybe she would forgive herself.

Wendy gave quick, straightforward answers to the questions about her own personal background. Then Joanna handed her an envelope containing a form listing the names of Philadelphia sperm banks. "You may keep this form and destroy it after you leave here. I'm not privy to the code numbers on this sheet. Please give the code number of the facility where you received the donor's semen."

Wendy hesitated. "How anonymous are my answers?"

"You're just a cipher fed into a computer."

Wendy sat silently for a few moments. "It's not that I don't trust you, Joanna, but I'm really uncomfortable with that question."

If only you knew how important this information is, Joanna thought. But she forced her voice to sound cheerful. "You don't have to answer it, then. Let's go on to the next."

"Thank you. You really are a sister under the skin." Wendy crumpled up the paper and tossed it into Joanna's wastebasket.

The next questions went quickly, with quick concise answers from Wendy. The traits she had chosen for the donor were based on a man she had admired as a child: her family doctor. "He was the kindest, most intelligent man I knew. Tall, with heavenly green eyes and brown curly hair. I guess I was in love with him. You know, the way young girls are."

Joanna nodded, trying not to reveal the catch in her throat as she asked the next question; and the next; and the next . . . and at last the final one: "Did the donor want to see the child or claim custody in the future?"

"Oh, no. Unless there's some medical reason down the road, I'll never know who he is. But I'm so grateful to him," she said, "for making this possible for me. With a baby I know my life will be complete."

As Wendy left the office talking about the baby and wearing a radiant smile on her round face, Joanna wanted to cry out, "Be careful. Please don't stay home alone tomorrow night!" But she couldn't say anything. The police would *want* Wendy to stay home alone. That was the only way they could protect her and flush out the murderer. They would wait outside of Wendy Green's house; and if she *was* the next victim on his list, they would catch him creeping up to her bedroom window and stop him once and for all.

Joanna did not have time to call Crosby or Jon before her next client entered her office.

"I'm sorry I had to delay you," she told Elinor Moore. "You know, in this business . . ." She spread her hands apologetically and smiled.

"I know you'd do the same for me if I had a problem," said Elinor, a tall attractive brunette who had carried her eight months of pregnancy unobtrusively thus far. "I hope the other woman's all right."

"A little nervous, but fine now. And how are things going with you?"

Elinor reported on her progress of the last three weeks, then the two women went into the examining room, where Elinor disrobed and Joanna helped her into a gown and checked her blood pressure.

After completing the fundal measurements—which determined how large Elinor's uterus had grown—and finding them normal, Joanna listened to the fetal heart sounds. She let Elinor listen, too. The woman's eyes misted over, and for the rest of the exam, she spoke of her awe and wonder at what was happening to her body.

"But it must seem so everyday to you. You deliver so many babies . . ."

Joanna stripped off her glove and patted her client's abdomen. "It never stops seeming wonderful. I live through it with every one of you. OK. You can sit up. Things look and feel just as they should." She helped Elinor sit up and handed her her clothes. "See you in my office."

A few minutes later, Elinor sat next to Joanna's desk. Joanna gave her suggestions for the last month-and-a-half, and told her to come back in three weeks.

"Any other questions I can answer for you?"

"You've been very thorough."

"I try to be," said Joanna. "But don't hesitate to call me any time . . ."

"There is one thing." Elinor looked mildly embarrassed.

"Go ahead."

"Well, actually it's not about me. It's about the woman who was in here before."

Joanna was bemused. "I don't know what I can tell you."

"Oh, nothing about her problem. I know you can't tell me anything confidential . . ."

"I'm glad you're aware of that."

"Well . . . I just wondered if she's some kind of celebrity or something?"

"What makes you ask that?" Joanna couldn't imagine that anyone would mistake pie-faced Wendy Green for a celebrity.

"Well the doctor that came from your office . . ."

"What doctor? I'm the only one here this afternoon."

"Well, he came from this end of the hall."

Joanna said, "That's possible. The staff elevator's here."

"Maybe that's where he came from. It's just that what he said made me think he'd been in your office. He seemed to know your client." Elinor looked embarrassed again. "Maybe I'm being presumptuous."

"No, not at all. What did he say that made you think Wendy might be a celebrity?"

"Wendy. Yes. He said Wendy Green."

Joanna nodded tensely. Who knew that Wendy was there? She hadn't even told her receptionist before Wendy showed up. "That was her name. What did he say about her?" Joanna's mouth felt dry.

"Just that I'd know the name in a few more days when it made the news." She spread her hands weakly, as if out of words.

"Go on. What else did he say?"

"I shouldn't have asked you. The whole thing's none of my business." She folded and unfolded her hands in her swollen lap.

"No. Please go on. What you're telling me is important." Joanna picked up her pen and gripped it tightly in her clammy hand.

"Well," Elinor said, looking above Joanna's head as if searching for words, "he said he was your partner. You worked together with two patients, and this

Wendy was one of them. She was going to make some kind of medical news, like the other one already did."

"Yes," said Joanna in a barely audible whisper.

"Then he is your partner." Elinor sighed and sat back. "I'm glad. You know, I hate to say this, Joanna, but he scared me at first. Something in his eyes . . ."

"The color," said Joanna.

"Oh, no. Not the color. They were a beautiful color. It was something else. You know how some people's eyes . . ."

"A beautiful shade of green . . ."

"Yes."

"Tall, with dark brown hair. Curly hair."

"I didn't see his hair. It was under the cap. But he was tall. Then I guess he's what he says he is." She sighed again and smiled. "I was silly to be scared of his eyes, I guess."

"No," said Joanna.

Elinor looked puzzled.

"He does have scary-looking eyes. Even I was once scared of his eyes. There's something about them, isn't there?" She put her pen down on her desk and looked into Elinor's eyes and forced herself to smile. "But I wouldn't worry about that. And to answer your question, I wouldn't expect Wendy's name to be in the news. For a while I was afraid it might be. But now I'm certain it won't. My partner spoke out of turn. You'll have to forgive him." She rose.

"I hope *I* didn't speak out of turn," said Elinor as she hefted her pregnant form into a standing position.

"Not at all. You did just the right thing. I'm glad you did."

After the woman left, Joanna slumped into her chair. She sat for several minutes, as fear and bewilderment washed over her. Then she picked up the telephone and called Crosby.

"He just left the office. This is Jones. Can I help you?"

"When is he coming back?"

"Tomorrow morning."

"But it's important."

"Lady, everything's important. Including a good night's sleep. The lieutenant's been on duty since five this morning. Don't you think he deserves a night off? If I can't help you with whatever it is, you'll just have to call back tomorrow."

She made a fist and pressed it against her desk. "I don't know you. I have to talk to him."

"As I said . . ."

"I know what you said. I can't wait till tomorrow. My name is Joanna Michaels. I'm leaving my own office now. Here's my home number." She gave it to him. "Please get in touch with Lt. Crosby as soon as you can. Have him call me there."

"The midwife?"

"Yes."

"Why didn't you tell me in the first place? He was hoping to hear from you."

"I'm sorry. I've been under a strain all day, Officer Jones."

"Sergeant. We've all been under a bit of a strain, Ms. Michaels. And we don't exactly need someone like you to add to it. I'll tell the lieutenant." He hung up.

She slammed down the phone, angry at him for his rudeness and at herself for losing her composure. What if he didn't call Crosby? She didn't relish the thought of having to call Jones back. And she couldn't wait until tomorrow.

She picked up the phone again and called Jon.

"What's keeping you? I thought you'd canceled your appointments," he said.

She could hear soft snuffling sounds in the background.

"I did. I'll be leaving soon."

"Joanna, you sound terrible."

"How's Cassie?"

"I'm giving her her bottle now. She eats like a horse."

"She's all right."

"Yes. Oh, I think the move upset her. But Louise brought her over and set up your spare bedroom to feel as much as possible like the one she was used to. And I fed her a bottle earlier today, so at least she got used to the feel of me." He laughed. "But it's going to take me a while to get used to the feel of her. I'm not sure I'm cut out to be a father."

Joanna was silent. Her thoughts whirled as she listened to the sounds of her daughter feeding.

"Joanna, are you all right?"

"No."

"What's wrong?"

"I can't tell you now. As soon as I get my head together, I'll come home."

"I'll come get you."

"No! Don't leave the apartment."

"I'm sure Louise will come over and watch Cassie," he said.

"No. Don't leave her with anyone. Not even for a minute. And don't take her out of the apartment. And don't let anyone come in." She knew she was being irrational. How could Kevin have guessed about Cassie?

He was silent a few seconds. Then he said, "All right. But hurry. I don't like the way you sound."

She hung up the telephone and looked down at Elinor Moore's chart on her desk. She still had a few notes to make, but her hand froze on her pen. She buzzed her secretary.

"Ginny, I have to leave Mrs. Moore's chart unfinished. I'm sorry. I'll file it in my desk till I get back."

"That's all right. Oh, and don't worry about coming in for the weekend. Walter Flame, the second-year resident, will fill in for you. I'll smooth things over with your clients about giving them a doctor instead of a midwife."

"Thank you," said Joanna, blunted to the humor intended by her loyal employee. "Ginny, did you see a doctor talking to Elinor Moore in the waiting room?"

"Yes."

"What did he look like? Have you ever seen him here before?"

"He was tall, that's all I know. With all the guys in scrub suits coming from the staff elevator, I've ceased to notice them. If you hadn't told me he was a doctor, I'd have thought he was another expectant father getting off at the wrong floor. Except this one didn't ask me for directions to the cafeteria, and he didn't look confused."

"Did you see which way he went after Wendy Green came out?"

"He went back to the staff elevators. Seemed to be in a hurry."

"Thank you, Ginny."

The receptionist hesitated. "I thought he might be a new resident. You know Jordan Martin is always starting new residents. And with you having to take time off . . ."

"Yes. OK. I just wanted you to know about Mrs. Moore's record."

"Sure."

It was after six when Joanna left her office. Most of the employees' reserved slots in the underground parking garage had been vacated. She recognized by the color of the stickers on their bumpers the cars of the medical and nursing staff. Next to Walter Flame's well-tended sky-blue Saab, she saw an unfamiliar tan Pontiac with a temporary parking tag tucked into the rear window. She was appalled anew at the Martin Center's lax security, considering the growing public fear over the Cradle murders.

Had the Pontiac been checked out by security? She doubted it. The security officers had taken to relaxing at their television monitors, leaning back with their feet up on their desk and a cup of coffee in one hand while the cameras scanned the parking lots, stairs, and elevators.

She glanced up at the slowly oscillating security camera in the corner and wondered if it was focusing on her . . . and if anyone really noticed.

She got into her car and started the engine, then took a deep breath before putting it into gear and backing out of her space. Time to shake her fear. Time to start thinking clearly again. Time to realize that Kevin had never been following her at all, had never known about Cassie. He had been following the women who'd been *artificially* inseminated with his semen, killing them and their children. Why? Why, why, why would he do it?

"Life's a bitch," she said out loud. "And then you die. Or kill yourself. And all your children!"

Her hands clutched the steering wheel as she drove up the ramp to the Walnut Street exit from the parking lot and made a right turn. His voice, as on the day she left him, rasped in her ears like the chattering of the still heavy rush-hour traffic: *There won't be anything left.*

Her own voice answering, cruel, uncaring: *You never happened. There won't be a trace when you're gone.*

And then his snarl, his pulling away when she felt a moment of remorse and was ready to take it all back.

But it had been too late. She had added her insults to a long string of injuries that women had visited on him in the past. She had chosen to have Cassie, knowing what it would do to him if he found out. She had hacked away—unknowing of course, but hacked away anyway—at what had been left of his self-esteem before she met him. She should have seen it. She of all women should have seen what was happening to him. But instead she had run away.

Now Kevin was going to kill himself and not leave a trace. Exactly as she'd demanded.

She sped toward her apartment, as if by driving too fast she could escape from the picture of Kevin. She felt the hairs rise on her nape, as if he were behind her, breathing on her neck. She elevated her eyes to the rearview mirror, expecting to meet his. She knew he would always follow her, never let her forget. Never let her forget that if she had not left him, all those woman and their babies would still be alive.

But he was not there. All that followed her was a long line of rush-hour traffic. The tan Pontiac was too far back for her to see.

"No!" she cried out loud. "I won't let you do it, Kevin. I won't let you kill me with guilt. I won't be one of your victims."

She parked behind her apartment building and hurried in and upstairs. Jon was waiting, carrying Cassie on his shoulder, hopping about the room in a dance that was obviously meant to calm her. The more he hopped and whirled, the more Cassie cried.

Joanna grasped her eagerly; as eagerly, he gave her up. And in a few minutes Cassie was quiet and soon fell asleep in her arms.

Joanna looked up and realized she was in her own apartment and wasn't quite sure what to do.

"We put her crib in the second bedroom," Jon said.

"Everything's changed."

"Yes," Jon said.

She took Cassie to the small room. The crib was wedged into a corner next to a sofa bed meant for guests. A soft evening breeze from the window across from it stirred the mobile suspended from the foot of the crib and carried the smell of baby powder to Joanna's nose.

She sniffed. "It smells like she belongs."

"We wanted to make her feel at home."

She nodded and put Cassie into her crib on her belly, and pulled the light blanket up to just below the reddish whorl of hair on her neck. Then she and Jon tiptoed out of the dim room.

"What about you?" he asked.

She looked up at him, brow knit.

"Do you feel at home?"

She shook her head. "Too much has happened. Too soon. I wasn't expecting . . ."

"Frankly, I don't feel at home, either, Joanna."

"I'm sorry. I made an awful mistake, didn't I?"

"Yes."

"And I have to live with it. The rest of my life."

"That's right."

"But you don't."

He sighed and crossed to the kitchen. "Louise left us dinner. I'll put it in the microwave."

"I'm not hungry. You don't have to live with my mistakes, Jon. I didn't expect you to."

"I'll make myself something, then. How about a glass of wine?"

"That might help."

He went to the refrigerator and got out the jug of chablis. He poured each of them a glass, which he set out on the kitchen counter. Then he took a dish from the refrigerator and spooned out what looked like one of Louise's stuffed peppers onto a plate, and put the plate in the microwave oven. He turned a knob and pressed the start button. While the oven ran out its ninety seconds, he carried the wine glasses into the living room and set them on the cocktail table.

At the beep of the oven, he returned to it, opened it, sniffed and nodded. "You're sure you don't want any?"

It smelled good. But she was sure that if she ate it, it would merely upset her stomach, which had been grinding all day.

She shook her head and picked up her glass of wine. "Maybe later."

He brought his steaming plate to the cocktail table and set it next to his wine glass. He looked puzzled for a minute, then returned to the kitchen and got himself a knife and fork.

"Napkins are in the drawer below that," she said.

"I know." He returned with the implements and napkins, then lifted his glass to her. "To learning to live with our mistakes."

She said nothing, but took a sip of wine.

He studied her a moment. "You don't look as bad as you sounded on the phone."

"I came to my senses in the car."

"What happened?"

"Bloody Shoes is the donor."

He sat forward. "Did you tell Crosby?"

"He wasn't in. They're supposed to have him call me here."

"Jesus, Joanna."

"That's not all." She paused. It was so hard to say. So hard to believe.

"Kevin is Bloody Shoes."

He put down his wine glass. His hand trembled slightly. "Kevin Willman?"

The telephone rang. She nodded as she went to get it. He followed her.

It was Crosby. She told him what happened with Wendy. Then she said, "I know who the murderer is. His name is Kevin Willman. He's a surgical resident at University Hospital."

"That fits."

"You got the list of women from the sperm bank? You didn't even need me to drag Wendy into this."

"Hold on, Joanna. What we got from Harrington was a clue left by the old woman that was killed last October. We had it all along, but we didn't know what to do with it. She'd opened a record in the computer, then closed it before she could finish it. All it had in it was the color of his hair and eyes and how tall he was. It fit with your theoretical Bloody Shoes."

"But did you get the list of women?"

"Dr. Harrington wasn't as cooperative as I hoped. But he did give us a list of all the donors that had green eyes and brown hair and were tall. He conceded that one of them might have killed Sarah, if not the other women. So we pulled out the three that were medical students at the time they gave semen. That narrowed it down to four. One of them is this Willman."

"He's the one. He's Bloody Shoes."

"How do you know?"

She told him about Elinor Moore.

"Then you saw him?"

"Not this time. I saw him the last time Wendy Green was in my office. I thought he was following me then, but it was Wendy he was after."

"Why would he be following you?"

She hesitated. "It's personal."

"Did he threaten you?"

"Not then. Look, Lieutenant . . ."

"Why don't you call me Bill, Joanna. I'm off duty."

"Bill, then. I told you all I can. I know Kevin Willman is the man who was following Wendy Green today; and now I know it was Wendy he was following the other time. If he was on the sperm bank list, then he's the one. And she's his next victim."

"Right. He's a nasty guy, eh?"

She said nothing.

"Well, you can relax now. You've saved us a lot of trouble. Us and those other three guys on the Harrington list. Nice job, Joanna. Rest easy. And give my best to your horse doctor friend."

She held the receiver for a while after he'd hung up. At last, she set it in the cradle. She looked up at Jon who had been pacing the kitchen as she talked.

"It's Kevin. There's no doubt it's Kevin. He killed them all, starting with the woman in the sperm bank."

"Why didn't you tell Crosby about Cassie?"

"It's irrelevant."

"Irrelevant! He's out to kill all his children and Cassie's one of them."

"But he doesn't even know she exists."

He grasped her arms. "How do you know? Maybe he does. Maybe he's doing all this, talking to your clients, showing up at your office as a warning to *you*. It's one hell of a good way to terrorize you. Get even with you."

"I *know* he doesn't know."

"He followed you to the Roberts funeral."

She paused for a moment. "True. But I don't think he was following me. He was checking out the results of his handiwork. You're hurting my arms."

He let go of her. "Joanna, it's not worth the chance. If he does know . . ."

"Then the police will follow him here instead of to Wendy's house tomorrow night."

"If he waits till tomorrow night."

She shrugged. "Whatever. Whenever. It's obvious he's after Wendy for now. He told Elinor Moore that she was the one who'd be making news. And the reason he had to tell her was that Wendy's the last one before Kevin kills himself. He wanted Elinor to know. Because he wanted *me* to know. But not yet. Not till after he was dead."

Jon studied her for several seconds, then pulled her to him. "My God, Joanna. You *were* right to lie about Cassie. To hide her. And we've all been blaming you . . ."

"David's the only one who blamed me."

"No. I've been sitting here all day blaming you. Thinking how unfair you were to Cassie and Louise and David and me." He held her so tightly she could hardly breathe.

"You had a right to blame me. I was unfair to all of you." She extricated herself from his arms. "It was all so subtle I've never been sure . . . maybe he wouldn't have done anything at all if he'd known I was pregnant. There was just something about him. It was there when I met him, but it seemed to go away after I stopped him from killing himself. That was when I . . . started sleeping with him." She looked up at him.

His eyes gave her tacit approval to continue.

"He was a virgin. I'm sure of it. I had to teach him every step of the way."

"Unusual for someone who's been through med school."

"Unusual period in this day and age."

"Right. We're the generation that invented it."

She smiled.

"He had problems about women from way back. It fits," he said.

"Women and children. And I thought I could cure him. But then he began to fall apart. At the same time I found out I was pregnant." She took a great swallow of wine.

"Great timing," Jon said.

"I've been thinking about this all afternoon and . . . My God, it's all my fault. If I'd just stayed with him, this wouldn't have happened. I could simply have had an abortion. I didn't have to have his baby."

"It isn't your fault. The man's sick. Whatever it is that made him that way, sooner or later he'd have done something awful. Thank God you never told him about Cassie."

"I wonder what he'll do when this is all over and he finds out. Will I have to change my name and move out of town, so when he gets out of some prison or mental hospital he doesn't come after me and Cassie?"

"That won't happen. They'll never let him out."

She shook her head and picked up her wine glass. "Who can be sure?" She tipped her glass to him, her hand still trembling. "To learning to live with our mistakes," she said.

Chapter Twenty-one

The cradle will fall

"It LOOKS MORE like April than May," said Wendy's next-door neighbor, Donna, as the two women met on the gravel driveway between their two houses.

Wendy nodded and ducked into her car. She struggled to collapse her umbrella without getting herself pelted by the rain. The umbrella flooded her lap and knees with the water it had kept off her head.

She laughed and pulled her knees into her car. "You can't win," she called to Donna. She pulled the door closed and put her key in the ignition switch. The engine turned over.

Donna, after starting to get into her own car, suddenly came around it and knocked on Wendy's window.

Puzzled, Wendy rolled the window down, and Donna, protecting herself with her umbrella, ducked down and leaned in. "Is everything all right with you, Wendy?"

Wendy's car stalled. "Everything but this car in wet weather. I can't wait till I'm rich enough to afford a house with a garage." Then she frowned. "Shouldn't I be all right?"

Donna looked to both sides and then whispered. "I don't want to upset you, but I've seen some strange cars around here."

"We get the overflow from the railroad station. You'll get used to it after you've lived here awhile."

"I don't mean that. I don't even have to set my watch anymore. I know it's five twenty-seven when the yellow VW pulls away from the curb. The proverbial wrong side of the tracks. That's not what I mean."

Wendy glanced quickly at her watch. Her neighbor, a secretary for a small metal working firm in Ambler, seemed to be a worrier. Always sure the people she saw in the Genuardis' supermarket were shoplifters; concerned that the clerks in the drugstores were shortchanging her.

Wendy reached for her key in the ignition.

Donna said, "You got home late from work yesterday. I saw you just as I was getting in."

"I didn't come straight home," Wendy said, trying to keep the annoyance out of her voice.

Donna looked from side to side again. "There was this strange man. I came out to get the paper in the driveway just a little after you got in. He was sitting there in his car at the curb. I think he followed you."

"That's silly. Nobody followed me. Look, I bet it was about five twenty-seven, and he just got in from Jenkintown on the train."

"No. He was some kind of doctor. With those wrinkled pajamas and a stethoscope around his neck. At first I thought he was dead."

Wendy hesitated a second. "You're letting your imagination run away with you. Look, I'll be late for work. You will, too. And you're getting soaked." She turned the key in the ignition and the car almost started.

"Damn!" She pumped the pedal a few times and tried the ignition again. "Oh shit!"

"Won't start? I bet somebody's been fooling with it."

"Oh, Donna!" Wendy took a deep breath. She dropped her hands in her lap and sat back, exasperated. Then she tried a few more times to start the car; it chugged and refused to fire up.

Donna said, "Come on. Get into my car, and I'll take you to work."

"But you'll be late."

"About time I was. Five years and never missed a day. They exploit me. They exploit everybody. There's all sorts of chemicals I breathe in. I'll probably get cancer. Come on."

Wendy sighed and got out of her car and into Donna's.

"I'll pick you up this afternoon," Donna said as she started her car. "You shouldn't be alone. Like I said, this guy was sitting there looking like he was dead. I mean, I actually thought he was. So I knocked on his window. And wow, was he a mean one. He sneered at me and nearly knocked me over when he drove off. Can you believe it?"

Wendy shook her head and tried to shut out her neighbor's chatter as she drove her the few miles to the school. She wished she didn't have to accept a favor from her, and wondered how and when she might be expected to return it.

Donna pulled up at the school in front of the flag pole.

"You really don't have to pick me up," Wendy insisted. "I can catch a cab. Or one of the other teachers will drive me home."

Donna leaned across the front seat and touched Wendy's arm as she was about to step out of the car. "You ought to be careful. I mean this is Friday. And you know about that guy."

"What guy?"

"The one that's been killing the mothers and babies."

"But . . ."

"Now don't try to hide it, Wendy. I mean, everyone knows you're pregnant."

Wendy stiffened and drew her arm away. "I don't think that's any of your business."

"And they say that killer's a doctor."

"I'll take a cab home. Thank you for driving me in."

"Suit yourself. I'm just trying to help," said Donna.

Donna's lips continued to move after Wendy slammed the car door, but her words were lost behind the rain-streaked window.

Wendy ran into the school without her umbrella, realizing she'd left it in her own car. She made it to her classroom just before the first pupils began to arrive, smelling of bananas and bologna and wet brown paper bags.

For most of the day the quick press of work distracted her from the unease that Donna had visited on her. But by the time the last of her charges left—dropping sheets of lined pulp papers that bore penciled scribbles and red checks from beneath their yellow hooded slickers—she felt as abandoned as the desks and chairs that surrounded her.

She hadn't thought at lunchtime to ask a colleague for a ride home. Now everyone but the maintenance man and the school nurse, Sherril, a tall dark-haired woman of fifty, fled before the final electronic bell stopped beeping. Sherril was finishing up some paperwork while she awaited a sick child's parent.

"You should have taken the school bus," the nurse said, after Wendy used her telephone to call for a cab. "I don't know how long I'll be."

"I never thought of it."

"You can wait here, if you want," said Sherril. "Don't you just hate this place when everybody's left?"

"Yes." Wendy looked at the little boy sitting sniffling and sneezing on the bench next to the nurse's desk. She could visualize a cloud of virus incubating in the humid air she was breathing. Involuntarily she dropped her hands to protect her belly. "I'll wait out by the door so the taxi driver won't miss me."

"They might be forever in this weather."

Twenty minutes later, with the taxi still not in sight, she felt her bladder begin to ache. At first she shifted from one foot to the other, craning her neck to look through the glassed doors. Finally, to make certain no taxi was in sight, she stepped outside in the blowing rain.

The wind clanged a tethered cable against the metal flag pole and whipped a soaked, crumpled notebook in against Wendy's ankles. The spiral spring of the notebook caught in her hose. The pages flapped against her legs like a huge wet moth. She cried out in fear and tried to kick it away. The spiral bit through her stockings and scratched her skin. A soggy piece of paper caught under the one-and-a-half inch heel of one shoe. She slipped on it and fell to the hard tile floor. Her books and purse went flying as she tried to break the fall. She twisted and landed on her abdomen.

Stunned, she almost lost control of her bladder.

Sherril, hearing her cry, came running.

Wendy lay still a minute, trying to catch her breath.

"It's OK," said the nurse. "You probably didn't break anything. But let me check anyway."

Wendy felt dizzy.

"Just wait till you catch your breath." Sherril knelt down and looked into Wendy's eyes. After a few seconds she asked, "OK now?"

Wendy pulled herself up into a half-kneeling, then a sitting position. She nodded her head. "I think so."

The nurse checked her arms and legs, then looked into her eyes again. "You didn't hit your head?"

"No. Really. I'm all right. Just a little shaken up. You'd better get back to that boy."

"He's fine. Let me help you stand up." She placed a hand under Wendy's left elbow and offered her own shoulder to Wendy's right hand.

Wendy rose shakily to her feet. She smiled sheepishly. "I really have to go."

"Use the john in my office."

Wendy followed her to the office. While she was in the toilet, she could hear the sick boy's mother complaining how she had to leave work early to come get him. The selfish whine of the woman annoyed her. Until she reminded herself that she might very well be in the same position in six or seven years. She had to get rid of her own old-fashioned ideas about what a mother should be.

"You all right in there, Wendy?" Sherril called through the door.

"All right." She left the washroom. She still felt an ache in her bladder, and lowered her hand down to it. She saw her books and purse on the nurse's desk. "Thank you for helping."

"You look a little pale."

"It's embarrassing, that's all."

"I'll drive you home."

"Well . . ."

Sherril picked up Wendy's belongings and thrust them into her arms. Then she got her own purse and raincoat, and ushered Wendy to her car. "You live in Ambler, don't you?" she asked as she started the car.

Wendy gave her directions. She felt anxious and irritable as the pang in her bladder radiated toward her back.

By the time they pulled up in the driveway behind Wendy's dripping, sad-looking car, she was sweating.

Sherril looked at her and knit her brow. "I'll come in with you."

"No. I'm all right. Really."

"No, you're not." The nurse cut her engine, put out her hand, and said, "Give me your keys. I'll open up for you. Then I'll help you into the house."

Wendy reached into her purse for her keys. They weren't there. She rifled around inside the handbag for a few seconds. "Oh, God, I must have lost them. Maybe at school when I fell."

"Oh, shit!" said Sherril. She started her engine again. "I guess we'll have to go back."

"This has been a bad day," said Wendy. The cramping had stopped, though, and she felt a little better.

"Amen," said the nurse. She turned her car back toward the school; but a block before reaching it, she suddenly turned into a residential street.

"Where are you going?" Wendy asked.

"Just hold tight a few minutes. I want to see something." After several turns onto side streets, she was in an industrial park.

"What's the matter? You're driving awfully fast."

Sherril said nothing. At last Wendy saw they were approaching the school again, but from an unfamiliar direction.

"I was right," the nurse said, as she pulled up in front of the building. "He was following us, but I lost him in the park. It's a maze in there. Anyone who doesn't cut through it every day like I do could spend a half-hour trying to get out." The nurse jumped out of the car, and disappeared for several minutes into the school.

She emerged waving Wendy's keys. "Peter was just sweeping them up from the hallway in front of my office. It's a good thing we're such good friends. He and I are usually the first in and last out of this place."

"Who was following us?"

Sherril pushed the keys into Wendy's hand. "I think he was parked near your house when we got there." She started her car again.

"How do you know he was following us?"

"Because he started out right after we did and took the same route."

Wendy shook her head. "You're as bad as my neighbor. He probably just came from the Ambler station. The parking's so bad there. We always have cars."

"He followed us into the park."

"He might have been going there. Or through there."

Sherril shook her head. "I don't think so. There was something about the way he seemed to be dogging us . . . Look, I just feel uneasy about it. Why don't you come home with me, just in case?"

"I don't . . ."

"I insist. Look, you've had a bad day and so have I. I live alone, and Friday dinners are lonely. I don't really mind you having a run in your hose and being kind of soggy. It would be a favor to me if you stay for dinner. I'll get you home early, and if anyone was following us, they'll be long gone."

Wendy paused before saying, "All right." Sherril was a nurse and she'd just felt another small twinge in her bladder. Of course, Sherril and Donna were crazy to think someone was following her. But dinner with a friend on a chilly, rainy Friday night did take the loneliness away.

Both the cramps and the rain had dissipated by the time Sherril brought her home. But the air felt chill, and the night was moonless and damp. Wendy locked the door behind her and watched through her window for several minutes after Sherril's car swished away. Seeing no one outside, she rechecked the lock, and went upstairs to take her bath in the chipped footed bathtub in the bathroom with its cracked linoleum floor.

She felt poorer in this house than she actually was. She had moved here when she decided to become pregnant. A house, however old, was a better place to raise a baby than an apartment. And, indeed, she had plenty of space here. The pine furniture given her by her parents did not completely fill the six rooms. Her father once had worked in building construction and told her the house was sound. He came over on weekends and helped her scrape off layers of old wallpaper and lift off the finish from the floors. Under the worn linoleum in the bathroom and kitchen, the floorboards were fine hardwood. Though the neighborhood had dissipated in the years just before Ambler's downtown redevelopment, these older houses were now being bought by young professionals like Wendy who couldn't afford to buy the new ones in Maple Glen or Fort Washington, but could afford to fix up and refurbish these gradually.

But on windy nights like this, the place creaked and the clammy air and darkness seemed to creep through the poorly lit, sparsely furnished rooms into Wendy's very soul. Suddenly she wished she hadn't moved here; and she almost wished she hadn't decided to have a child and raise it in a never quite finished house, in a never quite whole family.

"Stop it!" she said to herself as she pulled herself out of the tub and began to dry herself. "You'll be a good mother. You'll be a loving mother."

The door buzzer echoed from downstairs. She didn't want to see anyone; but the uneasiness that had been building up inside all day had not been relieved by her bath, and began to ratchet up as the buzzer rasped again and again.

She dried herself hurriedly, threw on her terrycloth robe, and ran downstairs. She turned on the porch light and pulled back the curtain on the glass-topped door.

"Wendy. Let me in." It was Donna.

"What's the matter?" Wendy said, as her neighbor pushed through before the door was halfway open.

"Where were you? I was scared stiff when you weren't home from work when I got here."

"With a friend."

"Did you call Triple A about your car?"

"I'll call my dad in the morning. His truck has a winch, and if he can't fix the trouble, he'll tow me to a place that can. Honestly, I *can* take care of myself."

"Close that door," Donna said, doing it herself.

"What is the matter, for God's sake?"

"I saw him again. That doctor. This time he wasn't dressed like a doctor. He was parked in front of your house again. He drove away as soon as he saw me. Got this ugly, mean look on his face."

"He's probably just a commuter."

"No. He's weird. I bet he's that guy."

A cramp spread through Wendy's pelvis. She caught her breath and stepped back to the overstuffed chair in the living room. She sank down in it.

"What's wrong? You look sick."

"It's nothing."

"Oh. Like I was saying, I'll bet it's that guy. He knows you're pregnant."

"Who told you I'm pregnant? It's nobody's business but mine."

"Somebody I know. She saw you at the Martin Center a few times."

"They do all sorts of things at the Martin Center."

"Yeah. But you're pregnant. You take all those vitamins and things. You got the prescription at the drugstore."

"*You're* the one following me around. I wish you'd leave me alone."

"I just hear things. I keep my eyes open. You ought to be glad I do. It's why I noticed this guy in the first place." She sat down on the sofa opposite Wendy.

Wendy put her hand to her forehead as another small cramp grabbed her.

Donna leaned forward. "Say, something *is* the matter with you."

"No. Nothing. I'm just tired. I was just going to go to bed. I really don't think anyone's after me. Please, Donna. Just go home. I'll feel better in the morning."

"I'm not going to go home. I'm going to stay here and make sure that guy doesn't come back again."

"What! No. I don't want you here." Wendy started to rise. Then she began to feel weak and sweaty again. She lowered herself into her chair.

Donna jumped up and came over to her. She grabbed her wrist. "Your pulse is just racing. Not on your life, I'm not going to leave you alone. Even if that guy doesn't come back, you aren't in shape to stay alone. Who's your doctor?"

"You mean you don't know?" Wendy said.

"There, your pulse is slowing down. Whatever it is must have passed. You must be coming down with something." She dropped Wendy's wrist.

"I'm sure it's just a virus or something. I'll be all

right." She got up and started walking toward the door. "I'll get to bed. Thanks for offering to stay."

Donna stayed her. "I'm not leaving here. You look awful, and I'm going to stay, 'cause I don't think you should be alone here with no car that works, feeling sick and being pregnant and some crazy guy on the loose. And the weather is lousy outside."

Wendy was overcome by a wave of tiredness which frightened her as much as Donna's dire warnings about some crazy man in a car. The leaden feeling in her arms that had dogged her since the earliest weeks of her pregnancy took hold of her. Donna was right. She didn't want to be alone. "All right. You can stay. But I'm exhausted. I'm going up to bed."

Wendy passed in and out of a fevered sleep. Each noise and odor in the small, damp house triggered its own dream: She ran from her burning kitchen, pursued by flames, and woke to the acrid, sulphurous scent of Donna's burning eggs downstairs. She sped in her car through a rainswept section of the Schuylkill Expressway, skidded onto the shoulder and stalled, grabbed the door handle and shook it, then realized she was trapped in her car. Crowds of gray-faced strangers rushed from the road and clawed at her windows. She threw her hands up to her throat and watched helplessly as a dead doctor came through the crowd and opened the door and leaned over her with his stethoscope dripping blood. She sat up and moaned in the darkness, her heart hammering not quite loud enough to shut out the sounds of the train squealing into the railroad station.

She fell back onto her pillow. The egg smell was gone and the house was oppressively silent now that the train had pulled away. She hoped that Donna had gone; and she hoped she had stayed. In the dark her digital alarm clock glowed red, the colon between the minutes and hours blinking away the seconds. It was only a little after nine. Shouldn't it be much later? She watched the pulsing colon till her eyes closed again.

Outside the rain began again. The tree outside her bedroom window beat its arching branches against the screen. She ought to get up and close the window, but the heaviness behind her eyes held them closed. She ignored the loud banging of the branch against the clapboard; ignored the cracking sound of the screen blowing into her window; ignored the soft creaking of the floor as someone crossed the room to her bed and bent over her.

She did not know which came first: the sharp pain that ripped through her pelvis or the scream that tore through her brain. In the reflected beam of a flashlight, Donna's horror-stricken face swam briefly before her eyes.

Then, awash in a sea of her blood, she lost consciousness again.

Chapter Twenty-two

Saturday

"THE GOOD NEWS in Philadelphia," said the slick YJN (Your Journal Network) commentator, "is that apparently no Cradle murders took place last night. This could be the result of the new turn the investigation has taken since a national news broadcast featuring Dr. Leonard (pronounced Lee-oh-nard) Wolfe, the renowned psychiatrist, was shown a week ago.

"The bad news is that the killings may not have come to an end. Police authorities acknowledge that new leads developed during their investigations of the doctors who delivered the Cradle victims' babies apparently reached a dead end. Police are mum about the exact nature of the leads they were following. They did, however, hint that this crime may be somehow connected to another. And a YJN investigative reporter has uncovered a strange coincidence. A birthing center midwife who delivered the baby of one victim was seen at the funeral of another. This same angel of mercy was also seen emerging from the Society Hill apartment once shared by Grace Heard, the lesbian victim in the so-called Cradle murders. It might be worth noting that the birthing center she works at was recently involved in a scandal of major proportions. And the Cradle murders began within days of the time this midwife returned from a mysterious six-month leave. We have confronted police with this coincidence and with questions about where this woman was on Monday night during the riot at another victim's wake. They denied there was any connection, but said they *were* aware of our midwife's recent activities.

"To which YJN replies, 'Where there's smoke, there's fire.' "

Joanna sat riveted to her chair as Jon turned off the TV with a savage twist of the knob. "YJN—Yellow Journalism Network!"

"People believe it," said Joanna. She dropped her head into her hands.

The telephone began ringing seconds later. Jon took the calls, most of which came from reporters seeking confirmation of the story. Jon said he knew nothing about it; that they should call the police. When asked for his name, he identified himself as a friend.

After several calls, he switched on the telephone answering machine. "Let them talk dirty to that! Come on. We're getting out of here."

"We can't," she said. "What about Cassie?"

His mouth fell open. The telephone answering machine took another call.

"You forgot about her."

"I'm not used to having a baby."

"You don't. I do."

"Joanna, you're being unfair."

"Maybe. The point is, I can't just pick up and leave anymore. And we can't just carry her out there now. People will put things together. 'Mysterious six-month leave', then suddenly she has a baby."

"Your neighbors won't even know it's you they were talking about."

"They won't. Kevin might."

The telephone rang again.

Jon nodded and sat down? "What happened? Why did they reach a dead end last night?"

She heard the beep at the end of her message tape. Then she heard Crosby's voice. She ran to the phone and grabbed the receiver. "Lieutenant ... Bill ... wait! Don't hang up." She left the volume of the answering machine turned up so Jon could listen in.

"That bastard!" said Crosby. "That son of a bitchin'
bastard. He's screwed up three cases of mine already
with his so-called investigative reporting."

"What happened last night?"

"Well, you did manage to save your client's life," he
said.

"Then it wasn't a dead end. You caught him?"

"Not exactly. We tailed him to your client's place. A
couple of times. She came home in a car with a woman
the first time, but they left again, and he followed
them. I guess the woman saw him, because she drove
like she was trying to throw him off her trail. And she
did.

"Then your client came back home a few hours
later, and he was waiting. Then her next-door neighbor went over to her house and stayed till ten o'clock."

"What happened? Please tell me what happened!"

"Our guys had a chance to be heroes. The neighbor
put in a nine-eleven; the dispatcher knew we were on
the scene."

"He got in while you were there?"

"He never got in. "Our guys were in that house
before she even hung up the phone. Your client was in
bed in a puddle of blood, just within a couple of pints
of bleeding to death."

"How did he . . . ?"

"He didn't. She was having a miscarriage. We got
her to the hospital faster than the rescue squad
could've. So even if our friend Willman didn't act, you
saved her."

Joanna sat trembling by the telephone. Poor Wendy.
She wanted that baby so badly.

Jon ran into the bedroom and picked up the telephone extension. "You picked Willman up?"

"On what grounds, Doc?"

"He was following this woman."

"Well, we know that. But he never touched her."

Joanna felt weak. She didn't understand. "But . . ."

"Look, Joanna. You figured out he was following *her*. But you thought at first he might be following *you*."

"That was before we found out about the sperm bank. You know he was a donor there."

"That's all we know for sure. And he's a suspect in the Harrington murder. But there's something you didn't tell us."

Jon said, "Joanna . . . ?"

"I told you everything Jon and I learned about the fathers."

"Why would this joker be following *you*?"

"I told you I had a personal relationship with him."

Crosby hesitated. "How personal? Sorry, Doc. I have to ask."

Jon didn't reply.

"It was personal and intimate. And Jon knows all about it."

"What about that, Doc?"

"I'll leave it to Joanna to tell you. And please don't call me 'Doc'."

"Did this guy ever hurt you?" Crosby asked after a brief grunt.

Joanna said nothing.

"You can tell him at least that much," Jon said.

"He never physically touched me."

"But he threatened you?"

"No, not actually."

"So you left him. And you left town for a very long time."

Jon said, "Look Lieutenant, why don't you stop badgering Joanna. She went to Europe. Would you like to see the pictures? You're the one who should be doing the explaining. You know who Bloody Shoes is and you haven't even picked him up."

"You're a better-than-average amateur detective,

Isenson. But you don't have all the answers. We don't know who Bloody Shoes is. We only know Kevin Willman was following Wendy Green and that he gave sperm at a sperm bank where a completely unrelated murder occurred. We know that two of the victims were artificially inseminated, but we don't know squat about the others and we don't even know where the victims got the semen. The same for Wendy Green.

"We can't pick up a guy just because he followed a woman around. We don't even know what kind of relationship he had with her. For all we know he's in love with her. And he's never laid a hand on her that we know of. He's never laid a hand on anyone that we know of."

"But Elinor Moore said he told her—"

"Who's she?"

"Another client. He told her Wendy would be famous."

"Right. I know all that. That is, you *told* me that."

Jon said, "Are you saying Joanna made it up?"

Crosby said nothing for several long moments. "I'm not saying you lied about that, Joanna. It's obvious Willman had some reason to follow Wendy Green around. It's also obvious that you know something that you'd rather not talk about."

"What I'd rather not talk about is personal. It has nothing to do with this case. All the other things Jon and I learned *do*."

"You didn't learn that much. You conjectured a lot. And nobody's backing up your theory. The sperm bank won't let us know if any of the victims got Willman's sperm unless we get releases from the surviving spouses. And the husbands of the victims are still denying to a man that their wives were artificially inseminated by *anyone*'s semen. So the only one who is absolutely sure Willman is Bloody Shoes is *you*. And since you won't talk about this personal matter, it crossed my mind you have something against the guy."

Joanna was stunned.

"Wait a minute, Lieutenant . . ." said Jon.

"And another thing, Ms. Michaels," Crosby said. "You saw your client Thursday afternoon in your office. On Friday she has a miscarriage . . ."

Joanna couldn't believe what she was hearing.

"So though I got to give you credit for saving her life, it just kind of makes me wonder what you have to gain by having Kevin Willman picked up."

"Look, Crosby," said Jon.

"No, Isenson, you look. Maybe one of you can tell me why Midwife Michaels's car was illegally parked overnight at Montgomery Mall. And why a couple fitting your description bought punker gear at Spencer's an hour or so before the riot up 309. And why even the midwife's sister didn't know where she was all night Monday. And how a couple of punkers managed to do such a perfect cesarean section on a dead woman. That baby's doing fine, too, by the way. The father would like me to thank you."

"Oh, God," Joanna said.

Then she heard the telephone click twice as Crosby and then Jon hung up. By the time Jon took the receiver from her hand and replaced it in the cradle, its electronic beep kept time with her heartbeat.

"Come on," he said. "Get Cassie and give her her bottle. You can't stay here anymore. I'm moving you to my house."

Stunned, she abdicated all decisions to him. The sound of the phone in the background kept pace with his comings and goings. They turned the answering machine volume all the way down so they could hear neither outgoing nor incoming messages. The thirty-minute tape for incoming messages had run out. But that was all right. She didn't want to know who was calling or what they were saying anyway.

Jon made several trips in his car back and forth from his house. The baby's crib knocked down completely, but it took two trips in his hatchback car to get the whole thing over. The carriage and a few drawers of clothing required another trip. They wouldn't take Joanna's car; sooner or later reporters would trace her new address or track down her car.

Three hours later Jon arrived at her apartment for the final time.

"I don't know how many times I can move you and your kid around." It was a weak joke. "Why don't I just adopt the two of you?"

Cassie began to cry as she lifted her head from the blanket on Joanna's bed. When Joanna tried to calm her, she cried even louder. "We can't take her out like this!"

"Maybe she needs another bottle," Jon suggested.

"No. I just fed her. She's upset."

"That's because you are."

She whirled on him and thrust the baby at him. "*You* calm her down then. What do you expect me to be?"

He stood surprised, holding the baby against his chest as if she were some kind of explosive that would go off if he relaxed his grip. Cassie screamed louder still, as if she were indeed building up steam for an explosion.

"You've got to calm down," he said.

"*You* calm down. I can't. Crosby knows we did that section on Monday. And he accused me of lying about Kevin."

"You did lie about Kevin. To him, too."

Cassie's cries rattled like machine gun fire. Joanna grabbed her from Jon. "No. No! No! No!" She ran

from him into the living room. "Stay away. Go away.
You don't want Cassie. You don't want me."

He followed her, his face twisted with pain.
"Joanna. I'm sorry. I didn't mean it. Please. You have
to calm down."

The telephone rang in the background. The answering machine clicked.

"No. I don't want to calm down. I just want to . . .
to . . ." She pulled the baby to her and buried her head
against Cassie's. The baby's crying was tearless, but
saliva sprayed from her mouth. "Oh, God, Baby, what
have I done to you? What am I doing to you?"

"Please. Joanna." Jon was weeping. He raised his
arms to hold both mother and child.

Joanna began to sob.

He pulled her against him. "I'm sorry. I know why
you did what you did. Kevin was crazy and you were
the only one that saw it. Please."

Cassie stopped crying and for a moment seemed to
be holding her breath.

Then the apartment door buzzer rasped and she let
out a screech.

Joanna stiffened. "They've found me."

"You don't have to answer. I'll take Cassie out. You
follow later. I'll wait for you in my car."

The buzzer sounded again.

Joanna handed Cassie to Jon. "All right. But quiet
her first. Please, Baby, Mommy won't let anyone hurt
you."

Jon began to rock Cassie as he stroked her cheek
with his finger. She shuddered and coughed a moment, then turned her mouth toward the crook in his
fingers, coughed and sniffled, then made sucking mo-
tions with her lips.

"She *does* want her bottle," he said. "Look how red
her face is."

Joanna got a nursing bottle of water and handed it to Jon.

He put the nipple in Cassie's mouth. She shuddered again, then began to suck.

The sound of her sucking drew a knot free from Joanna's chest.

Jon nodded at her, then pulled the blanket up around Cassie. "OK, I'll start down now. You sit tight for about ten minutes. They haven't buzzed again. I think they gave up."

"Maybe they slipped into the lobby with someone else."

There were three sharp raps on the door.

"I guess this is it," she whispered. They waited.

Finally a woman's voice said, "Joanna. I know you're there. Please answer the door. It's Louise."

Joanna ran to the door.

"I've tried to get you on the phone ten times. I knew you must be hiding." Louise looked at Jon. "Where are you taking the baby?"

"To my house."

"Good idea. Can I move in, too?"

"Oh, shit! said Joanna. Her sister looked harried and worried. "They haven't been bothering you!"

"No. I doubt that very many people outside of some of your colleagues and some fast-thinking journalists even know what midwife he was talking about."

"Thank God," said Jon. "That gives us time."

Louise gently lifted the blanket from Cassie's face. "Dear thing. I miss you, Baby. Are these guys taking good care of you?" She brushed Cassie's head with her lips. "Nothing smells just like a baby."

Cassie stopped sucking on her water bottle a moment. Then she sighed and continued drinking.

Louise looked away and brushed a tear from her eye with her knuckle.

"So you want to come and keep your eye on us," said Jon.

Louise's eyes narrowed and glittered. She bit on her lower lip. "I want to get away from David."

"Oh, Louise," said Joanna. "No."

"Don't take any blame for this. You did what you had to do, and so did I. I don't regret that for a minute."

"Does he know you're here?" asked Jon.

Louise looked at him and then quickly away.

"Then you shouldn't be."

"How dare you say that! You're two of a kind, you and David. And you don't even have a claim on Joanna, let alone me."

Jon looked abashed and confused.

"What happened?" said Joanna.

Louise clenched her fists. "He's insufferable. When he saw that broadcast he gloated. Said you had it coming to you. That all his warnings about not getting involved were right. He jumped up after that guy finished his report and hooted and pounded his fist into his hand."

Jon's jaws worked.

Cassie started to cry again.

Joanna walked over and took her from him. She put the baby up to her shoulder and rubbed her back.

"He said that story you told us about artificial insemination was off the wall, or the police wouldn't have reached a dead end. That was the lead they were talking about, wasn't it?"

"No," Joanna said.

"So your theory wasn't right. Still, how can he gloat like that when you're practically being accused of murder on TV? And that Monday night thing. They should call you two heroes."

"You didn't. Anyway, the theory is right," said Joanna. "The police can't prove it, that's all."

Louise furrowed her brow. "But I thought you said that wasn't the lead that brought them to a dead end."

"They were following Kevin Willman."

Louise gasped and seemed to lose her balance. She recovered it and sat on the chair across from Joanna. Finally, she said, "Why were they following him?"

As Cassie drained her bottle and fell asleep in her mother's arms, Joanna told Louise the story.

Louise rose from her chair after hearing it. "Dear God," she said. "Oh dear God."

Then she turned and began to weep into her own hands.

The telephone began ringing again. The answering machine clicked on.

"What are we going to do now?" said Louise. And her face filled with terror as she said, "Oh, David—oh, David, what have you done?"

Chapter Twenty-three

Down will come baby . . .

KEVIN WAS SATISFIED with the outcome, even though nature had taken it out of his hands. He was satisfied, though Wendy might not die. She still might, of course, and that would be fine, too. He needn't stay around to make sure. He had done what he had set out to do. And he may even have been indirectly responsible for her miscarriage.

She had seen him, and he had frightened her. He

could take comfort in that. He had made her run and try to hide.

At first the fact that she had other women around to protect her frustrated him. He spent the whole afternoon chasing around or waiting around. The rain would have been a wonderful cover. It kept people in; and he could have climbed in her bedroom window with very little danger of being seen. Everything might have been over by early evening. But the rain stopped, and then this woman came by and saw him again, and he had to drive off. He had just come back when the woman from next door climbed the porch steps and stood at Wendy's front door, looking every which way before she went in the house. And she stayed there.

Kevin had had to park far away so she couldn't see him. He found a spot screened by some forsythia bushes, which gave him a clear view of the house. The woman appeared in one window as soon as she disappeared from another—usually she was downstairs, but a couple of times she was upstairs. He could see the blind move; she was trying to be cagey, but he was too clever for her. Still he knew better than to approach the house while she was on guard.

And she didn't leave. Not even after the police car and van came out of nowhere, and men ran up the porch stairs and brought Wendy out on a stretcher. It wasn't a rescue squad stretcher. The police who carried her out weren't parameds, just cops on a first-aid call—lucky they happened to be in the neighborhood when the call came in.

He heard the woman cry out, "Please. Don't let her bleed to death. Can they save the baby?"

"We'll get her to the emergency room."

"Save the baby?" one cop said to the other. "Shit!

There ain't nothing left to save. It's all back there in the bed."

And Kevin knew it was over, and he was satisfied.

He drove home. He took Wissahickon Drive and the River Drives and cut through University City. The traffic was heavy for late Friday night. He opened his car windows wide so he could hear the swish of cars passing by and the occasional squeal of his own tires as he took a poorly banked curve too quickly. He could smell wet pavement and diesel fumes and something rotting in the river. He could see the marinas on the east side of the river, with the racing teams' boats hugging the docks. Huge drops of water splatted onto his windshield from trees above. He laughed, and the tension ran from his forehead like the rivulets windwashed from the windshield.

It was over. Not a trace of his seed was left in the world. And by midnight not a trace would be left of him.

He parked in the rutted parking lot behind his apartment building. He reached into the console between the bucket seats of his car and took out the tape recorder. As he walked to the apartment, he dictated what he recalled of the day, all about Wendy, all about Joanna. Though he could not dedicate this last one to Joanna, he *could* let her know that he would have. That she had had the chance to save him and hadn't.

He also told her what he had done to Michael, how he'd almost consummated, "Right under your very nose. You should have seen it. You and your stupid sister should have figured it out."

He liked that. Good last words to leave her with. A reminder of their neglect and the agony that would stay with the boy through his whole life.

Three flights up, he opened the door to his one-room apartment.

For a minute he was surprised to see it—all ready
for his final act—the sofa bed folded out; the top
sheet neatly folded down to reveal the double-bowed
sag of the mattress. It would never torture his back
again.

The saline sack on the IV pole saluted him from its
watch station beside the bed. On the table beside it
the bottle of yellow pentothal powder waited. He eyed
it with a vague curiosity. How had it got there? Why
was it in his room?

Then he remembered, grew resolute. He pictured
the sofa bed as an operating room table, a patient
upon it . . . himself . . . in mortal agony, mutilated by
the cosmic accident called life, belly torn open and
bleeding, putrid organs spilling out.

He was surgeon and patient in the center of an
operating room gallery. Above, leaning forward, their
faces lit with fascinated horror, they watched.

Forest crooked his finger at him.

Elizabeth turned and hid under her umbrella.

His sister put her hand under the skirt of a hollyhock doll, then tore off its head and threw it at him.

His mother shook her head, then began to weep and
wail.

His father watched idly but saw nothing.

Katie screwed with a stranger and laughed.

Joanna came down from the gallery and put on her
scrub dress and scrubbed up her hands. She put her
arms around his neck and rubbed herself against him
and reached for his cock with one hand. With the
other hand she reached up for the snake of plastic
tubing that looped from the saline sack and wound
around the top of the pole. With the one hand she
drew the last drops of his milk; with the other she
released the first drops of saline into the pentothal
bottle.

Then she ran weeping and laughing from the room and left him to mix the potion.

His hand trembled as he dissolved the anesthetic in several ccs of saline and drew up the liquid into the large syringe, then injected it into the plastic saline bag through a valve. He was thinking he must keep it sterile. It would go into the patient's bloodstream. He was thinking he must flush the tubing to get out air bubbles and avoid an air embolus. He was thinking . . .

He had to stop thinking. It was mixed now, everything was ready beside the bed. Everyone was ready in the gallery. Joanna was waiting outside the door of his apartment. He could hear her sniggering. "Don't leave a trace," she said.

He glared at the door and glared at the faces in the gallery. "I'm not quite ready. I have to have my drink."

"Want some," they all cried together.

"Want some," Joanna called from outside the door.

"We'll all get drunk together," said Kevin.

He went to the refrigerator and got out a gallon jug of vodka. From the shelf above the pullman kitchen sink he took seven mismatched glasses. One for himself and everybody in the gallery except the stranger, who was too busy screwing Katie to want any. Joanna would get nothing. She'd already drunk him dry.

He set the glasses on the small formica table and filled them. The gallery emptied and the viewers jostled one another to be first to drink with him.

His ears rang with their voices as they closed in on him.

They rang with the sound of the door buzzer as Joanna begged to come in. He tossed down an ounce of the burning liquid.

The ringing grew more insistent. It was coming from the telephone.

He answered it to shut it up, to shut Joanna up, to shut all of them up.

"Kevin!"

He looked around the room. Everyone had fled, leaving their drinks untouched on the table.

"Sorry to call you so late. I've been trying to get you all day."

He looked around the room. It was his apartment, quiet, waiting for the end. The IV pole saluted. "Who is this?"

"It's David Horne."

"I don't know any David Horne."

"Joanna's brother-in-law."

"She can't come in. She's drunk me dry."

"What?"

He looked around again. No sounds came from outside his door.

"I don't want to see her."

"I don't blame you. But there's something you have to know."

Kevin's head ached. He looked at the beckoning saline bag, its tube complete with needle at the ready, the tourniquet folded on the table. "I don't want to know anything about her."

"This is important, Kevin."

"No." He reached out his finger to shut the telephone connection down.

"She had your baby, Ke . . ."

Kevin's finger cut off the end of his name. He held it there long enough to break the connection. Then he left the receiver off the hook.

Outside the door he heard Joanna laughing again as she rasped, "Don't leave a trace."

"I won't," he said. He walked resolutely to the bed and sat down and applied the tourniquet to his left arm. He pumped his fist several times and slapped the flat inner surface of his forearm till he brought up the vein. He flushed out the tubing one final time, then closed it off. A single drop of liquid quivered at the tip of the needle, life holding tenuously on. He guided the needle into his vein. It stung, life torturing him again. He released the tourniquet after sucking a small amount of blood back into the tube and watching it turn the liquid pink, life mixing with death.

Then he reached up to start the drip of death.

Suddenly Joanna rushed into the room, holding a baby in her arms. She thrust it at him and cried out, "No! Don't leave a trace!"

He tore the needle from the vein. His own blood washed over his arm and he watched it in fascination as Joanna stared and the baby shrieked.

He didn't know where she lived; so he had to follow her from the Martin Center. It was Monday before she showed up there. He called her office from a pay phone. They said she had appointments till five-thirty that evening and could return his call after that.

"No. I'll call back."

He didn't know what kind of car she was driving. He had to wait until she left and sit in his car in a visitor's slot near the exit and hope to see her drive by.

On Monday evening he missed her. On Tuesday, after performing early surgery, he called the center. She was scheduled to work until nine-thirty.

"What about Wednesday?" he asked.

"Aren't you the man who called yesterday?"

"Yes," he said.

"I'm sure she'll be glad to return your call, sir."

"No. I'll call her tomorrow. Will she be in tomorrow?"

"She's in from nine on tomorrow."

"On? Till when?"

"Well, she's booked all day. It would probably be better if you called back on Friday. But why don't I have her call you?"

"That's all right." He hung up. Wednesday should be the day she worked evenings. Why had she changed it to Tuesday? Oh, well, he'd be working until noon today. So it was all working out perfectly. He'd finish his thirty-six-hour stint, drunk with fatigue again, but he would drive to the center and park in a visitor's slot and set his wristwatch alarm for nine P.M. When she left at nine-thirty he'd be awake and waiting for her to pull out of the deserted parking garage.

It didn't work out that way. At seven o'clock that evening he felt somebody grab his shoulder as he slept in the backseat of his car.

He lay there confused for a minute.

"You can't sleep here, sir," the man said.

"I'm waiting for someone."

"Sorry, you'll have to wait inside."

He grumbled and rubbed his eyes. He sat up.

"You work here?" the security guard asked, eyeing Kevin's scrub suit. "Didn't I see you here before?"

Kevin blinked and yawned. "Resident."

"New, eh? Better get yourself a parking tag. You can park with the doctors next time."

Kevin nodded.

The guard took a book of tickets out of his jacket pocket. "How long you staying?"

"Nine, nine-thirty."

The officer nodded and wrote something on the ticket in his hand. He tore off the ticket and handed it to Kevin. "Here's a temporary tag, Doctor. Why don't you just drive up one level to the doctors' lot. Right next to the elevator. You can park there. I marked it good till midnight, OK?"

Kevin rubbed his eyes again and looked at the ticket.

"Put it in your windshield. I'll validate your gate ticket for you, so you don't have to pay. Nobody told you the system?" he asked. "They just throw you guys to the wolves."

Kevin smiled wearily. "Goes with the job, I guess." He yawned again.

"They shouldn't force you to work such long hours." The guard's hip radio began to spit static. Someone asked him if everything was all right in the parking lot. "OK here. Just talking to some overworked doc."

The radio spat some instructions. "Roger," he said. Then he turned back to Kevin and said, "OK, how 'bout just driving up to that level where we can keep an eye on your car. And no sleeping there, either. It makes the boys nervous." He sauntered off.

Kevin took a deep breath and drove to an unreserved spot in the doctors' section. He noticed the empty slots had the names of the physicians they were reserved for painted in the center. He parked and got down on his knees to look under the car in the space next to his.

"Can I help you, Doctor?"

He looked up into the eyes of a woman carrying a lab coat over her arm.

"I . . . just dropped my keys," he said, rising and jingling them at her.

She seemed to study him a while. Then she got in her car and drove away.

He looked up at the security camera that panned the entire section. Suddenly the place was alive with sweeping eyes. Following Joanna was not going to be as easy as he thought.

Suddenly it became easy. He lounged in a booth in the snack shop until he heard a public address message announcing that visiting hours were over at nine. Traffic in the corridors and elevators increased as visitors, volunteers, and service employees began to leave. When he returned to his car he could hear the echoed screech of engines coming to life; motors rumbled and tires hummed along the spiraled cement aisles that led toward the exit.

He ducked down in the car each time the bell above the elevator door signaled the lift's imminent arrival. Every time a car started up, he looked out to see if it was Joanna. At last he saw her face clearly as she turned it to check to her rear when she pulled out of · her slot.

Thirty-five minutes later he was parked across the street from a small townhouse in Willow Grove. He saw her disappear into it.

Over the next two days he watched and followed her and the man she was living with. He learned which room they kept the baby in by observing her standing in the window, holding the child on her shoulder. The light in that room went on twice during the night; through the open window, he could hear the baby cry just before the lamp lit. Kevin figured out how he would get in. He would not have as much time to plan as he had with the others. But he was in luck, for the house they lived in was the last in the row of townhouses, and the nursery window opened to the side of the house that was partially obscured by trees. Under the window was a patio with a long redwood table and two benches that could easily be arranged to give him a makeshift stairway.

Joanna and the man left both mornings at seven. He carried the baby and a large cloth bag labeled DIAPERS, ETC. in large, multi-colored letters. Kevin decided to follow him, to see where he worked, to see what he did with the baby.

The man went to the Pharmogenetix campus of buildings in North Wales, not far from the rock singer's apartment. Kevin watched from his car as he went into one of the buildings. He was about to follow him in when he realized he was still wearing his scrub suit and needed a shave; so he decided to drive back to his apartment, catch some sleep, and return in the afternoon to see what happened when the man and the baby left.

At four the man came out from another building and through the door of the one he'd taken the baby into. A few minutes later he came out with the baby and diaper bag in his arms, carried them to his car, and placed the baby in some kind of contraption in the backseat. He then drove straight to his house.

Joanna came home shortly after.

Kevin stayed until midnight, when all of the lights in the house had gone out. He returned the next morning just before seven, and again followed the man and the baby to the Pharmogenetix campus.

This time Kevin followed the man into the building and saw him hand the baby and diaper bag over to a smartly dressed young woman who took the child down the corridor.

As Kevin started to follow her he was stopped by a man with a badge identifying him as a security officer. "I'm sorry sir, may I see your employee ID?"

"I'm looking for a job."

"Oh, I see. Personnel is in the tower building across the road. But they don't open till eight-thirty."

"OK. Thanks. Can I wait here?"

The man hesitated. "I suppose you can sit in the lobby for a while." He pointed to some modern orange deeply upholstered chairs, where a young professional looking woman with a briefcase sat reading a magazine.

"Thank you," he said and headed toward the chairs;

then seeing Joanna's lover come out, he turned toward the door and followed him out. The lover got back in his car and drove to another parking lot near another building a hundred yards off. It was obvious that this building was extra tightly secured, so Kevin returned to Joanna's house again.

For three hours he watched the comings and goings of neighbors. Most of them, women included, apparently worked in professional jobs. One woman seemingly stayed home to receive a delivery from a furniture store. As soon as the delivery van pulled away, she, too, left.

A truck bearing the name of a housecleaning service drove up to one townhouse along the row. A woman emerged and unlocked the house; two other women carrying cleaning equipment joined her. A lawn service truck pulled up next to Kevin's car. Four men with lawn mowers and electric trimmers began their rounds.

The noise and the activity gave Kevin the cover he needed to survey the house. He had already determined which room Joanna and her lover slept in. Now he got a good enough view through ground-floor windows to determine the location of the living room, dining room, and kitchen.

His reconnoiter complete, he now had to await opportunity. So far Joanna had never been alone in the house with the baby. So far only the lover had been alone with the baby. Day care for the child must have been provided by the lover's employer under conditions too secure for a kidnapping. He would have done that if he thought he could—snatched the child from day care, then returned to the empty house to wait for its mother to return. But no. If the kidnap were possible, such a scheme left too many possibilities for something to get out of hand. He might have to wait longer than he wanted . . . but he would wait till the time was right.

He returned to Pharmogenetix. At four-fifteen several mothers with young children emerged from the day-care center. Shortly afterward the woman who had taken the baby from the lover yesterday came out.

Kevin was puzzled. Was the day-care center closed? Was the lover still in the other building? Kevin hadn't seen him leave. The lover's car was parked where he had left it in the morning. Had someone else come to pick up the baby? Maybe the lover and Joanna were going out for Friday evening.

Kevin grew angry. Joanna, like the other single women who carried his seed, was happy to cast the baby around from pillar to post, hire someone to take care of it during the day and someone else to watch it at night. Her selfishness appalled him. She tricked him into making her pregnant, as he always knew she would. Then she tricked him by keeping the child from him. And now she was neglecting the child. Poisoning its life before it could have a chance—a chance that no child of his could ever have anyway. She'd found a lover who would take it off her hands, pass it around while she did whatever she wanted, then entertain her far into the night.

Well, he had found out before it was too late. He would end her neglect, end the child's cursed life, and leave not a single trace. Not of him, not of his seed, not of her and her poisonous eggs.

Suddenly the lover came out of the building, carrying the blanket-wrapped baby in his arms. He fastened it into its carrier in the backseat of the car, and drove directly to the house. He ran inside with the swaddled baby in his arms.

Shortly after Joanna came home, the lover came

with her to the front door. Kevin saw the two of them embrace. Then the lover left.

Much to Kevin's surprise the man had not come back by dusk. He could see Joanna standing by the nursery window, the infant on her shoulder. He saw the light in the nursery go out at eleven o'clock as it had the past two nights. The light remained on in the living room. But she turned off the outside light over the front door, as if she was not expecting her lover to come back that night.

And so the opportunity had come, sooner than he had expected. On the last Friday night in May.

He reached into the console between the car seats and pulled out a small black leather case. He ran one finger along its sleek nylon zipper, opened it and folded the top back.

The steel handles of three scalpels, secured in leather sheaths, gleamed against their jet black backdrop. He stroked them, then chose the middle one as having the right heft and blade angle to do the job cleanly and swiftly.

He removed the knife from its case and slipped it into a smaller protective sheath that fit into his jacket pocket. He patted it before and after getting out of his car and again several times as he approached the side of the townhouse and opened the gate to the low picket fence enclosing the patio.

The fence was apparently designed more for privacy than security, as the gate had no lock and was not completely closed. It creaked though, when he opened it, and he ducked behind it for a few moments after he was inside.

Four feet away the slats of the vertical blinds moved inside the sliding glass patio door. He saw the gleaming nails of three fingers turn them aside, and a pale swatch of skin flash momentarily above the fingers before they dropped away and the slats fell back into place.

Still stooping, he pressed himself against the brick wall beside the door. He remained cramped there for several minutes. If she heard the creak of the gate, she might hear him move the patio furniture.

But then he heard a sudden burst of music from behind the door. He smiled. She did love her classical music, he recalled, and played it a little too loud for his tastes. Something he didn't miss after she'd left him.

To the sounds of Chopin, he built his stairway to the nursery and the sleeping infant.

First he lifted the seven-foot redwood picnic table and turned it so that one edge of the tabletop rested against the brick. He slanted the table at an angle so that its top, running lengthwise, formed a ramp toward the window and its crossed legs and their supports provided footholds. He tested the pitch a few times, readjusting the table until he was certain it was secure.

Then he placed one of the benches horizontally on top of the table legs closer to the window, till the bench set in firmly balanced. The second bench would bridge the gap between the table and the window. As he steadied it into place, he saw the light in a second-story bedroom across the street flicker on. Someone came to the window, opened it, and peered out.

Kevin ducked down behind the fence and held his breath.

Through the space between the pickets he could see the person reach up and pull down a translucent blind. A few moments later the light went out.

He stood and surveyed the few houses he could see from this vantage point. Yes, he might still be seen; for the trees provided only a screen, not a curtain. But

at this hour on a Friday night, few people would be
around to see him. Those who weren't out would likely
be in bed.

He crept back and tested his structure one final
time. It held and he started his climb. His foot
found firm support in the joists where the crossed
table legs were bolted to the top. The horizontally
mounted bench held his weight without shifting.
But the bench leaning vertically against the upper
story of the townhouse would give little support; he
would have to grip the mortar lines between the
bricks, and the edge of the sill to hoist himself from
here. His height gave him a definite advantage, and
he pulled himself up till he rested on the top pair of
crossed bench legs.

Inside, the music stopped.

His fingers clutched at the frame of the double-hung
window screen. It made a soft scraping sound as he
raised it. Below him he heard the patio door slide
open and then quickly close. A latch snapped. Then
the music started again.

He hoisted himself through the window and into
the room.

The sweet and sour smell of diapers mixed with
baby powder hung in the almost pitch-dark nursery
air. Only a slim sliver of the palest light filtered in
from beneath that closed door. In the darkest corner
of the room he could make out the shape of the crib.

He slipped his hand into his jacket pocket and drew
out the sheathed scalpel. With his thumb he released
the snap of the case. He felt the cool handle against his
palm, and stroked it before pulling it free from its
holster.

He stepped toward the crib. As he drew closer he
could see the baby swathed in a gown that enclosed
its hands and feet completely. A lacy cap covered its

head. It lay on its belly, its pink face turned toward him.

He didn't want to look at its face, he never had wanted to see their faces. He knew they would all look ugly to him; for he could see right through them to their rotten cores. He could see their warped souls writhing just beneath the surface. He could smell death in the quick rise and fall of their chests as he approached. This baby's breath putrefied the air in the room and made him want to gag.

He placed his hand on the head.

It sighed and moved. It was a tiny, scrawny thing, as ugly as he'd imagined, as ugly as the others.

He ran his finger down the side of its head, and around its chin to its throat. Then he lifted and turned the child, resting it against his arm so the head fell backward and exposed its neck fully to the blade of his scalpel.

He drew the knife quickly across the small throbbing throat and watched as the blood spurted out.

The infant made a small gurgling sound.

Kevin took a thin blanket from the bottom of the crib, wrapped the baby in it, and lifted it, sopping up the blood that poured over his arms and down the front of his jacket. He crossed to the door.

A soft light from downstairs beckoned him. The piano music floated up on it.

As he slowly descended the stairs to the living room he could see Joanna curled up in a chair, rapt in the music she loved, her back turned to him.

Chapter Twenty-four

. . . Cradle and all

JOANNA DID NOT listen to the music. She huddled in it and cocked her ear to catch the sounds beyond it. And they—unfamiliar creaks and groans of a house that wasn't her home—frightened her.

She didn't want to be here alone on a Friday night. But where else could she be? Her apartment would never have done. Cassie's room there did not overlook a shaded patio. Traffic screeched below it night and day. And a million eyes were always on its sheer granite walls.

She could no longer ask Louise and David to court danger on her behalf. And the danger was no longer in David's eyes alone. Now they all knew how real it had become. Wherever Joanna lived, it lived. Wherever Cassie slept, it kept its vigil, awaited its opportunity. Sooner or later it would strike. Sooner or later the knife would flash in the moonlight and its blade would gleam as the sick and evil man ran it in anticipation along his thumb.

And Joanna would be alone when it happened, as all his victims were alone. She did not want to be alone so soon, and on a Friday, her very first in this house. But circumstances conspired against her. Her will, her wishes, her fears could not sway the fate determined by the random and willful acts of others. She had made herself the target of those acts long before she even imagined they were possible. And she could not now cower or deny her responsibility. She would have to be alone at the final reckoning. And unlike his other victims, she would know that the reckoning would arrive.

So when Jon had to go tonight and leave her alone, so very much alone, so completely deserted in this house unfamiliar and strange to her, she had wept only for a moment.

"Don't worry," he said. "I know that's easy to say. But I've been right about everything so far, haven't I?"

She'd had to admit that was true. Since he'd moved her and Cassie in here on Saturday, not a single phone call from the media had disturbed them. The police convinced the reporters that she was in no way involved in the Cradle murders, and the story broadcast on YJN neither appeared in print nor was picked up by the more reputable local channels or networks.

Crosby let up on her too. In fact apologized to her, an act that seemed as difficult for him as it seemed genuinely motivated.

And Jon had been right, too, about her going back to work on Monday. He arranged for Cassie's care at Pharmogenetix as part of their overall plan. And that had worked well. Neither he nor she had to miss a day of work, though he must have been as distracted all week as she was.

The responses of her colleagues and staff at the Martin Center overwhelmed her. Even Dr. Jordan Martin brushed off the damage the misleading TV reports might have caused.

"I doubt it'll affect malpractice insurance rates," he said. Then a shadow crossed his eyes and he sighed and said, "We've survived much worse, you know."

The security staff were no less accommodating. They beefed up parking garage patrols and reported all suspicious occurrences—cars left late in the visitors' slots, transients hanging around, altered tempo rary tags. They'd caught YJN's so-called investigative reporter trying to follow her out of the lot in the tan Pontiac she'd seen the week before. Never had she felt more secure in the Martin Center.

Never had she felt more secure about Cassie's safety. In the arms of others—Jon, the day-care aides, even the company nurse who'd treated a minor sniffle with saline nose drops—the baby seemed to thrive. She even seemed to like her new nursery, oblivious of the doom that might await her there.

Joanna was not. Nor was Jon. They knew full well what might happen in that room. But an infant had to have a room. And that room had to have an infant in it. And Joanna had to live with that fear, all the while protecting her child above any other. Above even her own self.

So she faced the fear, more alone than she had ever been in her life.

The music could not mute her dread nor shut out the noises in the house. Sometimes the noises made her forget that she'd vowed not to react to them, vowed not to give in to the terror in her heart. Once, in a panic, she'd run to the patio door and opened it; and only at the last moment had she closed and locked it.

She'd stopped the music between records and cocked her ear. Was a screen being raised in the nursery?

"Stop it!" she cried aloud to herself. She challenged the demon that tore at her resolve not to be afraid . . . challenged him and won. She started the music again and turned up the volume.

Doom's everpresence upstairs set loose its overpowering magnetic force. It twisted her from her chair, wrested her arms and legs into motion, tugged her toward the stairs.

She tore herself from its grasp, backed away from

it, and hands trembling at her mouth, returned to her
chair, sat down, turned her back on it.

Her blood pounded in her temples. She would not
give in to the pull of the magnet. She would not turn
toward the stairs, though her ears, like her imagination, told her he was descending them. She could feel
his presence, smell his tension and excitement, see in
her mind the blood dripping from the swaddled infant.

She would not turn until she could smell the blood.

She would not turn until she could feel the heat that
rose from his excitement, till it merged with the heat
of her fear.

She would not turn until she could see the picture
in her mind round the corner of her physical eye.

Till she could hear his voice whisper . . .

"Joanna."

The sweat of her palms glued her hands into helpless fists. Her chest ached. She turned her head.

He held out the child in its dripping windings. A
loose end of pink blanket dropped from his fingers and
trailed blood down the front of his slacks and onto his
shoes.

She cried out and reached out her hands.

He placed the dead infant in her arms.

She drew it to her, buried her head in it, wept. "Oh
no, oh no, oh no!"

"You see," he said, "I don't want to leave a trace."

"Please," she said. "Please."

In his hand the bloodied scalpel began to twitch.
"But it has to be cradle and all."

"No, please." She stood up and, dead infant tight to
her chest, she began to back away from him.

He raised the scalpel, brandished it as he advanced
on her.

"No! Kevin, don't. You don't know what you're
doing."

"It's your fault," he said.

"Yes, yes. It is. But don't kill me. Don't hurt me." She turned her back on him and ran toward the kitchen, a room with only one access, a room with no door for her to escape through.

He did not run after her. He just came deliberately, relentlessly toward her.

At the doorway she turned to plead with him again. As he advanced, was almost upon her, she stepped backwards one halting step at a time.

He teased her with the knife as he worked her back through the narrow kitchen, past the breakfast bar, past the refrigerator and range, past the pantry closet into a corner.

She held tightly onto the lifeless burden in her arms, knowing that this had been inevitable, knowing that this tiny, helpless infant had had to perish whatever she had done to try to save it. She had begged for another way. But no one would listen. "Please," she begged now for her own life.

He lifted the knife with one hand and shoved her shoulder back against the wall with the other. Then he raised the scalpel, and, measuring with his eyes the angle the thrust must take if it were to be quick and merciful, brought it down into its final plunge toward her throat.

Chapter Twenty-five

THE PANTRY DOOR flew open. A hand quicker than Kevin's grabbed his by the wrist and twisted his arm around and up his back till his own knuckles pressed sharply into his spine between his shoulder blades. The scalpel clacked to the floor.

He cried out and his eyes widened, and he released Joanna's shoulders as another pair of hands seized his legs, grappled them out from under him.

Then he was down on his knees, someone else's knees in his back, below his both hands now manacled there.

Then they pulled him up to standing, and he glared at Joanna, pain and incomprehension paling his face.

She said nothing as they turned him and half marched, half dragged him from the kitchen, while she stood tight against the wall as if he still pinioned her there by the shoulders. And the blood of the infant still in her arms congealed against her skin and her clothing and her face where she pressed it against its head.

Jon ran to her. He grasped her shoulders.

She lifted her head from the baby and looked into his face, then once more down to the child.

"You're all right," he said. "It's all over." He pulled her to him, limp, bloody infant and all.

She began to cry.

He held her and let her cry. When she lifted her eyes again and looked up at him, he released her. He stepped back and reached out his hands. "It's over now. Give her to me."

Reluctantly, she relinquished her hold on the creature, who had been marked and doomed by her uncommon genetic heritage long before Joanna had ever seen her. She held her out to him tentatively.

He took her with gentle respect. "I have to take her back to the lab. I don't want to wait too long to get her under refrigeration. I'll have to autopsy her tomorrow morning."

"Cassie. Where is she?"

"Louise and David have her outside in the car. They knew you'd want to see her tonight, no matter what time it was over."

"I want to hold her. Right now." She looked at the browning blood on her arms, and put a hand to her cheek. "I have to wash it off. That poor chimp's blood is all over me." She paused. "On my hands."

"Not really. More on mine. Really more on everybody's, I guess. But she was cared for like a princess all her life, and was fully sedated so she wouldn't feel a thing. And she had her day in the sun."

She managed a reluctant smile. "You're cruel. Take her out of here. I still don't know how you can possibly do what you do."

He grinned. "I do it for the greater good." He turned to leave. Then, after opening the door, he turned back. "Louise and David have the portable crib in their car. They weren't quite sure how well you'd stand up under a harrowing night like this. Will you want to stay at my place or yours?"

She studied his face for a long moment. "Neither," she said.

"I'm sure, all things considered, David will let you stay there with Cassie as long as you want."

"Not their place either," she said.

He knit his brow. "Then where?"

"How about *our* place?" she asked. "Wherever that is."

"Well, you're coming on a little strong, I'd say.

But I'll think about it on my way to the lab and back."

"Don't take too long," she said. Then she looked up past his shoulder and saw Louise running down the walk holding Cassie.

She ran past her lover and grasped her baby in her bloodstained arms and buried her face in her hair.

A Message To Our Readers...

As a person who reads books, you have access to countless possibilities for information and delight.

The world at your fingertips.

Millions of kids don't.

They don't because they can't read. Or won't. They've never found out how much fun reading can be. Many young people never open a book outside of school, much less finish one.

Think of what they're missing—all the books you loved as a child, all those you've enjoyed and learned from as an adult.

That's why there's RIF. For twenty years, Reading is Fundamental (RIF) has been helping community organizations help kids discover the fun of reading.

RIF's nationwide program of local projects makes it possible for young people to choose books that become theirs to keep. And, RIF activities motivate kids, so that they *want* to read.

To find out how RIF can help in your community or even in your own home, write to:

RIF
Dept. BK 2
Box 23444
Washington, D.C.
20026

Founded in 1966, RIF is a national nonprofit organization with local projects run by volunteers in every state of the union.

A NOVEL OF
   UNSPEAKABLE HORROR...

DEATH ANGEL

ROBERT BLACK

A rural farming community in Depression-era
America is terrorized by a serial killer in this
harrowing first novel. As masterful as the
best of Dean R. Koontz, this riveting tale of
horror from Robert Black is one you won't
easily forget.

ISBN 0-517-00835-1 $2.95

**COMING SOON
FROM PAGEANT BOOKS!**